Kissing Under the Mistletoe

Kissing Under the Mistletoe

A ST. HELENA VINEYARD NOVEL

MARINA ADAIR

Text copyright © 2012 Marina Adair
Printed in the United States of America.

Published by Montlake Romance
P.O. Box 400818
Las Vegas, NV 89140

ISBN-13: 9781612185859
ISBN-10: 1612185851

DEDICATION

To my daughter, Thuy.

You were my Christmas wish.

Among the billions of people on this

planet, separated by over seven thousand

miles of ocean, we managed to find each

other. You, bug-a-boo, are my proof

that miracles really can happen...

CHAPTER 1

I t wasn't every day that your average girl got to watch her career crumble before her very eyes. For Regan Martin, that day had been on repeat for the past six years. To be reminded of it while she was wearing blinking plastic antlers and a shirt that said "Elves Do It Better," though—that was enough to make her snap.

The minute Regan spotted her Ghost of Christmas Past, looking primped and relaxed as he lurked behind the condiments aisle, she no longer had to wonder why her career had suddenly gone from Welcome to the Gordon and Associates Family to Don't Let the Door Hit You in the Ass on the Way Out in under three seconds flat.

Which was why she dropped another pint—make that a gallon—of Rocky Road into her cart and sprinted for the front door. She ignored the clerk reminding her that she hadn't paid and the Santa clanking his bell for charity.

Fishing her keys from her purse, Regan rounded Picker's Produce, Meats and More, passed City Hall, and was reaching the community Christmas display—complete with a Santa and all nine reindeer—when she came to a screeching halt. Because there, under the town's flapping red banner that said "Merry Christmas One and All" and parked next to her 1994 Honda Civic, was a mini-McMansion on wheels, license plate reading: DELUCA1.

Her passenger door was blocked by a cluster of old wine barrels filled with festive poinsettias, leaving Regan's car completely boxed in. She parked her cart alongside the shiny orange Hummer, sure to test out its ding-free bumper claim, and tried to shimmy her way between the vehicles. *Tried* being the operative word. She doubted even her daughter could squeeze through that space, and Holly was only five. But there was no way she was willing to ask the man who had made her professional and, in turn, personal, life a living hell to move his car. Especially since she'd just landed a new job.

She propped her knee on the hood of her car and was about to see if she could pry off the moonroof when she heard a loud rip.

She teared up as she saw that Gabe DeLuca's side mirror had snagged and torn the ass out of her favorite pair of "Bah Humbug" sweats—an early Christmas present from Holly.

"Shit." Regan shimmied back to freedom. "Shit, shit, shit!"

She slapped her hand over her mouth, looking around to make sure nobody had heard her foul language. At home that would have cost her a quarter for every swear word uttered.

Suddenly, "Have Yourself a Merry Little Christmas" started playing. Loud and mechanical, the annoying shrill was accompanied by a blinking elf's nose. Damn shirt.

Shit, another quarter. Make that two.

Pressing her lips closed, Regan swallowed back a frustrated scream and resisted the temptation to kick his car. No sense in ruining her shoes, too.

Was he serious? How high school could he get, stalking her all over the country? Sure, she'd made a mistake—a big one. Just thinking about it made her stomach feel hollow and her chest tighten to the point of pain. She had been nothing but stupid, entrusting her heart to a man who'd lied to her, played her for the naive fool, never telling her that he was married. As a result, she had unintentionally committed one of the most unforgivable sins ever: she'd become the other woman. It was why she would never trust another man. She had learned her lesson the hard way, tried to make amends, and was, from the bottom of her heart, sorry. But she'd been paying the price ever since.

Enough was enough. Gabe DeLuca, enemy *numero uno*, had cost her eleven jobs over the past six years. Eleven! At first she'd tried to be understanding and see things from his family's point of view, but she was fed up. The minute she'd gotten the call from Ryo Wines offering Regan her dream job, she had packed up her life and moved Holly away from her friends and everything that was familiar, with the hope that they could find a fresh start here in St. Helena—and that didn't include being pushed around.

Regan glanced at the ice cream, perspiring in the afternoon sun, and looked back at her car. She had been in town only a week, hadn't even started her new job, and already her constant shadow had found her. No doubt he'd followed her here to get her fired—yet again.

Grabbing her cart, she took one, two, three steps backward, and before she knew what had happened, she surged ahead, ramming her cart into the back of Gabe's overcompensation-with-an-engine. A gigantic crash echoed, sending ice cream flying over the top of the car and landing on the hood with a victorious splat.

She picked up the remaining tub of Rocky Road, ripped back the lid, and squeezed the container until the contents fell to the trunk with a thwack. Still not satisfied, she sank her finger in and then carefully scrawled across the back windshield: Bah Humbug Mother Fuc—

"Are you through yet?"

Regan froze, her fingers still in the Rocky Road, and closed her eyes. She didn't need to turn around to see who was standing there; she'd recognize that voice anywhere. She knew she should pull on the big girl panties, apologize, and drive away. Unfortunately, today she had opted for her Rudolph panties, and was sporting a sequined nose on her ass.

Reminding herself that Martin women were fighters used to crawling their way back up, and also that she'd always told Holly turning your back while someone was speaking to you was rude, she mustered what was left of her pride, brushed her bangs out of her eyes, and turned to face the man who had ruined her life.

His gaze dropped to her naked finger and back to her eyes.

"Actually, no, I'm not." She was just getting started.

Gabriel DeLuca glanced over at the woman glaring at him and all he could think was, *Thank God.*

Thank God he had been the one suckered into picking up the groceries for the weekly family dinner rather than his sister. Abigail, being the only girl among four brothers, was always protected. And that's what he was doing now—protecting his sister.

"They have classes for that you know," he said, pointing to the wreck of a car. It would take several washings to get all that corn syrup and refined crap off.

He couldn't really blame Regan, though. He was responsible for her career—or lack thereof. But he had to keep her away from his family and, most importantly, his sister. The last thing Abby needed, with Christmas only three weeks away, was a visible reminder of her cheating bastard of a husband, Richard, and his taste for extravagance and beautiful women.

Gabe had no idea why his brother-in-law's mistress was in his town. The last he'd heard she was still in Oregon, a safe five hundred miles from the Napa Valley—and from his family.

"Oh?" She marched straight over, stopping so close that he caught a whiff of something sweet and, even worse, something sexy. Without hesitating, she raised one sugarcoated hand and smacked him. Not in the face, like he expected, but square in the chest—a melted Rocky Road handprint seeped through his button-down. Her other hand slapped a stain onto the left side of his shirt, and then with a smile that, if he were being honest, was almost as sweet as the ice cream, she dragged both hands down his chest—like an idiot, he flexed.

"I know this guy, he specializes in managing rage. I can call him if you want, set up an appointment." Gabe pulled out his phone and started scrolling. "Actually, he's in Portland; you could stop by. On your way home."

"I'm. Not. Leaving." She punctuated every word with another finger-paint doodle before turning back to the trunk for a refill and adding, "So back off!"

Not going to happen, he thought. Gabe didn't know exactly *why* she was here, but it didn't matter. It had taken him five years to convince Abby to move home. He wasn't about to give her another reason to move away. This year, he'd have his whole family around the tree. Collateral damage or not, Regan had to go—now.

As if reading his mind, she picked up her purse off the asphalt, hiked it high on her shoulder, and started walking away from him. Her raggedy sweats parted with each step, flashing him a great view of her ass—and Rudolph.

Keep on going, he thought, hating how great she still looked. Not that he'd been following her over the past six years, but he *had* been keeping tabs on her to make sure that her past didn't affect Abigail's future in any way.

Damn. Even with ice cream on her cheek and wearing a worn-out T-shirt, Regan Martin was as gorgeous as ever. And his dick agreed.

Hell, he'd never faulted his brother-in-law's taste—just the fact that the bastard couldn't keep it in his pants after he'd said, "I do." He also hated how women like Regan, who got off on dating married men with big balances, walked away scot-free while the families they wrecked suffered forever.

He wanted to give her the benefit of the doubt, but how could a woman not know that the man she was sleeping with was married?

"What the—" Gabe jerked to the right, narrowly avoiding the flying object spiraling at his head.

"That would be Dasher," Regan yelled, winding up again and chucking what appeared to be a porcelain Santa. She missed him, but before he could get smug, the shatter of glass told him she'd hit her target. He turned to find Mr. Kringle's black boots sticking out the back window of the Hummer.

"You've got a pretty good arm." Gabe tucked his hands in his pockets and leaned back against the fender. He'd never really understood why he enjoyed irritating her. Only that when her eyes went wild and that fighting pride of hers kicked in, all the years of drama between them seemed like bullshit.

"Three years of college softball at Oregon State."

"Hold up, it's happening again. Your eyes are glazing over and looking hard." Something brown skimmed his thigh, taking out the right brake light. She reached for the third deer—Prancer, he believed.

"Yup," he said, shaking his head sorrowfully. "Had a dog with that same problem. Used to foam at the mouth, snap at people for no reason. I had to put him down."

Another reindeer came jingling his way. Fast, and aimed with lethal accuracy. She may have played softball, but he hadn't been named MVP and Goalie of the Year on his college soccer team for nothing. He ducked.

"This whole heartless-bastard thing you got going on is working," she called. "You show up, growl at my employer, and I get fired. Then you follow me to the next town, block me in, and effectively ruin *my* Christmas spirit."

"*You're* calling *me* heartless?" He laughed. Like her or not, she was the only woman he'd ever met who gave as good as she got. Well, besides his grandmother.

"Rubber and glue, buddy. Rubber and glue." Then, in response to the smug grin, she sent Vixen flying, denting the hood and scratching the fender.

"You're the one who slept with a married man. My sister's husband, if you need me to be more specific."

"Yeah, I made a mistake. And you've gone out of your way to make sure I can't hold down a job ever again."

"No, I go out of my way to make sure you never work with a company where your path might cross with my sister's."

"I've built my career on marketing wine. Your family *is* wine! So does that mean you'll only stop harassing me if I give up my career?"

"As far as I know, your career is seriously lacking."

At his words, all of her attitude faded and she just looked tired. Sad, vulnerable, and so damn defeated that his chest actually clenched. He didn't like being the asshole. Hated it, as a matter of fact. But when his parents died, Gabe, twenty-three and the eldest of five, had stepped in as head of the DeLuca clan, and, as such, his duty was to protect his family. Twelve years had passed and nothing had changed—his family was his life. And right now no one was a bigger threat to their happiness than the gorgeous brunette standing in front of him.

Regan lowered the last reindeer in defeat, her voice barely audible over the light traffic. "How many times can I say I'm sorry? I mean, just let me know what that number is so we can both move on and you can leave me alone."

He never made the conscious decision to approach her. His legs just started moving, his tension increasing with each step. He knew he was an intimidating man, but her being a little afraid of him right now couldn't hurt. She didn't need to know he would never harm her.

Actually, he hadn't even really ruined her career. Oh, he may have gotten her fired from her first job, but that was because the firm she worked for, the one that had given her the job based on Richard's recommendation, was handling their family's new label. And he may have mentioned her name to a few friends in the industry as persona non grata. Aside from that, whatever problems she'd had over the years were all on her.

"I meant what I said to you that night I found you with Richard." Even the memory made him want to punch something.

Instead of backing away like a smart woman would do, Regan stayed put; her pert nose rose higher in the air, if that was even possible, and she did her best to look down at him—an amazing feat since he was a whole head taller.

"I will stop at nothing to protect my family from any further pain," he continued, trying to ignore the panic filling her big blue eyes and the way she clutched the deer to her chest, rocking it as if out of habit. "So until I see those taillights of yours heading out of town, I will be at your side, watching your every move, making your life hell until you realize that a vacation in the wine country isn't worth it."

Regan must have squeezed a little too hard, because the deer's nose lit up and a cheery, "Merry Christmas to one and all," echoed across the parking lot.

"Okay, I give up," Regan said, shutting the last closet door. Their new house was only seven hundred square feet. With only two bedrooms, a bathroom, kitchen, and family room, there certainly weren't many places that could conceal a dripping-wet, three-foot-tall urchin who was doing her best to avoid bedtime.

Regan glanced at her watch. She'd spent the past fifteen minutes trying to find Holly, a time span that most kindergarteners would lose patience with. Not her kindergartener.

Holly had the patience of Job and the determination of a hall monitor in training, which explained the "Dirty Jar" sitting on the coffee table. It was two-thirds full and strictly enforced. Every dirty word or rude action resulted in a twenty-five-cent fine. Regan went through lots of quarters. When the man at the bank, who was exchanging her twenty for two rolls of coins for the second time that week, suggested that the Laundromat had a change machine, Regan told him the machine was broken. Which cost her a quarter for lying.

Regan sighed. She had put off paying her fine from three days ago.

Draping the dry bath towel on the back of the couch, she dug through her purse, found her coin bag, and mentally added: shoplifting, bad words, cart to fender, ice cream to windshield—and one surly DeLuca—vandalizing Christmas display, raising her voice. She pulled out her buck seventy-five and dropped it into the jar, adding another dollar for stealing Rudolph, who was shoved in the trunk of her car.

At the clanking of coins, a giggle erupted from the far side of the family room. Regan spotted dark little ringlets sticking out over the top of a stack of moving boxes, which had a large tree drawn on them in pink crayon.

She leaned to look around the box, and sure enough, there were wiggling, naked toes. Eyes closed and clutching her favorite stuffed kitty, PurrKins, Holly stood silent in a puddle of wet carpet, careful not to give away her hiding spot.

"Gotcha!" Regan smiled as Holly screamed and took off for the back of the house, her bare feet slapping the hardwood. She picked up the useless towel and followed.

Ten minutes and another round of hide-and-seek later, the sitter was waiting on the couch and Regan had managed to corral Holly into her bedroom. She pulled a red night-gown covered with white kitties wearing Santa hats over her daughter's head and brushed a kiss across her forehead.

Holly was old enough to dress herself, and normally, when there was a guest her daughter wanted desperately to impress, she insisted. Tonight, though, she let Regan brush her hair and teeth, not even expelling a single huff or puff when Regan pulled out the long-sleeved nightgown.

One look at the red envelope with glittery candy-cane stickers resting under Holly's pillow and Regan didn't have to question the stellar behavior. Taking in her daughter's smile and the way she'd organized her toys in the bin, her heart melted.

Holly was adjusting like a champ. She'd made it through the first week of new house, new school, new life. And she seemed to be doing all right. More than all right—she was happy. Which made Regan happy, run-in with Gabe DeLuca notwithstanding.

This move was just what Regan had hoped it would be. A fresh start for them both. And tonight represented an end to six years of professional hell. She was about to attend her new company's holiday party and, come Monday, Regan would awe them with her ideas for their new wine.

She smoothed her fingers through her hair, arranging it into a makeshift upsweep, a few curls left free to add a touch of softness to the overall look. "Hair up or down?"

Her mini fashion consultant poked her tongue out the side of her mouth, deep in thought. After much consideration, she exclaimed, "Princesses look better when they wear it down. It makes the tiara stand out more, I think."

"Hair down it is. Now hop up in bed. It's lights-out time." Regan pulled the blankets taut, tucking them snugly around Holly's petite frame. She brushed another kiss across her daughter's forehead, one across each eyelid, and a final one across her button nose.

She clicked off the bedside lamp. Holly looked around the room, her eyes wide with wonder at the twinkle lights that went around the ceiling. They might not be anywhere near unpacked, but her daughter had Christmas lights in her room. "This is the best house ever."

Their house, a perk of her new job, was a modest two-bedroom casita off the Silverado Trail. It had a bright kitchen, a gnat-sized bathtub, and stucco walls that were covered in fuchsia and scarlet bougainvillea. It also had a leaky bathroom faucet, avocado tile, and a tiny patio that passed for a yard. But who needed grass when your house was set in the middle of thirty-nine acres of Syrah vines?

And for Holly, who had spent a lifetime living in one-bedroom apartments, this place was like Disneyland. It was also the kind of house that they could call home. The kind of place Regan had dreamed of raising Holly in.

"So tell me about school." Regan sat on the edge of the bed, careful not to displace the red envelope, which had "Santa" scrawled across it in green crayon.

"I already told you." Holly's balled fists rubbed at her eyes and she snuggled deeper into the sheets.

"Then tell me again," Regan said, knowing Holly was bursting with excitement to repeat her week.

"I made a new friend, Lauren, who sings just like Beyoncé and she loves kitties almost as much as I do. And she said she would come to my birthday party since she's not going away for Christmas."

Regan smiled. Holly was truly her Christmas miracle. Born five weeks too early on Christmas Eve, she had come out a fighter. Just like her mama. Holly had always loved her Christmas birthday; she said it was special, because how many kids got a birthday present from Santa? But the last few years, Regan had come to understand that birthday parties around the holidays were hard to plan. People were out of town or busy decorating trees and making memories with their own families. Not to mention that living in a cramped apartment had made it all the harder to host any sort of gathering. This year, though, they could have a party right here, in their new home. With her new friend Lauren.

"My teacher, Mrs. Collette, is really nice except she smells like saltines and says 'shhh' too loud." Holly interrupted herself to explain. "A fact, not gossip, so it's not bad. Then today we had the tryouts for the Christmas musical, and I went out for the role of Christmas Kitty and the music teacher, Mrs. Dee, said my purring was 'purrrfect.'"

Holly demonstrated said purr, and it was pretty dang perfect.

"You know what I was thinking?" A long blink was Holly's only response. "Maybe next weekend we could go chop down a tree."

"Chop down a tree? Like a real one?" That got her attention. "For the front room?"

"Yup. I saw a banner for a Christmas tree fund-raiser in town. It sounded fun."

"I want a big one, like they have in the middle of town, with twinkle lights, white ones only, and snow. Real snow. It has to smell like camping and have Grandma's star on top. Maybe even birds in it. And when I come out Christmas morning, there will be presents with red and green bows all around and the birds will sing."

Regan was already making a mental spreadsheet of the cost. Then stopped herself. This Christmas was going to be perfect. She had a new, plush job and a little in savings. "How about tomorrow we measure the front room and then go and see what they have that might fit?"

"How 'bout we measure it now?" Holly suggested, eyes alert, already sitting up.

"Tomorrow." Regan placed a hand on her daughter's shoulder, steering her back down. "*Now* we go to sleep."

Holly stared at her, clearly trying to think of a way to buy just five more minutes of awake time, but not even one of the million or so excuses she usually used came out. With a resigned sigh and a good-girl bat of the lashes, she folded her hands under her cheek and feigned sleep.

Realizing she was stalling too, Regan gave one last tuck to the sheets and stood. *Tonight's party will be fine*, she tried to convince herself. Fun, even. And with Christmas only three weeks away, what better way to beef up the yuletide spirit than a holiday party?

She kissed her daughter's hand and gave it three little I-love-you squeezes. Holly squeezed back with her two me-too grips.

"'Night, sweetie."

She'd crossed the room and was about to shut the door when the sleeping Holly spoke. "I forgot about the best part of my week."

"What's that?" Regan asked, even though she already knew the answer.

"When Mrs. Schultz said I could have a kitty of my very own. Not like in Newberg where I pretended that Miss Tuffett was mine, but one that sleeps in my bed and watches TV with me."

Regan's throat closed. One of the concessions she'd made to compensate Holly for leaving all her friends behind was the promise of a kitty of her very own. Last year, after Regan had finally gone under, financially speaking, they had been evicted from their apartment and forced to move to the other side of town and rent from a landlord who wouldn't allow pets of any kind. Holly had resorted to feeding a stray cat their dinner leftovers.

However, Jordan Schultz, Regan's new boss, current landlord, fast friend, and the first woman to take a chance on her in nearly six years, had merely waved her fingers dismissively at the request and said a cat would be a great addition to the house, instantly making Holly the happiest girl in the world.

Regan's eyes rested on her sleeping daughter and conceded that she was the luckiest mom in the world.

CHAPTER 2

Regan debated changing her order from a Sangiovese to a shot of Jack. The invitation had specifically said "cocktail attire." Apparently Oregon's definition and the Napa Valley's differed.

It had taken four laps around the lobby, three visits to the ladies' room, two pep talks, and a partridge in a pear tree for Regan to muster the courage to walk into that ballroom. She'd decided that her simple red sheath wasn't dressy enough and her heels not name brand enough and was making a beeline for the circular, rotating glass door when she passed the hotel's Christmas display.

Beautiful crystal ornaments, which told the story of the Twelve Days of Christmas, sparkled under the massive chandelier. Regan's eyes fell on the partridge ornament, and immediately she thought of Holly and her Christmas tree wish. Swallowing her nervousness, Regan marched into that party, determination locked and loaded.

From the outside, the Napa Grand Hotel looked like your typical high-end boutique hotel: a ten-story, stone-faced structure with marble end casings and ornate windows and doors. Once inside Regan couldn't decide if she was in a ballroom, a hotel, or on one of the sets from *Titanic*. And the man in the corner surrounded by security was quite possibly Francis Ford Coppola.

"There you are. I was beginning to think you'd passed out in a moving box. I was about to send in Search and Rescue," Jordan said from behind.

Tall, poised, and impeccably dressed, Jordan was the epitome of fashion. Her shoulder-length red hair was sexy in that effortless way Regan had never mastered. To accomplish the same look she would need a gallon of hair products and enough tease to cause permanent scalp scarring.

"Thanks for the gift basket—oh, and the use of your daughter," Regan said. Jordan had not only come over, welcome basket in hand, which had enough smelly cheeses and Ryo wines to get an entire house of Kappa Gamma Sigma trashed, she had also bribed her teenage daughter, Ava, into babysitting Holly tonight.

Jordan waved a hand, her lips making a raspberry sound. "You have to know what our wine tastes like to really sell it. As for the sitter, you are doing me a favor. This way I know Ava's new *friend*"—she threw air quotes around the last word—"isn't at my house, trying to get into her pants. As far as I'm concerned, she could be your live-in nanny if it means she doesn't round third before Christmas. Oh, look, the reason we all came."

A jacketed waiter circled through the crowd with a tray of wine-filled goblets. Jordan removed one and handed it to Regan. "Here, drink this and everything won't seem so overwhelming."

"Really?" Regan took a gulp. She didn't feel any different unless you counted the peppery zing, which woke up her taste buds and tickled her nose.

"No, not really, but it takes the edge off. A few of these and everyone will start to resemble famous people. Or past lovers."

Regan felt eyes burn through the back of her dress, caress their way down the length of her, and settle on her hips. Twisting her body slightly, she looked over one shoulder.

She couldn't tell the shape of his lips, the color of his eyes, or even who he was—the distance was too far and her last job hadn't included eye care in the benefits package. But her nipples apparently had twenty-twenty, because they went into full party mode.

The man shifted slightly, as if he, too, was ready to party. That was a bad sign. Because men did not—repeat, did *not*—fit into her five-year plan. There was Holly, her career, and creating a home. Period. None of those included the penis-carrying members of society.

That didn't mean she couldn't add him to her dream bank, though.

"Quite a sight to behold, isn't he, dear," said a woman who looked so regal she could give Queen Elizabeth a run for her money. Her accentuation of the hard consonants and rolling of the vowels screamed Italian origins—as in Italy, not the local pizzeria. The nonchalant way she wore her vintage Armani advertised that she came from old money.

"Excuse me?" Regan asked, but it came out more an apology than a question.

"The gentleman that you are currently ogling," the woman clarified, her eyes resting proudly on the man in question. "My grandson."

Regan opened her mouth and stopped. Caught sizing up anyone, let alone someone's grandson...talk about embarrassing. Should she apologize, deny, or perhaps qualify? Denying would cost her a quarter, qualifying would be even more embarrassing and cause her to say something that would no doubt cost her multiple quarters. Apology it was, then.

"Oh, stop gulping, dear. He's quite a specimen—takes after my side of the family. With three brothers equally as stunning, I've gotten used to women gaping at them in front of me." Her hands made a wide gesture, encompassing every woman in the room. "He's a bit too stubborn and way too responsible for his own good, but he has potential. A lovely choice on your part."

"What most people miss," Jordan jumped in with a smile that came from speaking of someone you admired and loved, "is that behind that impressive portfolio is an honorable and generous man." She leaned in and whispered, "With the most impressive package. I mean, look at him. Hands down, best ass in the Valley. If I hadn't played ballerinas with him as a kid, I would toss him in the nearest stall."

Regan turned for a better view of the man's impressive package. But he was gone.

"When Steve left me, I was a wreck. No marketable skills other than managing a house and playing hostess. He took me on as his assistant and—" Jordan paused, collecting herself.

Assistant? As far as Regan knew, Jordan was managing director of Ryo, which, according to Regan's research, was a female-owned-and-operated company.

Before she could question the information, or the identity of the mysterious man, Jordan spoke. "Let's just say he made me and Ava feel like part of the family."

"Well, since I don't have his naked baby pictures on me to complete this touching moment, why don't you tell me who this lovely child is?" the older woman said.

"Oh." Jordan shrugged, totally unfazed by her lapse in etiquette. "This is Regan Martin, marketing guru and appointed savior for Ryo Wines. Regan, this is Chiara Amalia Giovanna Ryo, founder and president of Ryo."

"You can call me ChiChi, dear." The older woman extended her arm like royalty. Regan didn't know whether to shake it or kiss it. She settled on a shake.

"As soon as I phase myself out of the day-to-day operations at Ryo, you will report directly to ChiChi," Jordan explained.

During the phone interview, Jordan had explained that she'd been brought on to hire staff and set up operations for the winery. Once the company found its footing, she would take on a smaller role, leaving Regan with plenty of opportunity for lateral growth. It was another aspect that had attracted Regan to the position.

"It's nice to finally meet you," Regan said, still pumping the woman's hand.

"I was thinking the same thing," the older woman said with a smile. "And Holly is just precious."

Jordan must have seen the look of confusion on Regan's face. "In addition to making a mean Syrah, ChiChi is also the chairwoman of the Community Action Committee, which means she heads up any and all community events and a lot of the arts programs at Holly's school."

"Right now we are working on the Christmas musical. And if that busybody PTA will leave me alone, it will be brilliant," ChiChi said, frowning at a group of ladies standing at the bar wearing entitled gowns and designer attitudes.

"The musical is all Holly can talk about. She was so excited about tryouts, she's been practicing her purr all day. And she just loves her music teacher...Mrs. Dee? I was afraid when we moved midyear that it would be hard on her, but everyone has been amazing. It really has made the transition so much easier," Regan gushed, all in one gigantic breath.

She felt like Holly, all big eyes and blabbering on, but she couldn't help herself; she was talking to the woman who had made this move a success. So she did what she always managed to do in these kinds of situations. She went on. And on.

"I can't even begin to thank you for recommending Holly. I know how long the wait list for St. Vincent's Academy is, and after you called them, they moved her to the top, and, well..." Regan forced herself to be quiet, afraid she'd burst into tears. ChiChi had single-handedly gained Holly admission into a school that Regan could never afford—and offered to pay for the full tuition as a benefit of working for Ryo Wines.

"One less vineyard brat to ferment the barrel. And she's quite the linguist. Most children today can't even speak one language properly, let alone three. Her grasp of French is remarkable, spoken like a true Parisian, and her Spanish..." ChiChi paused, leaning in to Regan. "You can let go of me, dear."

Regan released her death grip on the woman and blushed. "My mother made me take French in school and only spoke Spanish at home. I guess I wanted the same for Holly."

Actually, she wanted more for Holly. Regan's mother had been 100 percent Mexican, a Spanish-speaking cleaning lady with no degree, no papers, and no identity other than "illegal." And stubborn to a fault. The only thing Regan inherited from her diplomat French father was a few extra inches, piercing blue eyes, and the understanding that she was unwanted.

Regan was adamant that Holly have a childhood filled with opportunity and roots—and, above all, one where she knew that she belonged.

"Excuse me, but I believe this is our dance," a deep—she refused to say sexy—voice cut in from behind.

Startled, she whipped around and tried to convince herself that she was not staring down Gabe DeLuca for the second time in less than a week.

His request came off as cordial, but the reprimanding hand shackled around Regan's wrist was pure asshole. She pulled back. His grip tightened. Not enough to hurt, but rendering her unable to break free. Furious, she hit him with a look—a hard one.

But it was difficult to appear fierce when facing a mountain of angry testosterone. Gabe wasn't just angry, he was hot. She hadn't seen it the other day because she'd been thrown off by his smart-ass smile. She had only ever seen his snarl. And he was snarling now. Even though it should piss her off—which it did—it also made her panties wet.

Okay, time to pull it together, Regan!

She jerked with enough force to disengage her arm, rubbing at the strange tingling left by his fingers and cursing her hormones. That was what happened when young, healthy women avoided men for six years. They went sex-crazy.

"I know she's exquisite, Gabriel. But you know better than to manhandle a lady," ChiChi scolded, though she appeared to be smiling at the sparks flying between the two.

Regan wanted to tell the sweet older woman that it was loathing, not lust-inspired sparks, but she was afraid it might be a little of one and a sleigh full of the other.

"I apologize, Nonna." Gabe smiled—the first honest smile Regan had ever seen from him.

Nonna? *Grandmother?*

Gabe's eyes softened and he leaned down and gave ChiChi a kiss on both cheeks, pulling her in for a hug. Regan felt a strange tug of longing watching the obvious flow of affection between the two.

"Jordan, you look gorgeous as always." Gabe glanced around the room and grinned. "Incredible job tonight. You should be proud."

Regan blinked. This man who she thought didn't have a nice bone in his body was actually quite charming, and his fondness for the two women was genuine. What surprised her, though, was the way the women embraced him. It spoke of mutual admiration and heartfelt respect.

Great, the man was admired and endearing.

"I'm surprised to find Miss Martin here," Gabe continued. "Astonished really."

"Likewise," Regan snapped, crossing her arms.

"Careful." He leaned in, lowering his voice. "Your eyes are going all shifty. Sure you don't want the number for that anger management class I told you about?"

"What is wrong with this world? Anger management classes!" ChiChi snapped. "Just the other day Gabriel took me to the market to buy the meat for dinner and some crazy destroyed my car. Santa was thrown through my back window, and they still haven't found poor Randolph."

"You mean Rudolph," Regan casually corrected, going for innocent.

"The rest of the world has Rudolph. St. Helena has Randolph," ChiChi said as two of her fingers moved from forehead to chest, shoulder to shoulder, while mumbling something about the Father, Son, and the Holy Ghost. "A cardinal sin, I tell you! They should lock that crazy up."

"I agree," Gabe said, crossing his arms, which pulled his tuxedo jacket tightly across his chest. A chest that had absolutely nothing to do with the way her mouth went dry. "Don't you agree, Regan?"

"Yup," Regan mumbled, polishing off her second glass of wine in one gulp, surprised that Gabe hadn't ratted her out—and making a mental note to drop a whole roll of quarters into the Dirty Jar.

"You two know each other, then? How *interesting*," Jordan said with a little too much enthusiasm.

"Interesting," Gabe deadpanned. "Regan and I go way back." His stormy-blue gaze flicked to her hands and back to lock on her eyes, sending a shiver down her spine. "Now about that dance."

"I'll sit this one out, thank you though," Regan replied with a serene smile, in direct contrast to her eat-shit-and-choke-on-it bat of the lashes.

Gabe might have laughed if he hadn't been scanning the room for his sister. Between Richard's wayward dick, his sticky fingers, and last year's grape-ravaging frost, Abigail had had to claw her way back from bankruptcy—fiscally and emotionally. She'd spent the first four years after Richard left in Santa Barbara, avoiding the family, her friends—anyone who knew what had happened, which was pretty much the entire Napa Valley.

Then, two years ago, ChiChi convinced her to go in as partners in a new winery. With ChiChi heading up wine production, Abby designing the winery and handling the build, and a team of amazing women running the day-to-day operations, Ryo would become the only female-run winery in the DeLuca family.

Abby had finally agreed, under the conditions that her name stayed off the paperwork and that she could do the preliminary designs from her house in Santa Barbara. Over the past year, Ryo Wines had become her baby, the project that pulled her through a difficult time in her life.

Tonight was to be Abby's big moment, her I'm-back-and-stronger-than-ever party. It was her chance to prove to herself, and to everyone else, that she'd recovered from Richard's blow—it was *not* going to become a reminder of what a bastard he was.

"Too late for that, don't you think?" Gabe said. "Besides, they're playing our song."

"We don't have a song."

"No, but we do have an audience," he said softly, his eyes going from his grandmother to Jordan and back to Regan, who was now looking panicked.

"A dance," ChiChi said, clasping her chest. "What a lovely idea. You two go catch up, and I will entertain Isabel."

Isabel, right. Isabel Stark was blonde, stacked, and the woman ChiChi had blackmailed Gabe into bringing as his date tonight. She was a head of the local PTA, heir to the newest cork empire in the Valley, and had her recently divorced sights set on Gabe, who was not interested in anything other than a good time.

He looked around the room and found Isabel standing by the bar, looking entitled and irritated, right where he'd left her when he'd spotted Regan. At *his* party. Laughing with *his* family.

"Thank you, Nonna. And Jordan, remind me to give you a raise. You did a fantastic job tonight." To avoid his grandmother discovering just who Regan Martin was, Gabe extended an arm. "Shall we?"

When Regan's eyes met his, they were wide with understanding. Smart girl. She'd pieced it all together. Ryo Wines may not bear the DeLuca name, and he might not be allowed to set foot in their production house because he lacked the right number of X chromosomes, but it was still a DeLuca company. And his employees were loyal to him and his family.

"It was, um, so very nice to meet you, ChiChi." She set her wineglass on a passing tray and turned to Jordan. "Gabe is right, Jordan. It really is a wonderful party. Now, if you'll excuse me, it seems I have a dance."

Head high, Regan walked right past Gabe and headed straight for the exit. And straight for Abigail.

"Dance floor is this way." He clasped her arm firmly and led her back to the room, ignoring her protest and the pointy heel digging into his big toe. He'd have thrown her over his shoulder if it meant avoiding a scene.

"What makes you think I'd ever want to dance with you?" She jerked her arm away.

"How about because we are going have a conversation. The one where I remind you how you fucked over my family, and you promise to waltz your sweet little ass back to Oregon."

"I don't know how to waltz."

"Great, because this is a rumba." Wrapping his arm around her waist, he slid his hand down the exposed part of her back. Shit. She was soft and smelled incredible and was so damn sexy he went hard immediately.

Gabe spun her out and back in, then gently swayed to the music. To anyone else it would appear as though they were a couple enjoying a friendly dance. No one would notice how Regan's knee rose up within striking distance, her nails digging into his chest, while Gabe's arms tightened around her like a vise.

Unfortunately, his body couldn't help but notice her dress, red and silky and hugging every curve. Or the way their bodies brushed against each other. Or that when he looked down he had a damn-near perfect view of black lace and the most incredible cleavage he'd ever seen.

Based on the cold glare coming off Regan, which was enough to freeze his nuts off, she knew exactly what he was staring at. He looked at the walls, the band, anywhere but at her. Not that it helped. The woman smelled like gingerbread cookies and sex, and all he could think about was getting her under the mistletoe three feet away.

"We have to stop meeting like this, Vixen."

Her eyes narrowed into two rage-induced slits and she opened her mouth. Gabe placed his finger against her lips. "Careful now, it looks like you're getting ready to say something you'll regret later."

She bit his finger, smiling when he jerked his hand back. She wouldn't be smiling if she knew that his hand wasn't the only thing that jerked.

"Actually, I was going to say thank you for not ratting me out to ChiChi about the car." *Asshole* went unsaid. So did *liar, liar, pants on fire.* "So if you could please tell her that the crazy lady said she's sorry. That she didn't know it was her car."

"Are you saying you wouldn't be sorry if it had been mine?" He took her in a close embrace, this time sliding his fingers between hers while guiding them even farther toward the back of the ballroom.

"No. Yes. I don't know."

Gabe laughed and "Vixen" looked ready to bite again.

"Is this funny to you? Screwing with my life?" Even though she didn't miss a step, her words came out low and steady and full of fury. "What was your plan, to hook me with some fake job offer, make me leave behind everything I know and love so you could you get me down here and publicly humiliate me? I have a red Sharpie in my purse if you want to draw the letter *A* on my forehead and get it over with."

Gabe stopped dancing but didn't release her. "I have no idea what you're talking about."

"Don't lie to me." She stepped back, ignoring the couple that nearly toppled over her and the other three who had slowed their pace to listen in. "Look, I get it. You hate me and want to ruin my life. Well, you win, mission accomplished. At least have the balls to own it!"

She patted down her sides as if desperately searching for a pocket. When she came up short she dropped her head back with a dramatic sigh and mumbled something about dirty language and being a lady.

"What are you looking for?"

"A quarter," she huffed, and Gabe swore she stomped her left foot.

He reached into his pocket and offered her one, but she just stared at it, her shoulders slumping. When she looked up at him, her expression was one of defeat.

"Do you have any idea what your stupid game has done to my life?"

Gabe looked around the ballroom and found everyone staring back. He saw her throat working hard, her eyes blinking rapidly, and—shit!—she was about to cry. He hated when women cried. Especially ones who he was certain were too tough to cry. And especially if he was the a-hole who was the cause of those tears.

"Regan, I swear I had no idea that you were the marketing VP Jordan hired. She told me ChiChi had found the perfect person for Ryo, showed me the mock-ups, and I signed off."

He'd been so blown away by the proposal that he hadn't even asked questions. It should have struck him as odd that there wasn't a name on any of the mock-ups, but it wasn't his company—wasn't his call. ChiChi had declared that *this* was the person she'd chosen to take Ryo to market; Gabe signing off was a mere technicality.

It was also a necessity. Ryo was heading into its first harvest, and they needed a marketing strategy—fast. But *he* needed his managing director back. Jordan had been on loan to ChiChi for nearly five months, three months longer than the agreed-upon time. Her only goal now was to get Ryo staffed and operating smoothly so that she could get back to what she was paid to do—making his life easier.

"You expect me to believe that out of all of the people who work in the wine and marketing space, I was selected purely on the basis of my talent?" Regan asked.

"And you expect me to believe that you coming to my hometown had nothing to do with screwing with my sister?"

"I had no idea you even lived here. And your people called me, Gabe. Not the other way around. I researched Ryo Wines after my recruiter contacted me with the offer. It was a startup winery, owned and operated by women, and in no way could I tell that it was connected to your family. I would have never accepted the job had I known." Either she deserved an award or she really was as confused as Gabe, because he almost—almost—believed her. "But it doesn't matter, does it? I'm still out of a job, and Abigail is once again protected."

"Yes, you're fired. And believe me when I say that Abigail will *always* be protected."

"Lucky her." The words were spoken so softly Gabe barely heard them. But he couldn't miss the look in her eye. It wasn't anger or envy. It was almost admiration, underscored with longing.

They continued to silently face off as a crowd gathered. It looked as though ChiChi had invited the entire Napa Valley who were now witnessing what appeared to be Gabe making an innocent woman cry.

Regan must have felt the weight of the stares because she straightened her shoulders and, with the best screw-you flick of the hair he'd ever seen, glided toward the back exit, the fabric of her dress hugging that heart-shaped ass with every step. She rounded the bar and disappeared into the hall, leaving Gabe to wonder what had just happened.

She was the one who should be apologizing. So why was he feeling like he'd just told a preschooler that Santa is a lie? That woman was the most confusing person he'd ever met. Whenever he was around her he felt off balance. Which was the only reason he could think of why, after he started chasing her down like some stalker, he found himself apologizing. To her!

"Regan, I'm sorry. There was no master plan to mess with you. It was just dumb luck. We've used the same staffing firm before, and there wasn't any information connecting Ryo to the DeLuca name because ChiChi wanted this to be her and Abby's thing." She kept on walking. With her taking three steps for each one of his, he caught up quickly. "Look, to make things easier, you can just drop the keys in the mailbox when you leave town."

That got her attention.

She stopped and slowly turned to face him. Her eyes were red-rimmed. Like she'd been crying.

Damn it.

"The keys?"

"To the cottage. You can just drop them in the box."

At his words, Regan gasped and then took another breath, until she was breathing too fast and too hard. Gabe was doing some heavy breathing of his own, because Vixen was about to hyperventilate and all she kept saying was something about a kitty of her very own.

"Easy there." He took her by the shoulders and her skin was cold and clammy. Steering her down the hallway, through the back doors and into an open courtyard, he lowered her to an empty bench. The night air was cold, but that wasn't what was causing her to shake. He took off his jacket and wrapped it around her.

"You still with me?" He knelt down and, taking her wrist, pressed two fingers to her pulse. "Regan, I need you to look at me."

But when those baby blues went blank and her lower lip quivered he regretted asking, because something inside of him hollowed out and he found himself wishing they'd met under different circumstances.

After several *long* seconds, her breathing slowed and he could almost feel her fight to gain composure.

"You okay?" he asked, feeling her pulse return to normal.

"I think so." Still a little dazed, she rested her forehead against his shoulder. "I'm pretty sure I would have fallen, so thanks."

"I think this is the first time we've been this close and you haven't yelled at me or tried to inflict bodily harm," he teased, keeping a careful watch on her.

"No, it's not," she whispered, looking up at him through her lashes. "The night we first met."

She was right. In fact, that night Regan hadn't spoken at all. She'd only watched him and Richard, her eyes wide and filled with tears as they got into it about Abby. Even as Gabe dragged that cheating ass out of the restaurant, Regan had remained silent.

After he was certain Richard was headed home to face his wife, Gabe had chanced one last look inside the restaurant. Regan sat alone, staring down at a small, unwrapped box, tears streaming down her cheeks, making *him* feel like the ass.

Kind of like he felt now.

Once again, he reminded himself that it was all bullshit. None of this should be his problem. It wasn't his fault Regan chose to sleep with a married man or that Richard didn't have a loyal bone in his body. Except that it was. If it hadn't been for Gabe, Abby would never have met Richard.

"You think you can stand now?"

"Of course," she said, lifting her head and easing her hand out from under his. "I understand that the cottage is a perk for the marketing VP, which I no longer am. But could you give me a few days to find a new place?"

"How about next weekend. Is that long enough?"

She merely nodded.

What the hell was he doing? He was supposed to be getting her out of town, not offering her a way to stay longer. Then he took in her position, found himself eye level with the most perfect set of breasts, and blamed everything tonight on his dick.

Keeping her away from his sister for the next seven days would be difficult, but keeping his hands off her would be hell. Which was why, even though he felt like he was kicking a litter of puppies, he said, "It would probably be best if you settled down somewhere else after that. I wouldn't imagine you'd find living here...well, there won't be any warm welcome."

And just like that the fire flickered in her eyes, her shoulders went back, and she stood. Had he not straightened with her, she would have taken him out in the process—and smiled while doing it. Even though she was only about five foot four in heels, she somehow managed to stare down her nose at him.

Sworn enemy or not, this woman drove him crazy, and he feared he was starting to like it.

"Thank you for the extension," she said, not an ounce of vulnerability visible, making him wonder if she'd faked the entire panic attack to get extra time in the house. "I don't think you have to worry about my feelings, since I don't believe any welcome could be crueler than yours."

CHAPTER 3

"Wait? She's still here?" Marco asked, resting his pool stick against the wall and dropping onto the nearest bar stool. Gabe's middle brother could barely hold his head up and his eyes were bloodshot. Gabe felt for the guy—he'd recently sunk all of his money into renovating a local hotel. Whereas Marc's sleepless nights came from having more sweat equity than the liquid kind, making it a slow and risky venture, Gabe's stemmed from one fiery brunette with exotic eyes who seemed damn set on ruining his life.

Gabe faced down his brothers over the green felt top of the pool table and pinched the bridge of his nose. "She's still here."

That was the reason all four DeLuca brothers had decided to meet here, at the plaster-sealed wine cave that sat smack in the side of a mountain and doubled as the town's watering hole.

The Spigot was the only place in St. Helena that served something out of the tap, and since it wasn't off the main highway, tourists didn't know it existed. It was loud and dirty and a cash-mandatory, shoes-optional kind of place. And it fit his mood perfectly right about now. Because they needed to come up with a plan—fast.

"I talked to Rocco over at Chiappa Vineyards. Regan interviewed there yesterday."

"And?"

"And the position was no longer available." Gabe leaned down and broke. Not a single ball went in.

"Your game is crap." Trey, the youngest brother, aimed and shot. The one ball went in the right corner pocket, the three ball in the left.

"Tell me about it," Gabe mumbled.

Over the past few days, Regan had interviewed at six different wineries, all owned by friends of Gabe's, and all with the same result: position officially closed.

Gabe stayed true to his promise that wherever Regan went, he'd turn up. Monday, she was having lunch with Alessandro of Graziano Vineyards over at the Martini House. She had just pulled out her portfolio and had Alessandro drooling over her ideas—and her toned legs that were exposed from red-tipped toes to well past midthigh as she leaned over the table to point out some detail—when Gabe sat down and asked if he could join them, effectively ruining Regan's lunch, and her interview.

On Tuesday, while Regan was taking a tour of The Cellar, the premiere wine cave and distributor in the Valley, Gabe showed up to talk with the owner about their new inventory. The DeLucas being one of their biggest customers, Regan's interview was delayed—permanently. Just yesterday he'd been at Picker's Produce, Meats and More, buying some beer and burgers for the Niners' game when he rounded the chip aisle, headed for the buns, and came across the best set he'd ever seen in the produce aisle. Encased in a tight black skirt and offset by a pair of pointy black heels, Regan was squeezing a cantaloupe and looking like some X-rated corporate type with her hair wound up in a complicated knot. All that was missing were the glasses and briefcase.

Instead of slapping a restraining order on him, like most women in her situation would have, she asked him how many quarters he had. When he pulled out five, she chucked two melons at his head and let loose three derogatory words about his sex, then turned on those spiky heels and stormed out, her hips swaying with anger, each step doing stupid things below his belt.

Gabe needed a night to clear his head, and that meant no Regan. Plus, he and his brothers needed to figure out what they were going to do with the woman who was stubborn enough to try and make St. Helena her home.

"So, what cup size are we talking?" Marc asked.

Not the image Gabe needed. But he answered. "Definitely C."

"Was hoping you'd say D."

"Why?"

"Because a woman fitting your description with a full C just walked in and is headed straight for Jordan and Frankie."

"Holy shit," Trey said, his eyes glued to the front door.

Game face firmly intact, Gabe turned in his chair and— Sweet Mother of God. In her tight gray skirt, mile-high heels, and nothing but leg in between, Regan was, in a word, edible.

She gave a cute little wave, and Jordan—the traitor— waved back. So did Frankie and just about every man in a ten-foot radius of their table. Not that Gabe blamed them. Regan wasn't just beautiful, she had something exotic about her that made it impossible not to stare. And everyone was staring. Including Gabe.

"You've been holding out on us," said Nathaniel, the second oldest and, until that moment, Gabe's favorite brother, setting down a pitcher of beer while ogling every delectable inch of Regan.

"Holding out?" Gabe shot for the six ball and missed. "That woman is crazy and unpredictable."

"And hot as hell." Marc leaned back, rocking his stool against the wall, a smug grin on his face. "And here I felt bad for you, spending your days following around some *crazy* woman. She could throw her cantaloupes at me any day of the week."

"For all we know she showed up here to extort money out of us somehow," Nate said, kicking the legs of the stool, which almost sent Marc to the floor and won back Nate's role of favorite sibling. "She knows Abigail is our soft spot. She might try to use that."

Abigail was more than their soft spot. She was their only sister. Which meant that from the time she could walk, Gabe and his brothers had threatened, bullied, or intimidated anyone who even considered looking cross-eyed at her. When she grew boobs and guys started sniffing around, the DeLuca brothers rallied, beating the crap out of every douchebag who tried to get in her pants. Not much had changed over the years. Until Richard.

"And if she shows Frankie her portfolio, Frankie'll hire her in a second," Gabe said, knowing it was true. The woman had skills. And they weren't limited to seduction.

"Frankie would hire her just to screw with us," Nate said, staring at the table.

Francesca Baudouin was the granddaughter of Charles Baudouin, a man who knew his grapes and who, in a desperate attempt to win over the woman of his dreams, had declared his love for ChiChi on the day she married Gabe's grandfather. Fists were thrown, secrets exposed, and the two men walked out of the chapel sworn enemies. Although this generation had avoided the feud, old habits were hard to break. If hiring Regan would screw with the DeLuca clan, Frankie wasn't above it.

Except that people in St. Helena protected what was theirs, and feud or not, the DeLuca name was as old as the vines in the valley. And Gabe knew that Frankie was secretly looking into buying a plot of land to start her own boutique winery. The only other company interested was his...because the plot sat directly between the DeLuca and Baudouin vineyards. Both families had been after that land for over sixty years.

"What if we make Frankie an offer she can't refuse?" Gabe ventured.

"No way." Trey had lined up the five ball for the right side pocket, but when he placed the stick on the table, all that easygoing charm he'd mastered from years of selling the family wine vanished. "I see what you're thinking, and there's no way we're giving up that land. The only thing Nonno asked for when he passed was that the Baudouins never own that land."

"What part of Abigail and Regan meeting don't you get? Hell, the only reason they haven't run into each other is because I've spent the entire week following Regan." Which was messing with his head. Every time she got refused for a job, her stubborn chin would shoot up, her determination would increase, and it was the biggest turn-on in the world.

"Gabe's right," Marc said, flagging down the waitress and ordering a round of scotch before continuing. "If Regan gets that job, then she's here for good."

"You say that like it's a bad thing," said Nate, the resident expert on risk to exposure. Game over, the brothers set their pool sticks down and gathered around the table.

Only two years younger than Gabe, Nate was the self-appointed arbitrator of the family. Over the years, he'd perfected the art of balancing Trey's tendency toward wanderlust, Marc's need for high-stakes living, and Gabe's desire for order. His talent for analyzing calculated risks made him one of the most acclaimed viticulturists in the country. And a big reason DeLuca wines were in such high demand.

"We've been searching for Richard for five years, with no luck," Nate began.

Hunting him down was more like it. As soon as Abby went from victim to suspect in the investigation, Gabe and his brothers hired a guy who specialized in tracking down missing things—thieving SOBs included. Richard hadn't just broken their sister's heart; he'd cleaned out their company's account. Not only was his sister still married to that bastard, since one couldn't serve divorce papers to someone who couldn't be found, she had been left to pick up the pieces of a failed winery and explain to the investors, many of whom were family friends, that they had all been played.

Gabe knew exactly what that felt like. Richard had played him too.

The summer before grad school, Gabe's father had set up an internship for him on a vineyard outside Tuscany, working for a family friend. Richard was apprenticing under one of the winemakers and offered to show Gabe around. He defied rules, took huge risks, and was making his own way in the world of wine—something that Gabe admired, but because of his family name and responsibilities, he could never do.

When the summer ended, Richard convinced Gabe to get him a job at a DeLuca vineyard in Santa Barbara. After Gabe's parents died, Richard stepped in to help run things down in Southern California. The year Abby graduated from college, she was fresh off of a breakup and Richard swooped in. And when his best friend said he wanted to build a winery with Abby, Gabe had lined up the investors—no questions asked.

"Think about it. Why would we chase off the last person to see him? At least before we get some answers. For all we know, Regan is the key to nailing Richard."

"You want me to back off?" No way would Gabe let Regan stay here in St. Helena. He'd just gotten Abby home.

"I'm saying we do whatever it takes to find Richard. And if that means capitalizing on whatever is going on between you two, then—" Nate shrugged.

Gabe blinked. "Nothing is going on."

"Really. Then why are you two straddling the line between eye-fucking and strangling each other?"

Gabe was about to tell Nate to shut up when all three brothers looked over at Frankie's table. Regan had just taken a sip of her wine and her tongue poked out to lick her lips. Gabe heard someone moan. Unfortunately, it was him.

As if hearing him, Regan's head snapped up and they locked eyes. There was a charged beat during which neither one broke contact. The longer they stared, the harder it was to remember that this woman had slept with Richard. Then Regan's gaze dropped to his mouth, jerking back up when Gabe grinned. Making sure to let her know she'd been caught checking him out, he sent her a wink.

Her face folded into a frown and her big blue eyes narrowed. His lowered to take in the silky number she wore, whose top button had come undone, and he saw her swallow—hard.

He couldn't help but smile. Vixen wanted him. Almost as much as he wanted her.

"Let's say I give her a reason to stay," he said, shocked that he was even considering this. "What makes you think Richard still talks to her?"

"A guy doesn't forget a woman like that," Nate said.

And that was quickly becoming Gabe's problem.

"I was sure you'd get it," Jordan said, taking a long swig of wine. "Juliette said they had an opening, and your work is phenomenal. I don't understand what happened."

"Gabe DeLuca happened," Regan mumbled, then finished her wine in one gulp and seriously considered, not for the first time this week, doing something immature, like sticking Randolph right up Gabe's ass...

"Regan." Jordan sat back in her chair, her brows raised, lips pursed in disbelief, reminding Regan of the time she'd been called into the principal's office for shoving Sarah Carter's face in the toilet. Sarah had told everyone that the only reason Regan got into St. Joseph's Academy for Girls was because her mom cleaned the toilets. So Regan wanted to let Sarah see just how clean those toilets were, and that her mom and her career as a cleaning lady were not up for discussion. "I've known the DeLucas since I was a kid. They can be stubborn and annoying, but they don't have a cruel bone in them."

Jordan had also never slept with their sister's husband.

"He showed up at every interview, Jordan. Every single one." Regan worked hard to soften her voice. "I know he's your boss, which makes it that much more amazing that you still want to be seen with me let alone help me find a job, but the man has it out for me and he won't be happy until I am homeless and broke."

"Over a failed marketing campaign?" Jordan scoffed. "I don't think so."

"Is that what he told you?" Regan had to swallow. She also needed another glass of wine. Maybe the whole bottle.

Why would Gabe have lied?

"Don't tell me you were former lovers?" Jordan leaned in, eyes wide with interest. "Because if so, I want details. All of them."

There was no point in lying. Regan had never hidden what she'd done, and her mom had raised her to own up to her mistakes, to learn from them. These women had every right to hear the truth about who they were aligning themselves with.

"We were never lovers." Although, Gabe had been appearing in some pretty steamy dreams lately. "But what I did wasn't very far off."

"Oh my God, you slept with Trey." Frankie looked horrified. "I mean, he is way closer to your age. But he is such an asshat."

"No, I dated Richard for a little over a year."

Jordan was the first to react, her eyes going hard. "You're the one?"

And here it goes, Regan thought.

"Shut your face," Frankie exclaimed, her hand over her chest, the first feminine gesture Regan had witnessed from the winemaker. The chipped nails and thorn-scratched hands ruined the effect. "You slept with Abby's husband?"

"Yes, but before you crucify me and tell me what a slut I am, or that I'm a home-wrecker—" She'd heard it all before. "I had no idea he was married." Something the rat bastard conveniently left out when expressing his undying love and sliding that diamond on her finger.

"How could you not know?" Jordan countered. "Their wedding was all over the society pages."

"I lived in Oregon. I was trusting and stupid and nineteen. I had no idea who Richard was, other than this handsome, sophisticated man from Italy who made me feel special." *And wanted to take care of me.* Something Regan would never let happen again.

"You were nineteen?" Frankie slammed her palms on the table, silencing the entire bar. "He must have been, what?"

"Thirty," Regan whispered, hoping Frankie would take the hint and lower her voice. She didn't.

"Talk about daddy issues."

They had no idea. "Sophomore year of college I interned with the National Vintner's Historical Society for the summer. Richard was my mentor. It was a rough summer, my mom was sick and, well, I found out about Abby the night Gabe found out about me."

Regan had been five months pregnant. They'd been at the restaurant celebrating that they were having a girl.

"Oh. My. God! Is Holly *Richard's?*" Jordan whispered.

Regan nodded. Trusting Richard had been the biggest mistake of her life. Too bad she hadn't been the only one affected. Their relationship had not only broken up a marriage, it put Holly in a place no child should ever be in—unwanted by a parent.

It also got Regan wrapped up in a business venture she should never have been a part of. But she got Holly out of the deal. And that was what was important.

"Richard isn't involved in Holly's life." At all. "He pretty much took off after..."

She looked over her shoulder at Gabe. A slow churning started low in her belly, and when he winked in that I'm-watching-you way, it dropped south. She hated that he hated her, but she understood why. Even more, she hated that she wanted him. How sick was that?

"And pretty much, that's why Gabe is out to ruin my life," she said, turning back to the table.

"Ruin your life?" Frankie snorted. "Girl, you screwed with *the* DeLuca Darling and you still have all your appendages. Impressive. I mean, in the third grade I accidently nailed Abby in the face with a pile of grape pulp."

"How do you *accidently* nail someone in the face?" Jordan asked.

"I was aiming for Trey, who retaliated by holding my head in a vat until it turned my skin blue. Nate pulled us apart, eventually, but we all looked like Smurfs for our school pictures." Frankie glared at the DeLuca table before going on. "And that was before the accident."

"Accident?"

Jordan remained silent, as if speaking of the DeLucas to "the enemy" was a betrayal. Maybe it was. But when she crossed her arms and sat back, purposefully distancing herself from Regan and taking with her any warm fuzzies they had shared, Regan's heart sank to her toes.

Is this what living here would feel like every day? No matter how much she had changed or how many times she tried to right her wrong, was she going to be a constant disappointment?

"I was in college, so Abby must have been sixteen or so. Her parents were driving her back from a music recital when a car veered over the divide on Silverado Trail, killing them."

"Oh, my God. That is horrible." She wondered how old Gabe had been and how losing his parents without warning had affected him. She'd lost her mom to cancer, and it was the most painful experience of her life, but at least she'd had time to say good-bye.

"It gets worse," Jordan finally spoke. Any sign of judgment was replaced with sorrow—for the DeLucas. "No one found them for hours. So Abigail was stuck in the car with her parents as they..." She trailed off, her eyes misty. "They were such a great family. The whole town felt their loss."

Which explained why people were so willing to denounce Regan at one man's request.

"Gabe was back East in grad school," Jordan went on. "The funeral hadn't even ended and already he was thrown into his father's shoes, figuring out how to run a pretty massive wine business and making sure that what his family had spent a century building didn't fall apart."

And that his family didn't fall apart, Regan silently added. This was not what she needed to hear. The more she learned about Gabe, the harder it was to stay angry at him. And the last thing she needed was to start feeling some kind of kinship with the man who had caused her so much pain. She knew what it was like to lose a parent. More importantly, she could connect emotionally with how hard it was to be responsible for a family at such a young age. The only difference was that he'd had his grandmother and siblings and this town. After her mother died, Regan had no one. And just as Gabe would do whatever it took to protect what was his, so would she.

"I've been on the receiving end of the DeLucas' games, and when riled they can be jerks. Ruthless jerks." Whatever emotion was filling Frankie's face went much deeper than childhood pranks. "Intentional or not, they blame you for breaking up their baby sister's marriage. Watch your back."

"If what you say is true, then why would you ever want to come here?" Jordan asked, and Regan shrugged off the slap of her friend's doubt like a pro.

"It didn't take long before everyone in the wine industry in Oregon had heard some rumor about me. Finding steady work has been really hard." She swallowed. "So, when I got the call from my recruiter offering me the job at Ryo Wines, I jumped on it. I had no idea that it was a DeLuca company."

Regan gave one last glance over her shoulder at Gabe's table. He was deep in discussion with the rest of his party, who were all tall, dark, and seriously hot. If the identical black hair and dark mahogany eyes weren't a clue, the sheer amount of testosterone wafting off the four men was as good as a DNA test. That was the DeLuca clan, most likely plotting her downfall.

Gabe looked over. This time there was no arrogant smirk or condescending gleam. She searched his face looking for the truth, for some kind of explanation as to how she'd gotten here. She was used to his anger, but the idea that he would cause her to sacrifice so much just to make a point didn't feel right.

"Ryo is a female-owned and -run winery, ChiChi's brain child. She wanted it to be separate from the DeLuca umbrella. But it's still a DeLuca company." Jordan's face softened. "The DeLucas pretty much run the valley, Regan. There have to be other places you could move."

Regan pulled out the letter she'd kept in her purse all week, the one she'd reread after every devastating blow. It was the same one that Holly had asked her to mail, that she had opened at the cost of a quarter for spying, and that held the words which made moving to a new town impossible.

She stared at the rudimentary letters and, with a sigh, slid it across the table. Even upside down they made her heart hurt for the little girl who had already missed out on so much.

> Dear Santa,
>
> I know youre really busy so you dont have to brings me anything this year cuz I already gots what I wanted. A forever home with my own room and a yard that gots grass and a best friend Lauren. She loves kittys almost as much as me. If you wants you can come to the St. Helena

Community Christmas Muzikal cuz each
kid gets two tickets. I hope I get to play
Christmas Kitty and purr. Mrs. Dee says
I purr really good.

Merry Christmas,
Holly Martin
St. Helena, California

"Oh, honey." Jordan patted Regan's hand. Not that
Regan made a point of using her daughter for sympathy, but
in this case, she'd make an exception. "And here I thought
keeping Ava a virgin until Christmas was going to take a
Christmas miracle."

"Miracle or not, Holly is going to grow up here. She is
going to play with her new friend. And there is no way I am
letting that man chase me out of town. I want this Christmas
to be perfect for Holly. Last year we didn't even have a tree."

"Which is why if I could hire you, I would. Just to stick
it to the DeLucas," Frankie said, way too loud. "But my family outsourced all of our marketing to a company in France
a few years ago. It's cheaper than having someone in-house."

Regan was devastated. She had been sure that having
drinks with the DeLucas' biggest competition, combined
with Jordan's stellar recommendation, would guarantee her
the job. Problem was, there was no job to be guaranteed.

Which brought up a whole new problem: in the Valley,
no job meant no willing landlords. Regan had to fix one
mess before she could fix the other.

"Working for the Baudouins would be like firing the first
shot," Jordan reasoned. "If Regan is going to make a life for

herself here, she has to find a way to get on Gabe's good side. If the head DeLuca accepts her, then the town will follow."

Jordan turned to Regan, her expression serious, exposing just how difficult a task this was going to be. "The DeLucas' reach goes a lot further than wine here, Regan. They own half the businesses in town. And what they don't own, their friends do or they're on the board." Like ChiChi reigning supreme over Holly's school. God, what a mess. "You going to war with him publicly will only hurt *your* family, not his."

Jordan was right. And as far as Regan was concerned, Holly had already suffered enough. So if it meant Regan had to let go of the anger and resentment and the dream that involved her knee and his nuts, then so be it.

"Okay, get Gabe to tolerate me, win the town over, find a job, a new forever home that allows kitties, and all before Sunday when I have to turn over my keys to that ass—"

"Mary over at the Barrel Buyer is looking for an administrative assistant," Frankie cut in, saving her a quarter. "It doesn't come with corporate living or a car, and it's not as sexy as marketing, but it's a job. I'll give her a call and see if she can meet you tomorrow morning."

"And you know you could always crash with me and Ava. The more people in the house, the greater the chance that my daughter won't get a lump of coal and a box of condoms in her stocking."

Regan couldn't form words past the emotions in her throat. Not ones that would express what she was feeling, anyway. She'd only just met these ladies and here they were, putting their reputations on the line to get her interviews.

Offering her places to stay. For the first time in forever, she didn't feel so alone.

"Oh, no," Frankie said, leaning back as far from Regan as she could. "You shed one tear, and I'm out of here. I'm serious. I do not do crying."

"I'm not crying," Regan sniffed.

"Then what the hell is that?" Frankie's hands swirled to encompass Regan's entire face.

"This is the look of a woman who is too happy and too mature to take a pool stick to that behemoth, gas-guzzling man-truck in the parking lot."

Regan could single out Gabe's car at more than a hundred yards. Not a difficult skill, since it had shown up at every interview she'd had.

"And a happy holiday to you too, Vixen," came a voice behind her.

CHAPTER 4

Gabe dragged a chair over from the next table and dropped into it. This was his town, these were his friends, and Regan needed to understand that. "Thought I'd come over and see how St. Helena's newest resident was faring."

Actually, he'd come over to see if his brother's plan was even possible. Not that he would ever sleep with a woman to gain an edge on anything. It wasn't how he was raised. But Nate had a point. Gabe had met Regan once, and, six years later, he could still remember exactly what she had looked like, exactly what she had smelled like. If Richard kept in contact with anyone from his past, it would be her.

"Jordan, Frankie," he acknowledged. When he looked at Regan, heat flickered. He wondered if she was experiencing the same stupid attraction that he was, or if she had a bad case of heartburn.

"Gabe." Her smile was all sunshine and roses, but she spit out his name like it was a four-letter word. Yup, she definitely had it bad for him.

"Regan?" He feigned surprise. "I almost didn't recognize you with that smile on your face. You look so serene and... tame. You must have called my guy."

Regan pressed her lips tightly together, but he still heard a faint "Bah Humbug" come from her general direction.

"If you'll excuse me, I need to be getting home." Smile back in place, she grabbed her purse off the chair. Gabe was supposed to be winning her over, seeing if becoming friendly enough for her to open up to him was even a possibility. A hard task when all he wanted to open were the next two buttons on her blouse.

"Ah, and here I came all the way over here to buy you a drink."

"Maybe another time," she said, smile still holding. "It was—" She stopped, slapped a hand over her mouth, and looked at the other two women, who, eyes wide, cheeks straining, and heads nodding, were definitely sending her all kinds of signals. None of which he could understand.

Big surprise there, buddy.

"It was...?" He prompted her to finish.

"That's all, it just was." She stood, ready to leave.

Now *his* brothers were sending him various kinds of signals, all of which had a matching hand gesture. He knew the only way to play this was to pretend that he wanted her to leave. So he leaned back in his chair, rested his feet on *her* chair, and sent his brothers a cocky nod before wiggling his fingers at Regan in a smart-assed buh-bye.

Game on.

Regan growled. Swinging her purse, she whacked his loafers off the chair and reclaimed her seat. She signaled the waitress and looked him in the eye. Man, she was sexy when she was spitting mad.

"You know what, *Gabe*? I'll take that drink. In fact, let me buy *you* one as a token of my thanks for all you've done for me over the years."

"Ah, there's the girl I know and love." He sat forward and pressed his fingers into her forehead, pulling and massaging until he ironed out the wrinkles. His other hand tugged her lips up into a smile. "Much better."

She swatted his hands away and was about to swat him in the junk when Jordan cleared her throat. Both women were giving Regan a reprimanding wag of the head.

Batting her eyelashes she leaned into Gabe and asked, "What can I get for you? Wine? I hear the new DeLuca Zin is fantastic."

That's more like it. She was set on staying. His friends were back where they should be—in his corner. The other DeLucas were all but high-fiving him from across the room. And if Regan leaned any farther forward, he'd be able to see right down her shirt.

Time to volley.

"Actually I've got a beer over at my table. I came over to let you all know that there's an APB on one missing Randolph."

"Wait, is he the brown one with the red nose?" Regan deadpanned.

"Yes." Gabe leaned forward, making sure to take up all of Regan's space. "He is also a treasured town mascot."

"I heard about that," Frankie said, her face scrunching in anger. "Some idiot destroyed the town Christmas display.

People are pissed and I don't blame them. Every kid in town looks forward to getting their picture taken in the sleigh on Christmas morning."

"I heard they're offering a reward for his safe return." He spoke directly to Regan, who swallowed.

He knew she still had the deer, and he wanted to put the pressure on. A woman like Regan would know something was off if he suddenly went soft. Plus, he'd seen her mad and he knew riling her up was the quickest way to get her to open her mouth. It was also the quickest way to gain information. And if he was lucky, it would win him another glimpse of those Christmas panties.

"You wouldn't happen to know anything about poor Randolph, would you?" Gabe raised a brow.

"Why are you asking me?" Regan said, her voice close to a shriek. "I'm new here."

"You *are* the town vixen." He leaned in, tucking a strand of hair behind her ear.

She closed her eyes and he watched her mouth silently count to three—make that ten—then she dug through her purse. She dropped two bills on the table for her wine and smacked a quarter against his chest.

He eyed the coin and smiled. "What's this for?"

"For *not* saying, 'Have a good night!'"

The next day, Regan finally composed herself enough to pass for a woman who hadn't just spent the past ten minutes bawling her eyes out in the bathroom of a wine distribution center.

She had just finished her last interview, the ninth since Monday, and all she needed was *one* person to believe in her work. She'd foolishly thought that maybe, just maybe, Mary would be that person, the one in town who saw beyond the gaping holes in her employment record and her lack of a degree.

She'd even dropped her rates to the point of slave labor. The administrative assistant job at the Barrel Buyer was the last shot she had at staying here, at giving Holly her Christmas wish.

Hands steady, breathing regulated, Regan splashed some cold water on her neck and face and pulled her purse high on her shoulder. At least Mary had had the professionalism to pretend to peruse Regan's portfolio before giving her the it's-not-you-it's-the-nature-of-the-industry speech. Never once pointing out the Gabe-sized target Sharpied on her back.

Serene smile in place, Regan smoothed her skirt down and, forcing her lips higher at the receptionist's offer of Christmas cheer, shoved through the door and raced out of the office, making sure to drop a dollar in the red charity canister by the exit.

Cold air blasted her while a fine mist of rain trickled down, turning what had been a professional updo into more of a drowned-cat look. Using her portfolio as an umbrella, she clicked her heels down the lamp-lined sidewalk.

The town looked exactly like the photos she and Holly had seen online, only with a little extra spirit from Santa's helpers. Twinkle lights and joyful reindeer decorated nearly every storefront. People smiled and nodded and "afternooned" one another, inquiring about the kids, what the rain would mean for next year's harvest, and if they would be in town for the Christmas musical, as though everyone here was one big family.

With its world famous wines, picturesque downtown, and tourists flooding the streets during the summer and fall months, St. Helena was one of the most visited spots in the Napa Valley. But when winter rolled around, it belonged to the five thousand residents who were lucky enough to call it home.

Regan had hoped to call it home—was still determined to find a way to stay. But her options were running close to empty. She had switched tactics, adapted to her new situation, but the outcome was the same.

Pulling her jacket tighter, she hunkered down and pushed into the rain. What she needed was a Christmas miracle. Just one. Because she wasn't leaving until the big old fat man in red ho-ho-hoed.

She ducked between two garland-covered trees and dodged puddles as she passed the Grapevine Prune and Clip and Stan's Soup and Service Station, coming to a full and startling stop by the town Christmas display.

There, blocking the north corner of Hunt Avenue and surrounded by a million lit candles and enough poinsettias to decorate the Vatican, stood ChiChi, red umbrella in hand, and St. Vincent's Academy's upper-grade glee club singing a haunting rendition of "Grandma Got Run Over by a Reindeer." Regan took in Santa's chipped hat, Dancer's broken hoof, and the spot where Randolph should be standing—except that he was still in her trunk. In his absence was a gilded frame with an aged photo of Randolph standing next to…was that Gabe with glasses, freckles, and a cowlick? Good God, he wasn't kidding when he'd said Randolph was the treasured town relic.

Regan had tried to return the deer last night, but a suspicious gray bun kept peeking out of the window above Pricilla's Patisserie. Afraid she'd get caught red-handed with Red Nose himself, Regan figured it would be best to wait another day or two. Apparently she'd figured wrong. The town had gone into mourning mode.

Not wanting to get caught near the scene of the crime by the sweet woman whose car—and granddaughter's marriage—Regan had destroyed, she whispered some "excuse me's" and slunk past the glee club. Dodging their plastic swaying antlers and shimmying Santa gloves, she reached the other side of the formation and released a deep breath.

"Well, isn't this a surprise," ChiChi said, twirling her umbrella as she tiptoed over a puddle to catch Regan. "Just the woman I was looking for."

"Me?" Regan squeaked. "Why?"

With her round face flush from singing and a halo of gray hair bounding around her cheeks, ChiChi looked more like Mrs. Claus than a wine heiress. But her tone was so stern, Regan felt like she had just been called to the principal's office.

"Yes, dear. I was hoping you could come a few minutes early when picking up Holly. There is something I wanted to speak with you about."

"Me?" Regan repeated, searching her face for some clue as to whether or not Gabe had told her exactly who Regan Martin was. Or if this was the meeting where Regan discovered that Holly's scholarship was no longer valid, since it came with the job.

When the woman just smiled, open and warm, Regan felt herself relax. The idea of disappointing someone who had been so wonderful to her and Holly made her stomach ache. She would eventually have to tell ChiChi who she was, but for now it felt nice to have someone look at her like she was a good person.

"No need to panic." ChiChi patted her on the shoulder. "I wanted to ask you a favor. Why don't we say two o'clock in the theater? I have a little office right off the dressing rooms. That will give you time to grab a cup of coffee and warm up a smidge. Plus, Pricilla makes a peppermint latte that is just shy of heaven."

Regan followed the woman's eyes across Main Street to Pricilla's Patisserie. The two-story brick-faced building had a welcoming red-and-white-striped awning with little dancing elves in the window. It also had the most beautiful cakes in the window, a poster of David Hasselhoff in Christmas garb taped to the door, and a smell wafting out that wasn't even a little shy of heaven.

Regan was cold, wet, and close to tears—a latte sounded perfect.

"Ask for the Christmas Crawl. Pricilla uses homemade schnapps instead of that peppermint crap that the kids like."

"See you at two, then," Regan said as ChiChi smacked Regan's tush and sent her out into traffic with a wink.

She hopped up on the curb and, setting her portfolio case down, pressed her face to the glass and practically had to wipe the drool off the corners of her mouth when she spotted the display case full of chocolate. Light, dark, semisweet, raspberry-filled, white, white with peanut butter, and—sweet baby Jesus—Rocky Road truffles.

Eyes on the goal, she pushed open the door, stepped inside, took one look at a way-too-familiar and way-too-incredible backside in worn denim and walked right back out. She sprinted back across Main Street, cutting around the community park near the town hall, through a puddle that looked sole-deep when in reality it came up to her ankles, all the while with the rain slapping at her face. She flung open her car door, vaulted inside, turned the key, and...

The engine didn't turn over. She tried again.

"Not today!" She thumped her head against the steering wheel several times before letting it rest there. She was soaked, she wanted chocolate, the Grinch had made her forget her portfolio case on the sidewalk, and now her car was flipping her the bird.

She wanted to scream. Actually, she wanted to wad up her consignment-bought suit, shove it in her clunker of a car, and light them both on fire. And if Gabe DeLuca happened to be hiding in her trunk next to Randolph—well, merry freaking Christmas!

Taking off her jacket, she climbed out of her car, her heels sinking into a full gutter of water. Muttering under her breath, she yanked open the hood and disconnected the terminals of the battery.

"You're a mean one, Mr. Grinch," she hummed while scraping off the corrosion that had formed around one terminal before replacing it and doing the same to the next.

She had just hit the chorus and was maneuvering the clampy doohickeys back into place when something musky and sexy skirted past her nose.

She froze, afraid to breathe in any more male. Because with just that one scent, her thighs quivered and the day got that much worse.

Hoping that maybe he would go away if she ignored him, she checked the oil level and the coolant. He only moved closer, proving just how shitty her luck had been lately. Satisfied that the battery was the problem, Regan, resisting the urge to wipe her greasy hands down the front of his pristine shirt and certain she wouldn't dissolve into frustrated tears, spoke into the engine. "Go away."

Gabe leaned around her shoulder and peered under the hood, his body brushing up against her back and doing all kinds of yummy things to her front.

"I believe this is yours." A black portfolio case came into view.

Without looking at him she grabbed her case. "Thank you. Now, go away."

When he didn't move, she slammed the hood shut, his hands jerking back just in time. She smiled—serenely. She wasn't going to let him ruin this already ruined day.

She turned around. Gabe didn't budge, except to block her in further, leaving her wedged between two hard bodies with no place to go.

She frowned.

He smiled. It was a sweet smile of victory that made her stomach squeeze and her palms go moist. Then he looked over her with those deep caramel eyes and something altogether different went moist.

"You're cold."

She followed his line of sight to her blouse, which was white and wet and about as practical as tissue paper in the rain. When she met his eyes, he smiled...again. Crossing her arms, she held her tongue, swallowing a select word or three that desperately needed saying, and mentally replayed Holly's letter.

Slowly.

Centered, she finally spoke. "Mary over at the Barrel Buyer sends her best, by the way. She deemed me unqualified to file papers in under ten minutes." Gabe was so close that she took a step back and bumped into the hood of her car. She forced herself to lean casually against the grille, going for composed. A least she hoped she pulled off composed.

"Mary is a Baudouin, Vixen." He reached out and rested a palm against the hood on either side of her hips, caging her in. Ever so slowly he leaned forward, his arms brushing against the side of her breasts, his lips coming so close to hers that she thought for one crazy, exciting, idiotic second he was going to kiss her.

When he spoke, his breath tickled her mouth. "Which means she is genetically predisposed to screw with my life. Me discouraging her to hire you would have guaranteed you the job. That ten minutes, that was all on you."

His heart was truly two sizes too small.

Gabe looked down at the woman who moments ago had been all piss and vinegar and watched as her shoulders sank and her eyes went flat, making him feel like the biggest sack of shit north of the equator.

Regan was a fighter. But right now she looked a little lost and a lot scared. And no matter how many times he told himself that none of this was his fault, he couldn't get past how devastated she'd been over losing that cottage. Then he remembered why he'd come here.

The game had changed and he was supposed to do whatever it took to keep her here. In St. Helena.

"Look, about the cottage. Sunday is just two days away—"

"I am aware of that. Now, if you could please tell me how much the monthly charge is for the cottage, so I can prorate what I owe you." A blatant "screw you" cut through her polite polish.

"Don't worry about it." He'd never rented out the property, never had a need to.

Not to mention, there was no way in hell Regan could afford two weeks there. Cottage or not, it was one of the oldest historical buildings in the Valley, surrounded by one of the finest vineyards in California.

"It's only fair. You lost income waiting for me to arrive and then I spent the past two weeks there. I don't want you telling people that I ruined an account for you *and* left you high and dry."

So people had been talking. Probably Frankie.

In the spirit of fairness, Gabe shrugged and threw out a random, but *fair*, number. He crossed his arms, waiting for her to get all riled up so he could enjoy the show. But she sat there wide-eyed and mute, her expression washed white. Shame rose swiftly, pounding in his head until it began to ache. What the hell was he doing?

"Listen, about the rent, let's just forget—"

"Would you prefer to give me an address to send the check or just handle this through Jordan?" Her voice wobbled, but he could hear her pride kicking in.

Not wanting to screw this up any more than he already had, Gabe reached into his pocket, extracted a business card, and offered it to her. She took the card, careful not to brush fingers, placed it in her handbag, and sidestepped him.

Opening the door, she leaned over the steering wheel and turned the key. The car sputtered to life, black exhaust expelling from the tailpipe as the keys vibrated from the over-idling of the engine. Wanting to apologize, Gabe placed his palm down on the door frame just as Regan grabbed the handle to open it wider. It slammed back shut.

"What!" She spun around. "What more do you want from me?" Her voice shook and instead of anger, something else entirely shot through his body. This was the moment he and his brothers were waiting for: Regan stripped down to the point where she would talk. All he had to do was push.

But in this instant Gabe didn't care about Richard or the affair or the big picture. He couldn't think past this insane connection he felt or how every time he looked at her it was like someone had kicked him in the gut.

They stood silent for a long moment, the rain coming down harder, yet neither moved.

As the wind gusted, a few wet strands of hair clung to her lips. Gabe reached out, tucking them behind her ear, his finger lingering. He felt more than heard Regan's breath catch, and he knew he was in trouble because his chest was doing some catching of its own. Especially when she worried her lower lip, making it fuller, redder, and wetter.

"The truth, Regan," he whispered gruffly. "That's all I want and then this will end. For both of us."

She stood there, open and vulnerable, her finger tracing the top edge of the side mirror, and nodded. They both knew he was talking about so much more than their rivalry. Just like they both knew that whatever was happening between them, if allowed to grow, would only wind up hurting some-one—most likely Regan.

She studied the ground for a moment, shifting her weight, then looked up at him through rain-spiked lashes. "Do you want to hear that I was stupid? That I gave my heart to a man who lied to me? That for the first time in my life, I was happy that my mom had died so I wouldn't have to see the disappointment in her eyes? Would that make you feel better?"

No, it wouldn't, and it didn't. Because he could see that she had been crushed by Richard. Worse still, Gabe had made her life even harder.

"You'd think business trips over Christmas and Easter would have been a sign that something was up. But I was in love," she croaked out. The look of horror and pain in her eyes was genuine, and at that moment he knew he had made a mistake.

"I didn't cheat on your sister, Gabe. Richard did. I've never even met the woman. But I'm willing to bet she knew as much about me as I knew about her."

When he didn't move, didn't so much as respond, she sagged, her whole body giving in. And this time when her eyes met his, they were filled with tears.

"I don't know how many more times I can apologize. I'm so sorry for hurting your sister. Sorry for trusting Richard. You have no idea how much I've paid for that mistake. In a way, I actually understand why you set out to ruin my life. And your sister...she's lucky to have a family that cares for her so much." She brushed angrily at her cheeks.

Is that what he'd set out to do? Ruin a woman's life? A woman, he admitted, he didn't really even know?

Looking back, he'd only meant to scare her from trying to use her affair to extort money out of the family. He'd done it to protect Abby from more pain, to make up for introducing her to Richard. But when he looked into Regan's face and saw her dump of a car, her well-worn clothes, doubt began to weigh in.

Regan mistook his silence for censure. "Never mind, I don't even know why I bothered." She shoved at his hand, which still secured the door shut. "I answered your question. Now move. I. Said. Move!"

He did, and she jerked the car door open, its rusty hinges groaning under the force. She climbed in and slammed it shut. With the car in reverse, eyes forward, she cracked the window and said, "Life is messy, Gabe. It sucks and it's hard and people get hurt, but they move on. So do me a favor and figure out how long you need to get over this so I don't have to wonder if today is the day when *I* finally get to move on."

CHAPTER 5

At precisely 1:50 p.m., Regan pulled into Holly's school. Situated just east of the main part of town, behind St. Helena Corkery, and on the south side of one of the DeLucas' vineyards, St. Vincent's Academy looked more like a winery than a private school. The main building was faced with hand-shaped stone and boasted two massive wooden doors at its entrance and a front lawn that could easily host an RV-and-boat fair.

It was Friday and raining, and that meant that the parking lot was packed with high-end cars and moms wielding designer galoshes and matching umbrellas. Regan had just finished her second tour of the parking lot when she gave up and parked down the street by the school's Performing Arts Building.

"He's just one man. His opinion doesn't matter," she said, flipping down the visor. She gasped when she saw her face. Eyes red, nose even redder, she looked like a woman who had spent the last seven blocks bawling her eyes out. Which

she had. Because no matter how many times she told herself
that she could do this, that she wouldn't let some man hurt
her again, it didn't stop the tears from coming.

After a good blow of the nose and a new layer of cover-
up, Regan stepped out of the car and, dollar store umbrella
in hand, ran down the block. The wind blasted her, causing
her umbrella to bend backward.

By the time she made it inside the school, she was officially drenched and reality had set in. All she could do now
was find the bathroom, transform herself into some believ-
able form of successful mommy, and then face ChiChi. No
matter what the older woman wanted to talk about, Regan
understood that she would have to withdraw Holly from the
school. She was jobless, practically broke, and, come Sunday,
homeless. Talk about humiliating.

She passed the front office, the glass display case that was
filled with photos of last year's graduates in front of the Arc
de Triomphe, and had just opened the bathroom door when
something caught her eye.

Full-color flyers hung on each stall, one after the next,
all the same, spanning the entire length of the bathroom,
and making Regan's palms sweat.

"Missing: Randolph and Christmas Cheer. A $5,000 reward
for the safe return of St. Helena's most beloved mammal."

It even had the heart-melting photo of Gabe when he was
a boy hugging the ceramic statue. Dropping to her hands
and knees, she checked to ensure that every last stall was
empty. Coast clear, she scrambled to her feet and went to
work, ripping down one, then the next. She got to six when
she noticed that Randolph's sad little face was also plastered
on the insides of the stalls. They must have been posted by

the high school basketball team because some were taped to the ceiling, dangling like banners.

Hiking up her skirt, she closed the lid on the first toilet, crawled on top, and, teetering dangerously on her heels, gave a hard tug on the flyer just as someone cleared their throat. Frozen, hand in mid-rip, Regan turned to find herself staring down at not one but three gawking grannies. Besides their clothes, they looked like a trio of Mrs. Clauses: all with white hair. All with little round glasses perched on their noses. And all looking up at Regan like she had lost her mind.

Regan did what any grown woman would do when caught committing a crime. She stepped off the toilet, shoved the flyers behind her back, and slammed the stall door. Then she sat on the toilet lid and pulled her legs up to her chest.

Maybe if she closed her eyes and waited long enough they would forget that she was in there. And leave.

The seconds ticked by. Regan heard the squeak of someone's orthopedic shoes, followed by the clicking of kitten heels, getting closer. She shut her eyes and rested her head against her knees. She would wait until the Mrs. Clauses left, grab Holly, and e-mail ChiChi with the sad news. They could be halfway back to Oregon before the humiliation of the day's events even hit.

Then what? She had no job or house there either. No real support system. And she would be no closer to securing Holly's Christmas wish.

The stall door flew open, slamming against the wall with enough force to shatter the tiles. Regan opened her eyes and looked at the Mrs. Clauses, who were, surprisingly, smiling.

"Hi, ChiChi," Regan began, wondering how, if at all, she was going to get through this conversation. She had lost her last hope of finding gainful employment in this town. Holly was going to be devastated to lose her forever home with a kitty of her very own and a best friend.

And now Regan was a wanted deer-napper who had, for the second time in so many days, vandalized the property of the one person in the DeLuca clan who had treated her with kindness.

She opened her mouth to apologize, fess up, drop a ten in the Dirty Jar for her sins, when the smaller and rounder of the three, who was holding a basket of pastries and treats, pulled out a truffle and shoved it in Regan's mouth.

"Don't talk, dear, you might say something stupid," she said. And based on the Hasselhoff T-shirt, red boa, and life-altering truffle, Regan assumed that this was Pricilla.

"Oh. My. God," Regan moaned around a mouthful of chocolate and peppermint. "What's in this? It's incredible."

"If I told you, then I'd have to—" Pricilla sliced a finger across her neck, punctuating the gesture with added sound effects.

Regan smiled at her joke. The other women didn't.

The one on the left of ChiChi was dressed in a pair of sexually ambiguous pants and a green men's button-down. She studied the wadded-up flyers in Regan's hands while clutching a scraggly cat, who had an elf hat Velcroed to its head, against her ample bosom in a protective gesture. "Is there something you want to tell us?"

Regan felt the tears well up again.

"Lucinda, don't make the poor girl cry," ChiChi said. "She's had quite a day. Haven't you, dear?"

Regan nodded and wiped at her face with one of the flyers. Lucinda frowned at the pile of crumpled Randolph posters at her feet.

Regan gave an apologetic shrug.

"Yes, well, next time use toilet tissue." Lucinda reached into a denim fanny pack and offered up a gingham handkerchief. "It took us hours to make those flyers."

Regan accepted the cloth, relieved that the older woman was questioning her possession of the flyers and not Mr. Most Wanted himself. After a sniffle, she finally spoke. "I'm sorry, ChiChi. I know you wanted to meet with me about a favor, but—"

"Yes, I had assumed you would come to my office, though." ChiChi's maternal stare locked on Regan, who suddenly felt like she had been given a test and failed.

"Yeah, well"—Regan glanced at the flyers—"I got distracted, and I apologize." She swallowed. "For everything. I know you took a risk hiring me and an even bigger risk recommending Holly to the school. They were already at full capacity and made an exception because of you." She shifted on the toilet seat, the motion causing it to flush. "But things didn't work out," she yelled over the rushing water. "As I'm sure you've already heard I was fired, and so Holly and I won't be staying in St. Helena. So, if you could e-mail me the total costs accrued, that would be great." *Just great.*

All three women exchanged a meaningful glance that Regan couldn't decipher. Then they all smiled and walked closer. Regan wanted to lean back but was afraid she would set off the auto-flush again.

"Let us get this straight—" Pricilla said.

"You want her to bill you for two weeks that you assumed would be free." Lucinda poked Regan in the shoulder. She had surprisingly bony fingers for such a muscular woman.

"It was a perk of working for Ryo, but you intend to pay it back in full?" The corners of ChiChi's lips twitched with something Regan didn't understand, but somehow it reminded her of her mother.

Her fingers strangled the snotty flyers. She hated owing people money, but under the circumstances she saw no other choice. "To be honest, I'm not sure when I'll be able to pay you back, but if we could set up some kind of payment plan...I know that this is probably not a request you receive often, but if you could make an exception." Her throat closed on the last word, making it come out strangled.

"Quite the moxie," Pricilla said.

"Stubborn *and* honest."

"It's refreshing."

"I won't take up any more of your time." Regan stood, smoothing down her skirt, leftover rainwater trickling out the toes of her pumps.

"Sit," ChiChi ordered.

Lucinda's cat hissed, sending a reprimanding glare from beneath the fuzzy white ball at the end of his hat.

"Now, Mr. Puffins," Lucinda cooed, her voice dropping to a soothing singsong.

Over their blue-haired haloes, Regan looked around the room, taking note of the sole exit. Knowing the only way she could escape would be to take out a granny, she grunted and plopped back down on the toilet. Her heart plopped with her.

As if understanding her need to run, the three ladies fanned out, blocking the opening of the stall. *So this is what timeout feels like*, Regan thought, taking in how ridiculous she looked cowering on the too-small toilet.

"Because my bullheaded grandson acted so *incredibly* out of character—" ChiChi paused to smile, as if she found her words *incredibly* amusing. Apparently everyone but Regan saw the amusement, because even the cat was grinning.

Regan could think of a few select and more accurate words than bullheaded to describe Gabe but settled on a nod.

"You are out of a job. And we"—ChiChi glanced at her two friends, who appeared equally as worried—"are in desperate need of a new look."

Regan looked at the St. John's–wearing granny, then down at her own wrinkled and wet suit, and frowned.

"I was talking about the town's public perception," ChiChi clarified with a laugh that let Regan know just how bad she appeared at the moment. "We need to modernize our image without losing all of the tradition that makes this town special. Prove to the people that we aren't a bunch of crazy old bats. Those pushy PTA moms are driving us nuts with social media this and twatting that. The minute they figure out the only thing we know how to do on the Interweb is shop for men—"

"And book trips to Vegas," Pricilla added with an excited nod.

"Not to mention how we lost Randolph..." ChiChi trailed off and made the sign of the cross.

"There's already whispers of impeachment. Our mothers founded the Community Action Committee over seventy years ago, and this silicone, nannyfied, yoga pants–wearing posse—" Lucinda stopped, her hands shaking. The cat hissed. "This is war, Regan, and we need a secret weapon."

Regan scooted to the edge of the toilet. She could be their secret weapon. Last year she had consulted part-time with a high-end kids clothing boutique in Portland, helping them grow their social media presence and attract new clientele. Even though the contract had only lasted six months, she had quickly become a Twitter goddess, creating a black book filled with blogging mommies who could help spread the word, and she hated yoga pants on design alone.

"Hang on, honey," ChiChi said. "I see that got your attention, but before you begin dreaming of Fendi and fittings with Valentino, the actual budget for the position is...well, nonexistent really."

"That damn PTA took away our hiring power after we offered the summer dance instructor position to a stripper we met on one of our trips to Vegas." All three women went dreamy-eyed at Pricilla's words. "He had a marvelous cha-cha."

"PTA or not," ChiChi said, "without us the school's art program would have died out when the dot-com industry went into the crapper. So all we can offer you is a non-paid position, but according to our bylaws, members of the Community Action Committee gain free tuition for all of their offspring. You could build your résumé, and Holly would be able to stay here at St. Vincent's."

"This is so wonderful, but," *I slept with your grandson-in-law!* "I don't have a job or a place to—"

In went another truffle, this one milk chocolate and rum, cutting off all her reasons for why she couldn't stay.

"I would hire you back if I could," ChiChi said, wiping a chocolate smudge off Regan's cheek. "But the family made a decision and I was outvoted. No matter how much I adore you, we are Italian, after all."

Regan wished she was Italian. It sounded safe and warm.

"So I got on the e-mail this morning," Lucinda said proudly. "My cousin, Perkins, says you can rent his place. He owns the St. Helena Corkery."

"You want me to move my daughter into a corkery?"

"Goodness no, that would be silly," Lucinda said, stroking her cat. "He renovated the upstairs into an apartment for when Ruth kicks him out. It's nothing fancy, but it's clean, within walking distance to school, and available immediately."

"What happens when Ruth kicks him out again?"

"He'd sleep in the corkery," she said as if Regan were slow-witted. "Plus, we're Baudouins. The second Perkins heard that Gabriel was giving you a hard time, he offered the space. No credit check needed."

"But she's a DeLuca." Regan pointed her chin at ChiChi.

"I, my dear, am a Ryo. The second oldest family name in the Valley." Her tone told Regan to *never* make that mistake again. "And as such, I never took my husband's name. Created quite a stir in town. Although my husband loved my independent streak." She eyed Regan carefully, her expression turning thoughtful. "You remind me of myself when I was your age, which is why I'm telling you that there is a job at the Napa Grand Hotel with your name on it. Just say the word."

There went the tears again because, God, how long had it been since she'd felt like she had someone in her corner? Not since her mom died.

She closed her eyes and took in the moment, knowing that this feeling wouldn't last. Because they still didn't know who she was—the real reason Gabe had fired her. Not that she got to voice her concerns, because Pricilla shoved another truffle in her mouth.

"Don't fall to your knees yet," ChiChi said. "I believe it's in the house management department."

And just like that, Regan's heart started to ache, either from too much chocolate or from the fact that she was a single mother, homeless, with three hundred dollars in the bank and had just been offered a job as cleaning lady. Just like her mom.

Regan had worked hard not to become a statistic, to build a better life for herself. And here she was looking at a future of sore feet, backaches, and—she glanced down at her glossy nails, trimmed cuticles, soft, clean skin—chapped hands.

Her mother's voice played in her head. *Work is work, mija. As long as it's honest, puts food in your belly, and a roof over your head, there is no reason to feel shame.*

Could she do this? Sacrifice her hard-won dreams to clean toilets?

Yes, she thought without hesitation. For Holly, she could do anything. She would just invest in rubber gloves. Rubber gloves and masks, she amended. The risk of being mistaken for an H1N1 carrier didn't outweigh the exposure to all of the chemicals.

The one thing she was not willing to sacrifice, however, was her integrity. And she knew that she had reached the place in the agenda for her to pull on her big-girl panties and fess up.

"Did you know that Gabe fired me because I had an affair with your grandson-in-law?"

ChiChi snorted, waving her hand dismissively. "Of course, child. Richard always was fond of playing hide the sausage. Interns being his favorite opponents. Now, do we have a deal or not?"

A motor roared and sputtered, then kicked in from right behind Gabe. It was followed by a lot of pounding, banging, and finally Barry Manilow singing "Rockin' Around the Christmas Tree." Gabe rolled over, his face sticking to the leather, and almost fell off the couch.

"Crap," he muttered, pulling a pillow over his head.

"Language," ChiChi scolded from fifteen feet away. The pantry door slammed to punctuate her disapproval.

"It's Sunday." Gabe took in his slacks, button-down, the godawful time of the day and sighed. "And seven. In the morning." Which meant that he'd achieved less than three hours of sleep.

Between figuring out how to get Regan to stay while making sure Abby was insulated and dealing with the marketing disaster that was quickly becoming Ryo Wines, Gabe was spent.

"Which is why I'm baking my famous fruitcake."

Gabe cringed. ChiChi's fruitcakes were famous, all right— famous for causing heartburn and bringing fear into the digestive tracts of thousands.

There went the motor again. Giving up on sleep, and in desperate need of coffee, Gabe pushed himself up and ran a hand through his hair, which from the feel of it was a pretty epic case of bed head. He padded into the kitchen and poured himself a cup of coffee.

ChiChi stood at the island, elbow deep in dough. She immediately began tutting when Gabe leaned against the counter and she saw what he was wearing. Her white coiffed crop shook in judgment while she mumbled something about him needing a wife.

ChiChi had two goals in life: getting her some great-grandbabies and irritating the hell out of her grandkids.

Often they worked in conjunction. She also was known as the town busybody, meaning she was busy being in everybody's business. And if she was here, in his kitchen, on a Sunday morning, then something was up.

"What are you doing here, Nonna?"

"I already said, making a cake." She paused, her penciled brows disappearing into her hairline. "Well, not for you with that look."

"What look?" Gabe forced his face to relax. It wasn't working; just the smell of those candied cherries was messing with his gut.

"The look of horror you get every Christmas when I pull out *the* pan." ChiChi shot him the look that had been able to silence him and his brothers since they were babies. "Don't you believe for one minute that I don't know you toss out my fruitcake when you think I'm not looking. Now Marco"—ChiChi dumped a bowl of flour into the blender, a cloud of white dust covering everything—"he loves my fruitcake."

Marc hated her fruitcake. He fed it to his dog one year and had to get the poor thing's stomach pumped. "Then why don't you cook *that* over at *his* place?"

ChiChi stopped. She had flour on her cheek and molasses dripping all over his counters. "Are you saying you would rather I leave?"

Gabe walked over to his grandma, pulling her in for a one-armed hug and making sure to hold his breath since she had already opened the prunes. "Nah, Nonna. I was just surprised to see you here so early."

"I figured I'd cook you a nice breakfast and we could talk about Christmas. I miss my grandson."

"That sounds nice." Gabe kissed her forehead, not caring that she tasted like rum and cinnamon.

ChiChi smiled and went back to her cake. "Plus, if I made this at Marco's he would think it was for him. I'm making it for that nice young woman, Miss Martin."

Gabe choked on his coffee, the hot liquid scorching his throat.

This was exactly why he'd told his brothers that keeping Regan here was a bad move. The last thing they needed was ChiChi taking Regan under her wing only to be crushed when she discovered who she really was.

"I heard she's leaving town," he said casually when he'd recovered. "Probably won't be here for Christmas."

"That's a shame. I really like her."

"You like everybody."

ChiChi stopped folding in the currants and gave him a pointed look. "I don't like you all that much right now."

"What?"

He must have looked as shocked as he felt because ChiChi placed a hand on his cheek. He could feel the batter stick to his stubble.

"Oh, Gabriel, don't look so hurt. Even though you are a difficult person to like at times, I love you like you're my own."

"I *am* your own."

"I know." She patted his cheek and went back to those prunes. "Which is why I set you up with—what was her name?—the snobby girl who had the fat pumped in her lips and her—"

She gestured to her breasts, batter splattering on the floor, and Gabe closed his eyes.

Snobby? "You like Isabel."

"That woman is entitled and elitist."

Gabe held back a smile. Under her "One Hot Nonna" apron, ChiChi wore a designer pantsuit, diamond bracelet, and earrings that cost more than Vixen's car.

"I see how you are looking at me and stop it. I work hard and love hard, and I have earned every penny I have ever spent. That Isabel is a terrible mother and everyone in town knows that she's just looking for a father for her kids and a last name that will bring credibility to her daddy's plastic cork company."

ChiChi was the most independent, hardworking woman Gabe had ever met. Even though she'd married into the DeLuca family, she had worked that field every crush, and when Gabe's grandfather died, she'd stepped in to take over as head winemaker for DeLuca until Nate was old enough. To this day her opinion still reigned supreme when it came to creating new blends.

"Then why did you sucker me into taking Isabel to the company Christmas party?"

"Because she's had her eye on you since even before she lost that wedding ring of hers." ChiChi gave one final mix and then scooped the batter into the pan. It landed with a loud thwack. "I was afraid that she'd corner you when you were alone and use her synthetic wiles to get into your bed."

Her synthetic wiles had already been in his bed after husband number two walked and before number three entered the scene. And that was not something he wanted to relive anytime soon. Sure she was hot in that pampered socialite kind of way, but Gabe was looking for a good time and the last thing he wanted was an instant family. He'd already raised one and had no intention of signing on for another. "So you set me up with someone you don't like? That makes no sense at all."

ChiChi slid the cake in the oven, washed her hands, and, ignoring the disaster she had made of his kitchen, took a seat at the table, gesturing for Gabe to do the same.

"I wanted you to see what your life would be like if you didn't pull your head out of your backside. To show you how being selfish can spoil you."

Selfish? That pissed him off. If anything he was sel*fless*. The fact that his family kept overlooking what he'd given up really hurt. Normally it didn't bug him, but lately, ever since Regan had come into town, he'd started to resent it.

"When Mom and Dad died—"

ChiChi closed her eyes and made the sign of the cross. When she was done with her "God blesses" and "Lord rest their souls," he continued.

"I stepped into a position that I never asked for." Or wanted. "I walked away from art school, my friends, everything, so that this family could keep functioning. I became a parent to Abby, Marco, Trey, and, to an extent, Nate. I stepped in as president of a company that Dad had mismanaged for so long it was barely turning a profit, and lost—"

Jasmine. After all these years, Gabe couldn't even say her name out loud. It wasn't that he was still in love with her, it was that the one person who he'd counted on, had pictured building a future with, had walked. At the most difficult time of his life. Taking with her every dream he'd created for the future.

ChiChi patted his hand, her eyes soft with understanding. "We know what you sacrificed, how unhappy you are. You

may never say it, but you wear it on your sleeve as a badge
to remind us daily."

Did he? Gabe tried so hard to fill his father's shoes, to
be the kind of man his mother would have been proud of
and the kind of man his siblings could depend on, but he'd
never meant to make his family feel guilty.

ChiChi walked to the fridge, and when she returned she
had a glass of milk in one hand and was balancing a plate full
of Pricilla's pastries—including his favorite, a mascarpone
cheese danish—in the other. As with all Italian grandmoth-
ers, food was her solution to everything.

"Do you know when I fell in love with your grandfather?"

Gabe couldn't help but smile. He'd heard this story a
million times. "When Grandpa stole that Merlot blend you
were secretly making in your dad's cellar and placed it in
the Summer Wine Showdown." Because even in those days
a woman couldn't enter. "And when it took first place, he
told everyone that it was yours."

"That"—ChiChi sighed, clutching her locket that held
a photo of Grandpa DeLuca—"*and* he deflowered me the
same night. Your great-grandfather Ryo threatened to shoot
his balls off if he didn't make an honest woman out of me."

Gabe swallowed his bite whole.

Her expression fell serious. "That was why I married him,
Gabe. But I fell in love with him when he ate my fruitcake
and asked for seconds."

"Grandpa liked your fruitcake?"

"Don't sound so horrified." ChiChi laughed. "And no, he
hated it. But he loved me enough to let me fail, and believe
it or not, over the years it's gotten better."

Gabe's respect for his grandfather just quadrupled.

"What I'm saying is, stop smothering your siblings. Let them fail and find their way through the pain on their own. You're so busy running everyone else's lives that you're missing your own."

Gabe didn't think of it as running his siblings' lives so much as avoiding avoidable disasters. Nate, trying to pick up the slack after losing Regan, had hired a marketing team out of Chicago that was determined to make Ryo Wines appear like they belonged in a box. Marco was in over his head with his new hotel. Trey had made a life of new day, new country, new girl, and if he wasn't careful he'd wind up in an early grave. Abby was so trusting and sweet that she attracted every SOB in a pair of slacks and loafers. And now, with Regan in town and—

"See, there you go again. You're already plotting out how to save the family."

"I just don't want them to get hurt."

"And you think running Richard's mistress out of town will help Abigail?" ChiChi picked up a scone and, pinkie raised like a lady, took an enormous bite. "That sister of yours needs to own up to the fact that Richard was a cheat. She knew it and married him anyway. Can't spend her life blaming the sheep when she watched her wolf get clothed every day."

"You knew that Regan was Richard's mistress?"

"It's why I sent her the job offer. Poor girl deserves a second chance at happiness." She reached over and pinched his cheek. "Just like you do."

CHAPTER 6

"Okay, angel. Hands up and then we finish packing your room."

Regan pulled a pink T-shirt with two kittens across the front over Holly's head and slid her arms through the sleeve holes. With a quick twist of the wrist she began securing Holly's silky curls into two tiny pigtails resembling little chocolate fountains poking out on either side of her head.

"But the bird's nest," Holly said, her body shaking with excitement.

Last week they had discovered a hummingbird nest in the tree adjacent to the kitchen window. They hadn't seen any hummingbirds, but Holly still checked every morning.

"It will still be there when I'm done with your hair. The stiller you are, the faster I can go." Holly froze while Regan twisted the last rubber band in place.

When standing still became too much, she lifted her little arms and wrapped them around Regan's neck.

Regan crushed her daughter tight, breathing her in and sending up a silent thank you to her Mrs. Clauses. All of the uncertainty that had been churning since the night of the Christmas party had taken its toll.

You just have to make it through today, she thought. Because today was the last day of Regan's old life, the last day of her old dreams. Tomorrow was another day with new direction. And it would be worth it, she reminded herself, holding Holly even closer. The chance to raise her daughter in St. Helena would be worth every sacrifice: the long hours, toothpaste-stained sinks, and soap-scummed showers.

Holly wiggled out of reach, and without another word dashed down the hallway, her pigtails bouncing with each step.

Regan looked around at the cottage, with its two bedrooms, hardwood floors, and even the avocado-green tile, and swallowed hard. They were moving into a one-bedroom apartment with white walls, gray carpet, and venetian blinds. It would smell of carpet cleaner, paint, and bleach.

Not the end of the world. She could make this work. *Would* make this work.

"Two minutes, young lady. Then we need to pack up your books," she called.

Regan opened her underwear drawer and started tossing lace and satin—and a depressing amount of cotton—into a box. Not willing to admit that she was in serious need of some new lingerie, she stuffed the practical panties at the bottom of the box and draped the sexy and slinky ones over the top. She'd just folded the flaps over when the doorbell sounded.

Hoisting the box in her arms, she grabbed the tape and made her way to the front door. ChiChi had said she would come by to help keep an eye on Holly so Regan could take the first load to the new place. The thought of how wonderful her three Mrs. Clauses had been over the past two days made her perk up as she opened the door.

Her smile vanished and something entirely inappropriate began to burn low in her belly.

Even in faded jeans and a worn Stanford T-shirt, Gabe looked expensive and full of himself—and good enough to strip down and lick. His dark hair, still damp from a shower, was rumpled like he'd just run his fingers through it, and based on the shadow of stubble, he hadn't even bothered to shave.

Gabe DeLuca was a perfect specimen of the male sex. And suddenly, the only thing she could think about was sex. With him. And that incredible package Jordan talked about. Which she was currently gawking at.

Gabe cleared his throat and Regan jerked her eyes up, away from his prize-winning package to his face that was crinkled into a knowing grin.

"Morning, Vixen," he said in that low, you-know-you-want-me voice.

She scowled by way of greeting. His eyes dipped to the floor and Regan squeaked. Somehow in the process of mentally stripping him down, she had dropped the box and now her entryway looked like Victoria's Secret after a two-for-one blowout.

"Let me help with that," Gabe offered.

"I got it."

They both bent down at the same time, Regan scrambling to shove handfuls of panties back into the box, Gabe pulling them back out one by one to inspect them.

Satisfied that she had gotten every last scrap, Regan yanked the yellow demibra out of Gabe's long, lean fingers, dropped it in the box, slammed the flaps shut, smacked away his hands, and taped it securely. She stood, ready to give him an earful. Her day was stressful enough without having to deal with him.

Only, when she looked up she was speechless. Between Gabe's two pointer fingers, the elastic stretched tight, hung a pair of red panties with a big green bow and "Merry Christmas, Love, Santa" across the crotch.

His lips twitched. "I didn't know we were exchanging gifts. I think you have to be wearing it for the full effect, though."

Ignoring the way her toes curled into the rug, she snatched the panties and shoved them in her back pocket. "Do you have a reason for being here? Other than to bother me?"

"I was supposed to come bearing fruitcake, care of ChiChi. But—" Gabe picked up a pastry box off the porch bench. Oh, God, he brought doughnuts? She loved doughnuts. "I stopped by Pricilla's and picked up these instead."

"Why?" She tried to feign disinterest but found herself sniffing the air for hints of maple.

"Because ChiChi's fruitcake has been known to cause copious amounts of vomiting, and I didn't want you to accuse me of digestive assault with a deadly fruitcake."

Regan refused to smile. Even though, when Gabe wasn't getting her fired or kicking her out of parties, he was charming. And she *could* smell the faintest hint of maple. Oh, boy, she was a goner.

"No, I mean, why are you here?"

"I heard you were moving and—"

"Oh." Of course. Her heart sank.

Disappointed and mad at herself for feeling disappointed, Regan grabbed her purse off of the table by the door, riffled through it, and extracted an envelope with his name on it. Forcing herself to look him in the eye, she explained, "I don't have it all. But I hope this will be enough for now. I'll send you a payment every week until it's paid off."

Gabe just stared at the envelope. When he didn't make a move to take it, Regan leaned around him and stuck it in his butt pocket, making sure *not* to notice how firm his ass was, or how yummy he smelled, or how her heart picked up when his eyes lit with humor. Nor did she succumb to lust and give him a firm little pat on that incredibly pat-able butt.

"Look, Regan. I didn't come here to—"

Gabe's words were cut short by what sounded like a small herd of elephants stampeding down the hardwood floor. The thundering drew to a close, only to be replaced by a shrill squeal that was nothing short of pure, uncontained joy.

"Mommy, he brought us doughnuts!"

Gabe looked at the tiny bundle of excitement jumping up and down, and froze. His face went slack and his eyes widened with shock.

He didn't know?

Holly's hands alternating between clapping and pointing at the pink box in his possession only made his discomfort more obvious. Regan closed her eyes. This was not what she needed today.

Wrapping an arm around her daughter's shoulders, she pulled Holly into the shelter of her body and pinned Gabe with a glare, hard and determined. Neither spoke, but the message was clear: Mess with my kid and I will fuck you up.

"Mommy," Holly whispered, eyeing the Dirty Jar. "You should introduce me. It's only polite."

Regan nodded. "Holly, this is Mr. DeLuca. Gabe, my daughter, Holly."

She knew the moment he figured out who Holly's father was. It didn't take much. Holly was the perfect combination of her and Richard. At least physically.

"Nice to meet you," Holly said, sticking out a hand that had a brown smudge that looked suspiciously like peanut butter.

Regan sent a questioning glance at the undeniable evidence of pre-breakfast nibbling. Holly swayed nervously and quickly wiped the evidence off on her jean-clad legs before reoffering her hand. "Can I have a doughnut? It's polite to share."

Gabe's mouth opened and shut, his chest rising and falling faster than seemed healthy. With a single nod, he offered Holly the entire box of pastries. Sucker.

Regan almost felt sorry for him. Okay, she didn't feel sorry at all. It felt nice to see Mr. Laid Back squirm.

Holly peeked under the lid and clutched the treasured pink box to her chest. Eyes squinted, face scrunched in concentration, she tilted her head and studied Gabe—tall, dark, and undoubtedly feeling guilty as hell. Regan almost snorted.

After long deliberation, Holly eyed the Dirty Jar and frowned. "He didn't shake my hand, but he brought the ones with the pink sprinkles on top."

Regan smiled at her daughter's dilemma. The law was the law. But doughnuts were doughnuts. She also admired her daughter's ability to gracefully break the tension in the room. The moment Holly opened her mouth, Gabe's horrified expression faded and a charmed smile hovered on his lips. He squatted down and extended his hand.

"It's a pleasure to meet you, Holly. I seem to have left my manners at home." Holly easily accepted his excuse and hand, pumping it like a politician.

"He's sorry 'bout the bad manners, Mommy." Holly looked back and forth between the two adults. "Does he have to put a quarter in the Dirty Jar?"

At that Gabe raised a brow. "Dirty Jar?"

"Yup, whenever Mommy or I do something dirty or impolite we have to put a quarter in the Dirty Jar."

"Ah," he stood, pinning Regan with a look. "So, if your mom were to, say, call someone a bad name or throw a melon at someone's head she'd have to—"

"Pay fifty cents," Holly said proudly. "We collected enough quarters to go to the movies *and* buy popcorn when we got stuck in traffic moving here."

"I'll bet," Gabe said, hands in belt loops, rocking back on his heels.

"Holly, why don't you take those in the kitchen and put one on a napkin," Regan instructed.

Holly flew down the hallway, the box teetering dangerously in her greedy little palms.

"Do you need to go help her?"

"No." What she needed was for him to leave.

Gabe watched Holly disappear, then took stock of the Dirty Jar. His right eyebrow twitched, and the look he gave her was 100 percent Dirty Jar–worthy.

"Since I ran into you, I've practically paid for two years at Stanford for her." Regan laughed, but quickly realized that she was the only one laughing. Gabe looked pained and a bit constipated.

"Is she Richar—"

"She's mine." Richard may have donated the sperm, but that's where his influence ended.

"She's beautiful," Gabe said. "Like her mom." A heated gaze swept down her body and made its way back to lock with hers. His assessment wasn't filled with disgust but an appreciation so primal Regan looked at the floor and toed at the corner of the entry rug.

How was it possible to be turned on by the one person who had caused her so much pain?

"Why are you here?"

"I came to see if you needed help loading up."

"Of course you did." Too bad for him she was only moving two miles away. "Well, thanks, but no thanks."

She went to slam the door—in his face—when he shoved his foot in the doorjamb.

"Wait, that came out wrong. ChiChi mentioned that you got a place over by the school." So he knew. She frowned, mentally kicking herself for wondering how he felt about it. "I figured I have a truck that would make moving your things easier than trying to fit it all in your car. Plus, an extra set of arms always helps."

Regan remained silent, her eyes trained on his face, unconvinced. If she looked down at that extra set of arms, she'd give in. Because he had really nice arms. A nice chest too. And his lips—

"Also, I wanted to apologize for my behavior last weekend."

Regan found herself smiling, pleasantly stunned that the most irritating, high-handed man she knew was actually apologizing. To her.

Still, she wanted him to sweat it out.

"And the other day downtown." Gabe cleared his throat and ran a hand through his already messy hair. "Actually, I wanted to apologize for just about everything I've ever said or done since the moment we met."

Regan blinked. Twice, actually, and considered what to say.

She had rehearsed this moment a thousand times. Yet standing there, while he sincerely made his apologies, her scathing reply somehow stuck in her throat. Her anger faded and all she could think about was how his heartfelt contrition made her warm in places she didn't want to acknowledge.

"Did ChiChi make you say that?"

"No. I've been trying to say it for a couple of days now, but every time I get around you I end up making everything worse."

She knew exactly how he felt.

"That's the last of it," Gabe called out, biting back a disgusted grunt and dropping a box on the carpet next to the patio door.

Patio didn't even begin to describe the six-foot concrete square that sat behind Regan's apartment. Rolling his shoulders, he scanned the interior of her new home. This time he did grunt. No matter how she decided to dress it, the four sterile walls, two single-paned windows, and industrial sludge–colored carpet wouldn't amount to much more than a crappy apartment. Nowhere near the home that a little girl deserved come Christmas morning. Hell, he didn't even think there would be room for a tree once they brought Regan's furniture over.

Gabe made his way to the bedroom and leaned against the door frame, his body suddenly heavy. Holly was curled up in a sleeping bag on the floor. Her eyes fluttered shut and snapped back open, fighting naptime while Regan read from a book with a kitten on the cover.

Closing his eyes, Gabe listened to her hushed voice, which to him sounded sleep-roughened and husky, and it made him want to crawl into bed too. But only if it included Regan, naked and eight uninterrupted, kid-free hours.

She came to the end of the book, leaned over, and pressed a kiss to Holly's forehead, her jeans riding low and her shirt high as she bent over, exposing a tiny mark on her right hip that Gabe would have never guessed existed. Vixen had a tattoo. A little green bundle of leaves.

The distance made it impossible to determine for sure, but he was pretty confident that under those business suits and polished professionalism, she was sporting a holly leaf tattoo. He wondered what other secrets she had hidden and knew it would take a whole lot more than one night to discover each and every one of them. And he was up for the task.

When she'd answered the door earlier, face flushed from packing, hair pulled back into a messy ponytail, elbow deep in lingerie, all he could think about was what kind of panties she was wearing. And if they too had a big bow that he could slowly untie to get to her present. And who, if anyone, currently had their name on that particular box.

She, on the other hand, had looked like she wanted to punch someone. He'd bet good money that that someone was him. He considered puffing out his chest and offering her a free swing or two, on the house, to help her burn off some of that pent-up anger. Then he came up with a bunch of other ways to blow off steam and was about to tell her each and every one in great detail when Holly came bounding down the hall.

At that moment, Gabe realized that the only help he should be offering was to make the Martin ladies' lives easier, not further complicating it. Which was why when he finished helping unload, Gabe was going to wish them well in their new life, somehow explain to his family that Regan wasn't a threat, and do his best to stay away.

"Sleep tight, angel," Regan said.

"But I'm not sleepy," Holly protested, her lids halfway closed.

"Well, how 'bout I come back and check on you in twenty minutes, and if you're still awake, then no nap. Deal?"

"Twenty minutes!"

"That's my final offer."

Holly's eyes narrowed and her arms crossed as she considered her mom's compromise. With a nod she conceded, but her frown said that she was not happy about it.

Holly spotted Gabe in the doorway and her face lit up. "Mr. DeLuca. You gonna be here when I wake up?"

"I should be." He turned to address Regan, who looked so damn sweet holding her daughter that he forgot what he was going to say. She quirked a brow. He smiled back.

"I was going to call my brother, Marc. See if he'd meet me at the cottage and help me load up the rest of your stuff.

That way Holly can sleep, and you don't have to worry about the clouds opening up again."

They had been lucky. That morning there was a lull in the normal December showers in the Valley, making the move much easier than expected so far. By the looks of the dark clouds coming in over the mountains, though, their luck was quickly running out and they were in for a pretty bad downpour.

Regan's face went red. "There's nothing else left. We've moved it all."

Gabe looked at the bedroom, which, much like the front room, held only a few boxes and three suitcases. "But the furniture—"

"It came with the cottage. None of it was ours. But we're looking forward to camping out in our bedroom," she said with overdone excitement, tickling Holly in the ribs.

"Mommy says we're gonna camp on the floor, but we can't have a fire 'cuz it's against the law and dangerous." Holly folded her hands under her cheek, snuggling deeper into her pillow.

He looked at Regan. "Are you serious? You can't live in a sleeping bag." He regretted his tone the moment little Holly's face fell. He looked at Regan, expecting her to laugh it off because there was no way that they could live here. Not like this.

Regan didn't laugh. She didn't even smile. Instead her face hardened, and she gave him the same look she'd given him earlier when he'd first met Holly.

"Could you please wait for me in the front room?" Regan said, clearly dismissing him.

He went. But this conversation was not over. Mama bear claws out or not, there was no way those two were going to sleep here with nothing but a few clothes, a box of books, and a ratty old sleeping bag.

Regan leaned down for one last peanut butter-and-honey-flavored kiss. "Tonight, it's just you, me, and the great outdoors."

"Can we make s'mores?"

Regan thought of the microwave, mentally added graham crackers, marshmallows, and chocolate to her grocery list, and nodded. "And hot dogs?"

Holly nodded excitedly. Closing the blinds, Regan headed for the front room, soft breathing already emanating from the sleeping bag.

Her breathing, however, was coming fast and furious.

"What the hell are you thinking?" Gabe said the second the door slid closed. It was part statement–part question, and completely judgmental. "You can't let her sleep on the floor."

Regan marched across the room, glaring the whole way. "Don't you *ever* tell me how to raise my daughter. Do you think *this* is what I want for her?"

"I'm sorry, but it just can't be good." His eyes raked over the dismal apartment. It wasn't the Ritz, but she and Holly had survived worse. And they would survive this.

"Kids do it all the time at sleepovers. This is no different."

"Sleepovers don't smell like…God, what is that?" Gabe sniffed the air. "It's like wet dog or—"

"I live above a corkery, which aside from the smell—" Regan held her breath. It didn't smell like wet dog, it smelled worse. "Can be a cool place to live when you're a kid. But the minute you start questioning, she'll go from feeling like this is an adventure to feeling like she should be ashamed of her...of where we live." She couldn't stomach using the word *home* to describe their current living condition.

Gabe closed his eyes and took a deep breath. "You're right, I'm sorry. I didn't mean to overstep."

"I know this isn't ideal, but I am doing the best I can." Regan leaned against the wall, so tired that it took everything she had not to cry. Or hyperventilate. "Please...don't ruin this for us."

Gripping the back of his neck, Gabe stared at the ceiling. "Look, why don't I load up some of the furniture from the cottage and bring it over."

Like that was going to happen. Martin women made their own way. "We'll manage just fine."

"Let me help you. This is partly my fault."

"Partly?" Was this guy serious?

"Christ, Regan. I can't leave you two here in this—"

"Careful," Regan said, stepping forward again and poking him in the chest. "You're about to say something about my home. And I know that compared to your Armani McMansion this seems like a pathetic little dump. But it's my pathetic little dump."

The past week had drained her, played on every one of her insecurities. And being here with him, like he was today, had thrown her off balance. Gabe DeLuca could be charming, funny, even gentle when he wanted to be, which for her was more dangerous than the asshole she'd come to know and loathe. Problem was, reconciling him with that guy who'd been determined to ruin her life was becoming more and more difficult. And that made her nervous.

When he was going for the jugular, Regan knew how to respond. Because there, at least, she understood the rules. So of course Gabe had to go and say, "You're right, Regan. And I'm sorry."

"You've started saying that a lot."

"Only to you," he whispered, tugging on her ponytail and—oh boy—her stomach did a funny little flip right up into her chest. Not good.

"And I mean it every time. I am so sorry." He opened his mouth to say more, but instead of speaking he took a step closer.

Regan's fingers wouldn't listen to reason. They tangled in his shirt, pulling him even closer. She could feel the strong beat of his heart vibrate under her hand and wondered what it would feel like to fall asleep listening to that.

Gabe's head tilted to look at her hand, which was now splayed over his chest, and she felt his pulse speed up. His head didn't move, but his eyes flew to hers. They were the most intense shade of brown and so heavy with want that Regan felt her whole body actually tingle with awareness.

When Gabe reached out, his hand sliding into her hair and tipping her face to his, three things hit her all at once. First, she knew that he was going to kiss her. Knew that it would be the kind of kiss that would literally change the game. And once it happened there would be no stopping it.

Because—and this was where the second realization came into play—kissing Gabe would lead to one hot roll in the sack. And since the only kind of sack Regan owned had a zipper and a sleeping five-year-old, any sacking would be had in the bed of a man whose family—minus a meddling grandma—hated her. Which was a one-night roll straight into disaster.

Finally, Gabe would be an incredible lover. Although he was six-plus feet of muscle and sexy male, he also had a gentleness about him. She had seen it in the way he treated his grandmother and how patiently he sat while Holly carefully wrapped each and every toy in bubble wrap before letting him place it in the moving box. And she felt it now in the way his hands confidently held her to him, while his finger gently traced her lower lip.

This was a man who would ruin her. Not just for other men, but period. Because there was no future for them, and she was afraid that after him there would be no going back.

Knowing all that, Regan realized that she was in trouble. This kiss was going to happen, and there was nothing she could do to stop it. So instead of telling him no, she slid her arms around his neck and stepped flush with him, something quivering deep in her belly when his arm tightened around her waist.

"This is crazy," he whispered, and before she could agree his mouth was on hers.

Slow and gentle, his lips cradling hers. He tilted his head, taking the kiss deeper and making every single synapse in her brain fire simultaneously.

Holy Mother of God, the man could kiss. They hadn't even made it past first base and Regan's head was spinning. Which was why, she told herself, when Gabe eased back she found herself practically crawling up his chest with her hands fisted in his hair.

"Wow," was all she could manage, and even that came out breathy. Gabe smirked and she smirked back, until reality set in. And she understood how incredibly stupid they'd both just been.

He must have sensed her withdraw, because they both let go of each other at the same time and took a gigantic step back.

"We can't—"

"I know—"

"That was—"

"Hot as hell—"

"This can't happen again."

"Agreed," Gabe said with a decisive nod. Then he grabbed a stack of boxes and headed for the door.

"What are you doing?"

"Moving you back to the cottage," he said, halfway to the front door. "You can stay until you find something"—he shot her a look over his shoulder—"furnished."

Regan was on him in two strides. She reached for the boxes, but when he merely raised them over his head and out of reach, she wedged herself between his massive body and the door frame. "Are you offering me my job back?"

Gabe released a sigh, his shoulders slumping slightly. Not a good sign.

"I can't, Vixen. I can't risk you and Abby running into each other. Plus she's a partner in Ryo. ChiChi might be the face of Ryo, but Abby's the passion behind it."

"And you think me living in the cottage is going to solve that problem?" Regan's stomach sank to her toes. "Gabe, we live in the same town, we're bound to run into each other. Me and Holly living on Ryo's property is a guarantee that we will run into each other. A lot."

"Damn it, Regan. What do you want me to do?"

"Give me my job back," she said, tired of always getting the sucky end of the straw. Gabe dutifully went to the extreme to protect his family; Regan would do the same.

"Move in with me."

"What?" There was no way she'd heard him right. "You can't be serious."

"Can and am. I have way too much space for one guy and"—he looked around, genuine regret in his eyes—"this place is way too small for the two of you."

Regan shook her head, which was only adding to the ache that had been growing there since she'd run into him in the parking lot two weeks ago. If he kept looking at her like that, the ache would drop to her heart.

"Listen." He set the boxes down and, after prying her hands off the door frame, took them in his. "I fucked up. Big time. I never intended for you to end up here. All I was trying to do was protect my sister. Let me fix this." She opened her mouth, but he went on. "I've got three spare rooms. My place is so big, we won't even see each other. And Holly will be close to the school."

"She's close now."

"So are the local dealers and punk-ass kids who'll steal your tires."

"I know where I live, Gabe. And I don't need you to fix my life." Although if he kept stroking his thumb over her wrists, she might melt into a puddle at his feet. "You and I living in the same space—" She shook her head. "We just agreed that taking this…attraction any further could never happen."

"I never said that."

"Yes, you did."

"No. I agreed that you and Holly can't end up in a shithole again. I never said anything about not kissing you again." He wagged a brow. "Or sex being off the table."

God, sex. Something Regan had accepted that she would never have again. Between being heartbroken, her mom dying, and raising Holly, she hadn't had a man-made orgasm in six long years. But single motherhood didn't leave time for men, and Holly was her main focus right now.

Plus, Regan had already learned her lesson with regard to relying on someone else for survival. It was too hard when they walked away. And with women like her, they always walked away.

"I don't date."

"Ever?" He sounded shocked. And she guessed it did sound weird. She was only twenty-seven, and already she had resigned herself to the life of a retiree. Although, she'd worked at a retirement community for a few months and those people had sex. A lot of sex. Which made her next admission a bit embarrassing.

"Not since Richard. Holly is my number one priority right now. And think of how your family would react to you living with Richard's ex-mistress." His panicked expression proved her point. Even though it shouldn't sting, it did. "I won't put Holly through that. Or myself." Not again.

"I don't know how to fix this."

His voice broke her heart. Here was a guy, a surprisingly good guy, who just wanted to keep everyone safe. She admired that, even though she knew from experience that it was an impossible goal to keep.

"You already did," she whispered. "By making my kid feel like she matters. And helping me through a really hard day."

Slowly she extracted one hand and fished through her front pocket. She closed her eyes when her finger brushed metal. Taking Gabe's hand, she maneuvered it palm up and placed the item in it before closing his fingers around it.

"So this is where I say, 'Thank you, Gabe, for all your help.'" She stretched up on the tips of her toes and brushed his cheek with her lips, her hand still covering his. "And you say, 'No problem. See you around, Vixen.'"

The moment her hand was free of his, the weight was lifted, releasing her from the past. He had given her the moment she was desperate for, the day when she got to move on with her life, free of the guilt and regret. Regan wanted to smile, laugh, and cry—all at the same time. But she would wait until she was alone and Holly was in bed for the night.

Gabe opened his fingers and froze. His eyes flickered to her and back to the platinum and diamond band that lay on his open palm. It was as beautiful as it had been the night Richard slid it on her finger. Only now, when she looked at it, she saw it for what it was, a stunning piece of twisted metal and crystallized carbon.

"Why?" was all he said, but that one word held so much pain.

"I saw how you looked at it the night we met. You search my hands every time we run into each other. I figured Richard didn't get it at an estate sale."

Gabe's fingers traced the filigree scrollwork on the antique band. "It was my mom's. My dad got it for her on their twenty-fifth anniversary. Abby thought she had lost it. "

"Well then, I'm glad it's back with the right family."

She stepped back and held open the door. But Gabe didn't leave. Instead he studied her much like his grandmother had.

Yet the pain in his eyes when he looked back at the ring, clutching it as if he was afraid he might lose it, tugged at her heart. Because *that* feeling Regan connected with in a way that only someone who had lost something precious could.

"Now, it's your turn, Gabe."

She could tell he didn't want to leave. But she needed him to because she was one heartbeat away from falling for him.

"No problem. See you around, Vixen." He hugged her and Regan found herself clinging to his strength. Giving herself just a moment to pretend that she was the kind of woman a man like him would want to come home to.

He released her and then he was gone.

She closed the door and leaned against it. Something crunched as she pressed herself against the wood. Reaching in her back pocket, she knew that the tears wouldn't wait. Because her panties were missing. And in their place was the envelope with her money.

CHAPTER 7

By the time Regan and Holly arrived at school, Regan had a permanent twitch behind her right eye. Holly had spent the entire morning chattering on about the move, her new room, and her new friend, Gabe. She wondered—aloud and often—where he lived, if he had a pet, how he knew her favorite doughnuts were the ones with the pink sprinkles on top. Making Regan wonder what in the heck she had been thinking, taking him up on the offer to help her move. Not to mention that kiss. Which was why avoiding him was the best option.

"Lauren!" Holly yelled, dropping Regan's hand so she could wave her own excitedly at the blonde-haired girl who stood at the end of the hallway under a new batch of Missing Randolph posters. Lauren's little face went wide and she started jumping up and down, chanting Holly's name.

"Mommy! That's Lauren!" Holly tugged on Regan's coat, which was buttoned from knee to neck. She wasn't embarrassed about the polyester blend she had on underneath, but she also didn't want to advertise that she cleaned toilets. Not at Holly's school.

"She's in my class and she likes kitties too. We played together at recess. She and Summer and Chloe were pretending to be orphaned baby kittens in the wild, and she was really nice and let me play with them. It's Lauren!" Holly said in one long breath with no pauses, her voice elevating with each word.

"Yes, you've told me about Lauren." And Regan assumed Summer and Chloe were the other two girls who had joined in the jumping. "Why don't you bring them over and introduce us?"

Holly had barely made it ten feet before the three girls surrounded her, each taking their turn in giving her daughter a hug.

Regan's breath caught in her throat. This is what she wanted for Holly. This moment, right here. Friends. Happiness. Connection.

Roots.

And no matter how hard it got, she would do anything to keep her kid as happy as she was right then.

"It's the same thing at our house." A woman approached Regan. Dressed in designer slacks and ridiculously high heels, with sculpted blonde hair, she was the epitome of Napa Valley society. She also looked incredibly stuck up and vaguely familiar. Regan pulled her coat tighter. "Lauren talks about Holly nonstop. She's been hounding me for days about setting up a playdate."

Regan felt herself relax. Mommy talk she could do. It was something she had mastered early on in Holly's life. If she kept the conversation on the kids, people were too wrapped up in bragging to notice that Regan was at least a good decade younger.

"Holly would love that. She says Lauren is quite the singer."

"She gets that from my side," the woman preened. "Actually, all of my daughters have landed the role in the community Christmas musical. This is Lauren's year. She's purr-fect for Christmas Kitty."

Regan swallowed. "Christmas Kitty is the lead?"

"The play is called *Christmas Kitty Goes to Frogtown*," Lauren's mother enunciated slowly, as if *Christmas Kitty Goes to Frogtown* had starred Julie Andrews and won the Tony for Best Musical Featuring Felines and Faux Fur. "And Lauren will do brilliantly."

"I didn't know it was already cast."

"Oh, it's just a matter of semantics. And don't worry about Holly." Miss Actor's Guild leaned in, patting Regan on the shoulder. "All the kids understand that a Stark gets the lead. It's tradition. Not every girl can hold center stage, but the chorus members are just as important; they're the foundation of any play. Oh, and by the way, I'm Isabel Stark."

"Of course you are." Regan swallowed, taking Isabel's hand and shaking it. The woman was not only a stuck-up b—bad word, she looked familiar because she had been Gabe's date to the Ryo Christmas party.

Gabe, who had kissed Regan just last night. The same Gabe who had asked her to live with him—well, not *with* him but with him. God, she hated men.

"I'm Regan Martin."

Isabel gave Regan a long, thorough examination, her brows furrowing, which looked bizarre since her forehead didn't move. "Have we met?"

"I don't think so."

"Stanford, class of—"

"Nope." Try Clovisville High, class of not all that long ago. There went the unmoving forehead again. "Are you sure? You look so familiar and I never forget a face."

Maybe it was when I was dancing with your date? God, even if the woman grated on Regan's every nerve, no one deserved to see another woman dancing with their date. Time to say sorry. "I think we may have been at the same party—"

"Mommy," Holly called, she and her three friends bounding up, their little pigtails and curly poofs bouncing with every step. "This is Summer, Lauren, and Chloe. And we're the…" Holly stopped.

All four girls looked at each other for a quick second, their faces scrunched in confusion, then Lauren directed as they scrambled around until they were in a straight line, ranging from shortest to tallest, with Holly being on the shortest side and Lauren on the tallest. Isabel smiled proudly at her daughter's ability to lead.

"And we're the…" Lauren repeated Holly's earlier words.

"B." Holly punched her fist forward like she was some superhero. There was a blue *B* drawn on her knuckles.

"F." Summer followed with the announcement and fist pump.

"F." Chloe pumped.

"Sssssssss…" Lauren finished, dragging out the letter like a snake. All four girls slithered down to the ground before erupting into giggles once more.

God, she loved her kid.

Isabel, however, made a horrified gasp. Her hand, shy one wedding band, clutched at her surgically enhanced chest. "Lauren, you were always the *B*."

"But Holly's the smallest so we gave her the biggest letter. It's only fair." Lauren beamed. The kid obviously had a great father.

Isabel stood behind her daughter, eyes firmly on Regan. "She's been the *B* since Mommy and Me."

"Mrs. Abby said it was a good friend thing to do," Lauren said, her smile dimming.

Regan's smile did more than dim. "Abby?"

"Our music teacher," Holly said, looking at Regan as if she had lost her mind.

Her mind? No. But her breakfast? A distinct possibility.

"I thought her name was Mrs. Dee." Because the universe could not be that cruel.

"D," Isabel once again enunciated slowly, this time as if Regan was phonetically challenged. "As in DeLuca. Abby and I go way back. She was the *F* to my *B*."

"I didn't know she taught here. Wait, doesn't she live in Santa Barbara?"

"She moved back a few months ago and, no, she doesn't work here. The play is held in the school's performing arts center, but it is a community event, and the DeLuca family has always been amazing about giving back. And as you could imagine, I was ecstatic when good old Abs volunteered to run the musical this year. Just ecstatic. Isn't that right, Lauren?"

Lauren nodded hesitantly, her little eyes darting back and forth between the adults. She wasn't sure what was going on, but the girl instinctively knew that something was off in Frogtown. And that she had just been pushed neck deep in it.

Had Regan not been hyperaware of every adult in the hallway with dark curly hair and brown eyes, or scanning for every exit within a fifty-foot radius, she would have said something to break the tension. Instead she kissed Holly's head and hugged her tightly.

"I have to get to work, angel. See you after school."

"Aren't you coming to the parent meeting?" Isabel asked. "It concerns the Christmas musical. We're doling out what still needs to be done. Every year the parents rally together and volunteer for various positions. It's what makes St. Helena such a wonderful community."

Holly looked at the floor. She knew the drill. Working mommies didn't go to midmorning meetings. They didn't have time to make sets or sew costumes. They barely made it to the performance.

Regan wanted to go to that stupid parent meeting, just for Holly, but as it was, she was already going to be late for her first day of work. Not to mention, she would rather eat glass than face Abigail right now. She had no idea how much Gabe's sister knew, if she would even recognize Regan, or if she knew Holly was Richard's. The month after Regan discovered Richard was married, she had sent Abigail a letter apologizing and explaining that she hadn't known he was married. The letter had come back unopened: Return to Sender.

The meeting between the two women would take place, that was certain, but not here. Not with Holly in the same building and a hundred prying ears.

"I have work this afternoon. But"—she got down on her knees so that she and Holly were at the same level—"I would love to sign up and volunteer."

At that Holly smiled and planted a big, wet kiss smack on Regan's lips. "You're the best mommy!"

"Easy when I have the best kiddo," she whispered.

"I bet Mrs. Stark would be nice and sign you up on a real good committee," Holly said.

"Why, I would love to." Isabel beamed.

I just bet you would. Regan stood and watched the girls skip down the hallway, holding hands and humming.

Isabel leaned in, eyes still on her daughter. "The Costume Committee is in serious need of help. Since you won't be available for morning duties or afterschool positions, how about I put your name in for seamstress?"

The most time-consuming and meticulous position available.

"That would be lovely. Very nice of you to offer."

"My pleasure."

Regan shoved her purse higher on her shoulder and called out, "Holly, give Mommy a big purr before I leave."

Holly stopped, turned around, and let loose the cutest damn purr in the history of animal impersonations. Her face scrunched while her eyes went as big as saucers of milk. It was Tony-worthy.

Regan didn't have to look at Isabel to know that her jaw was dangling around those designer stilettos. The woman had gasped so hard that she had sucked all of the oxygen out of the building. Regan spun on her orthopedic heel, and with a "See you later," made her way toward the front of the school, smiling the whole way. Normally she never would have used Holly in a Mommy sparring, but...

"Chorus members are the foundation, my ass," she muttered.

With a smile, full-blown and broadcasting what a wonderful morning it had turned out to be, Regan rounded the hall and was passing the trophy display when the front door blew open. And there, surrounded by a glowing halo of sunlight, with auburn curls and those intense brown eyes that Regan was all too familiar with, stood Richard's ex-wife.

Abigail was petite in all the places that counted, curvy in the ones that said "woman," and with her big lashes and pert nose, was just about the most adorable thing Regan had ever seen. Abigail truly was the DeLuca Darling. Regan looked down at herself and was suddenly reminded how, once again, there was a distinct difference between...how had Richard put it in the end? Oh, yes...the kind of woman you marry and the kind you screw.

Swallowing back the residual hurt, Regan started forward. Her first instinct was to approach Abigail, introduce herself, and try to make this inevitable meeting as painless as possible for both of them. To assure the woman that she wasn't here to cause the DeLucas problems and convince her that Holly was an innocent in all of this.

She searched Abigail's face for some kind of recognition, some kind of clue to let her know how the woman wanted to handle this. Or if she even knew what *this* was. Regan had had six years to prepare, but—

Then the other door opened and in stepped two laughing, big, dark-haired, bad-ass Italians. Their laughs died instantly when they locked eyes on Regan.

Her right eye started to twitch again, and her nerves went on a full-scale war with her stomach. They weren't Gabe, the kissing jerk, but they were DeLucas and they were pissed. And Regan didn't have to guess who inspired those chests to puff out or those eyes to turn to slits.

Not willing to cower, she took two more steps forward and then, deciding she didn't have to fight them now as a united front, made a beeline for the nearest classroom door. She opened it and ducked inside, only exhaling when she heard their voices disappear down the other hall.

"Well, how nice of you to join us."

Regan spun around. The three Mrs. Clauses held court at the front of the classroom. Glasses low on their noses, each holding a ruler and laser pointer, they were doing some kind of presentation to a room full of parents and a small handful of—

Holy crap!

The whiteboard was covered with photos of the Christmas display, Santa sticking out of ChiChi's car, and enough evidence for a full-scale White House investigation. In the middle of the collage was a glossy 8-by-10 of Randolph. And studying Regan, with what appeared to be blatant suspicion, was the sheriff.

"Thank goodness you're here," ChiChi said, taking Regan by the arm and dragging her to the front of the room. All the parents stared. "We were just telling the sheriff here about the deer-napping of our beloved Randolph."

The sheriff was a short man with skinny arms, skinny legs, and a spare tire under his belt. He gave Regan a bear-with-me smile, which was difficult to see under his mustache, followed by a meaningful wink. At least the local law enforcement wasn't acting ridiculous about some stupid statue. A statue that Regan still hadn't returned.

Pricilla hugged her. "We were telling him how you—"

"—being our marketing and social media expert—" Lucinda added.

"—could keep the general public notified of the status of Randolph's case," ChiChi went on. "You see, the sheriff here just agreed to make this his top priority. They're going to arrest whoever committed this sinful act."

"Arrest?" Regan choked out.

"My manners." ChiChi shook her head. "Sheriff Bryant, this is Regan, Regan Martin."

"You can't be serious," Regan said, pumping his hand.

Sheriff Bryant's grip tightened and his eyes narrowed. "As a bullet. Now, Ms. Martin, you wouldn't happen to know anything about the disappearance of our town mascot, would you?"

Regan looked to Pricilla and opened her mouth, waiting for her friend to shove a truffle in before she said something stupid. Too bad for Regan, Pricilla seemed short on truffles at the moment. And Regan was about to be short on quarters.

Regan's no-nonsense shoes squeaked as she shuffled across the marble floor, walking as fast as she could without appearing to be in a rush. Head down, she darted through the vast lobby, edging past the reception desk, hoping not to be caught by one of her superiors while sneaking through the Guests Only entrance.

The lobby, usually calm at this hour, was clamoring with an overabundance of confused guests and designer luggage. Regan stepped around a Louis Vuitton pet purse that growled and almost collided with its owner, who was currently expressing her frustration at the lone girl manning the registration desk.

Rounding the corner, she pushed open a door—the dividing line between chocolate roses and breakfast in bed, and scrubbing tubs and sheet service.

"There you are," an authorial voice snapped from behind.

She stopped, straddling the threshold. Crap. Caught.

"Sabrina," Regan started, embarrassed that she was caught walking in late...again. It was only her third day at her new job. "I want to apologize for being late."

She had tried to return that stupid reindeer, only to be cornered by the Mrs. Clauses, force-fed a two-thousand-calorie breakfast, given an earful about the yoga pants posse and their secret meeting for world domination, and then sent on her merry way—Randolph still safely hidden in her trunk. Not that she could tell her boss that. So she fibbed.

"My daughter forgot her homework on the, uh, counter and we, uh..." She slowly turned around, but instead of finding her boss, Sabrina, with her shrink-wrapped uniform and perky attitude, Regan found Jordan, looking ever so amused. "What are you doing here?"

"You mean here, at the employee entrance, where you should be walking out of and not into?" Jordan said, her hands dramatically circling before zeroing in on her. "Where I'm not is at my desk searching the Internet for chastity belts since Mr. Sex with Wheels snuck into Ava's room last night. Which they make, by the way—chastity belts. I'll save the link for when Holly reaches fifteen. Although they look like they would encourage sex, not prevent it."

"And Mr. Sex with Wheels still retains the appropriate equipment to be a threat?"

"That was my next search, but I got called here before I could finish reading the instructions. Apparently, Marc had to go to Vegas. Something about Sabrina, a bachelorette party, an undercover cop, and bail."

When ChiChi offered Regan the job, she'd failed to mention that the hotel was owned by another one of her overprotective grandsons. Water cooler gossip was that Marco had bought the Napa Grand three years ago and turned a dilapidated hotel into the most exclusive luxury resort and members-only club in the Napa Valley.

Not that Regan had run into the middle DeLuca. Okay, she had successfully avoided him a total of eleven times in three days. So she was happy to hear he was gone. Would buy that events coordinator a round if she managed to keep him busy in Vegas for the rest of the week. Because all this sneaking around was exhausting.

"I get paid to make Gabe's troubles go away," Jordan continued, "and Marc is always in trouble. So I have two days to clean house, which makes me your boss. Again."

"Woo hoo," Regan deadpanned. "Because that worked out stellar for me the last time."

"*I* am an excellent boss. And you're still here, aren't you?" Jordan held up a finger in warning. "But don't you dare address me as Mrs. Schultz. It makes me sound divorced."

"You are divorced."

"Yes, well, it also implies I wear Ann Taylor and starch." She shuddered. "Now that we're done with the heart to heart, can I say thank heavens you're here. You *hable français*, right?"

"Oui," Regan played along, chuckling. She couldn't help it. Jordan was fast becoming one of her favorite people. She was straightforward, told it like it was, and made no apologies. She had also brought over a casserole the other night, along with a set of bath toys for Holly. Not to mention that her life was like watching some bizarre afternoon talk show unfold.

"Cute. Now, can you put this on and get to the front desk in"—Jordan thrust a garment bag at Regan in a panic, eyes bugged as she took in the chaotic lobby—"well, ten minutes ago?"

Regan eyed the reception-desk uniform.

"I know, not an Isaac Mizrahi." Jordan looked at the black nylon skirt and rayon blouse and grimaced. "Not even his Target line, but we work with what we're given, right?"

Jordan now studied her with the assessment of a fashion-consultant-slash-critic. Regan took the bag but couldn't help feeling that she too was another project where Jordan felt she was forced to work with what she was given.

"I have two days to get you out of the dungeon and into management."

"Management? Are you serious?" Her world just got so much better.

"That's my goal. So don't be late. Don't piss off any more DeLucas. And don't let Marc charm his way under your skirt."

Regan wanted to ask if the same rules applied for the oldest DeLuca, then remembered Isabel and changed her mind.

"Now, be a doll and strip." Jordan looked around at the clusters of irritated customers. "Well, not here. But what a crowd you'd draw. All those uptight Frenchies over there would hand over their best foie gras and forget that their reservations have somehow vanished and the wine convention they thought they were here for is actually scheduled for next week."

"How did that happen?"

"Because Marc has a tendency to hire personnel based on their bra size rather than their organizational skills. Which is why he's in Vegas and I'm here. And I need to get someone with brains in management so I can get back to DeLuca Wines and do *my* job, which is where you come in."

Jordan pressed her palm on the small of Regan's back and maneuvered her through the lobby before shoving her into an office. "Five minutes. Go." She clapped twice and disappeared, the door slamming dramatically behind her.

Oh boy. Not just any office. Marco DeLuca's office.

A massive mahogany desk sat in the middle of the room, staring her down. It was dark, imposing, and besides the stack of unopened mail, it was meticulously arranged. It was also intimidating. The kind of desk that people get fired at.

Over the past few years, Regan had learned a lot about desks with regard to their owners. And this was one desk she wouldn't want to tangle with. There it was, two weeks until Christmas and not one decoration or Christmas card was in sight. In fact, the only evidence of softness was the small collection of wire-framed photos that sat on a bookshelf at the rear of the room.

After skimming her fingers along the edge of one, Regan picked it up. The photo was at least twenty years old and screamed of the childhood Regan had always dreamed of. Two loving parents, an army of happy, dark-haired boys and a smiling little girl with auburn curls—all in red and green and all standing around Randolph.

"Stupid deer," Regan mumbled, placing the photo back.

Stepping out of her shoes, she peeled down her cleaning-lady polyester dress, draping it on the back of Marco's chair. She tugged her undershirt over her head and was reaching back for the skirt and blouse when a low sound of male appreciation came from the doorway.

"Need help with that?" Gabe leaned against the doorjamb as Regan spun around, the uniform slipping to the floor. Left with nothing but red lace and embarrassment for cover, she scrambled to hide all of her girly parts. Problem was, she had more girly parts than hands.

He took in her complicated updo, the little tattoo peeking out, and incredible bronze skin. Regan was the sexiest woman he'd ever seen. He had no idea why she was here, but as long as she stayed in nothing but that red lace, he really didn't care.

"No," she snapped.

"You sure about that? Mine cover more area." He held up his hands as proof. Regan's eyes went narrow, clearly telling him what she thought of his suggestion.

Gabe shrugged. Maybe she was right. She had a whole hell of a lot of curves. Then again, he never backed down from a challenge.

The don't-mess-with-me scowl on her face told him the answer was no. Too bad, because for the past seventy-two hours Gabe had spent his days figuring out how to get her in his bed, and his nights creating his own Dirty Jar versions of how things played out between them. They usually ended with him and Regan in a sweaty, tangled heap on her kitchen counter. Sometimes in his shower. But always with her screaming out his name.

A slow grin took over his face. Tonight, she'd be wearing Christmas red in those dreams.

Leaving the door ajar, Gabe took a step forward and Vixen backed up.

"Oh, no, you don't."

"Don't what?" He rounded the desk, and before he could even touch her, she'd picked up her clothes and darted around the other side.

"You *know* what! And can't you see I'm getting dressed?"

"Why? You look perfectly fine to me."

She rolled her eyes at the way he said *fine*. Or maybe it was how he took his time observing exactly how she was dressed. Either way, when he sat himself down in the chair, she gave a dramatic huff and turned away from him. She yanked on her uniform as if she was trying to break some world record for quickest dresser. Not quick enough that Gabe didn't get a chance to fully take in her backside, which was almost as impressive as her front.

He zeroed in on her ass and found himself wavering. Before he could stand by that decision, he'd need time to compare and contrast the two. A lot of time.

"Seeing as this is my brother's office, I think I'll make myself at home." Hands behind his head, he plunked his running shoes on top of the desk and leaned back.

This day was warming up to be incredible. After a hard workout, which had done nothing to help his growing problem, he'd stopped by Marc's office hoping to find an employee file on the latest disaster of the Napa Grand—the events coordinator who had a thing for dirty martinis and propositioning the wrong guy. Instead, he'd found his favorite new employee wrapped in Christmas red.

The polite thing would have been to give her a heads-up that she had company. But then she'd dropped trou, and he'd been rendered stupid. Because that was the only word that could sum up why he would willingly walk into a room containing a half-naked woman who he couldn't sleep with but couldn't stop thinking about sleeping with.

"Then, I'll go," Regan said, turning around and slipping the blazer over the untucked blouse. She grabbed her clothes, palmed her shoes, and, without another word, swept by him. Her eyes were shimmering. With anger or hurt, he wasn't sure.

Gabe cursed himself, stood, and stepped in front of her, blocking her exit. "Hang on. That was rude of me." He reached in his pocket, plucked out a quarter, and offered it to her. Then he thought about all of the places he'd imagined her naked and emptied his pockets on the desk.

Instead of a smile, when she looked up her eyes were on fire. "I met Isabel today."

"Okay."

"The one you took to the Christmas party."

He still had no idea where she was going with this. Then her face scrunched and his gut rolled painfully.

"You kissed me, Gabe. And you're dating another woman."

"It's not what you think," he said, hating the hurt in her eyes.

"That's what they all say." She looked at the floor.

"Not me." He curled his finger around her chin and lifted until he could see those baby blues through her lashes. "I have never cheated and I never will. It's not who I am." She still didn't look convinced. Not that he blamed her, if all she had to judge his sex by was Richard. "Isabel and I dated very briefly, several years ago. The week before the party, ChiChi told me I should take Isabel. In front of Isabel. I wasn't going to be rude and say no. So we shared a drink,

I danced with you, drove her home, and with a kiss on the cheek said good night. She's called a few times, but I told her I wasn't looking for anything permanent. End of story."

"Oh," was all she said, but he could tell that she believed him and was now feeling silly.

"Yeah, oh." He cupped her face. "And, Regan. I didn't kiss you the other night."

"Yes, you did," she argued. He loved it when she tried to argue with him.

"No, I didn't. *This* is a kiss." He gave her a hard, quick smack on the lips. God he loved those lips. Had been fantasizing about them all week.

"And *this* is what *we* did." With that, he covered her mouth with his, surprised when she didn't knee him in the nuts and instead kissed him back.

He started out slow, nibbling her lower lip and taking his time to thoroughly explore every inch of her mouth. She made a sexy little noise in the back of her throat, her shoes hit the floor, and then her hands were on him. They slid around his middle, her nails digging into his back, and when they dropped down to his ass he was lost.

Lost track of time. Who he was with. Hell, somewhere between her hands digging under his shirt and raking up his back, and him doing the same, only exploring her front, he forgot they were standing in the doorway of his brother's office, in clear view of anyone passing by, making out like two horny teenagers.

With a groan, he eased back, just enough that they could catch their breaths, but their foreheads and noses still touched.

"Can you see the difference now? Because if you're still confused I can show you again."

Her fingers fisted in his hair and she pulled him to her, obviously wanting another demonstration of the distinct difference. So he showed her. Twice.

"You smell good," she whispered, nuzzling his neck.

"I smell like the gym," he chuckled. She nuzzled deeper.

"Besides, anything is a step up from your apartment."

"It's not the gym, you smell like—" She stopped, pulling back enough to level him with a look, but she didn't move out of his arms. "We promised not to do that again."

"I never made any such promise." He kissed her nose. "Because making a promise I have no intention on keeping is a waste of time, Vixen."

"We can't...this won't...I have to get to work." She looked at him horrified, like she'd blown it, like she was about to get screwed. And not in a good way. "I work here. I was going to tell you. And then I saw...I should have called you and told you." When she exhaled, her breath was so weighted and shaky that it left him unbalanced.

He took in her starched white shirt, which had somehow come undone again, black pencil skirt, matching blazer with the hotel logo embroidered on the lapel, and smiled. "Kind of figured." He wanted to ask who she had seen but knew better than to push. He'd find out later. "It's okay, Regan, ChiChi told me the day you were hired."

Which was ridiculous, since Marc had been the one to come up with the idea of hiring Regan as a way to keep an eye on her, then slyly mentioned the opening to ChiChi. Gabe hadn't been a part of it, but he also hadn't stopped it. He figured Regan needed a job and was too stubborn to let him help her. What he didn't know, until that morning when Jordan had called him, was that his dickhead brother had given Regan a job as a maid.

"She also told me that if I were to upset you in any way, she'd pull out the wooden spoon."

That got a smile out of her and Gabe felt his chest relax.

"To spank you?"

"No, to bake me a fruitcake."

"So, when Marc gets home he isn't going to fire me?"

Did Regan really think that after last weekend he'd allow that? He still didn't have a solution that made everyone happy, but he was working on it.

"We're not going to cause problems for you, Regan." He tucked her hair, now a rumpled mess tumbling around her shoulders, behind her ear. "That, I can promise."

She showed genuine surprise at his confession. God, he felt like shit.

When they found Richard, he was going to kick his ass for breaking Abby's heart. Then kick it again for hurting Regan. Then he'd kick his own ass for doing equal damage to her life. And maybe Marc's ass while he was at it.

First they had to find the bastard. And what sucked was that his brothers still believed that the only reliable lead they had was currently looking up at him with those big lapis eyes. If his brothers were right, and his gut said that they were, where did that leave him and Regan?

"You are needed out on the floor. Now!" Jordan shoved her way into the office.

Regan jerked away, buttoning up her shirt and smoothing back her hair. And Gabe stood there like an idiot watching her. All the pressing in the world couldn't hide that she had just been loved. Oh, they hadn't made love—yet—but what was happening between them was way more than just kissing.

"Hello? Did you not hear me?" Jordan said again, her eyes darting back and forth between the two.

"I'm sorry, I was just grabbing my things." Regan leaned down and picked up her shoes.

"Not you," Jordan sighed dramatically. "Although you were supposed to be on the floor over twenty minutes ago." Her irritation zeroed in on Gabe. "You! I have been texting you for nearly ten minutes."

He shrugged, used to Jordan's dramatics. Whenever she complained about her daughter being a handful, he considered buying her a black tea kettle.

"Texts? I didn't get any."

As if on cue, his phone vibrated. Jordan picked it up off the floor and thrust it at him. He silenced it and set it on the desk. Regan, on the other hand, was bright red and doing her best to avoid looking him in the eye.

"Jordan, give us a minute, would you?"

"That's okay. We can talk," Regan mumbled to the floor. "You know." No, he didn't know. And he wanted to finish this conversation now. Before Regan made it all the way to the door, which was where she was headed. Fast.

Gabe reached for her but she skirted past, his fingers grazing her hand, which seconds ago had been all over his body. She hadn't made it more than five feet when she was shoved back inside, and right back into his arms, by three shouting ladies, a hissing fluff ball in Santa drag, an angry Frenchman, and a partridge in a pear tree. Literally.

The Frenchman held the crystal partridge from the lobby display.

"Get us some rope, Regan," Lucinda said, jabbing the businessman in the rear with an umbrella. "We can tie him up while we wait for the sheriff."

"Nobody is tying anybody up," Gabe hollered, snatching Lucinda's makeshift cattle prod and ChiChi's scarf for good measure, since she was holding it like a rope. Easing Regan out of scratching distance, since the cat was showing its claws, Gabe took the Frenchman by the arm and guided him to the chair.

"Now, would someone mind telling me what in the hell is going on?"

The entire room erupted into conversation. Well, conversation implied a two-way thing—this was more of everyone telling their side of the story simultaneously. At the top of their lungs. Besides him, the only one who wasn't yelling was Regan, who was still looking for a way out.

"Silence!"

Everyone froze, including the cat, whose hat was now covering its eyes.

"Jordan, please explain to me what is going on."

Jordan folded her arms and glared. "Check your phone. It's all there."

This, Gabe thought, right here, was why he spent so much time—what had ChiChi called it?—*smothering* his family members. Because when he didn't, he spent his days cleaning up his brothers' messes and dealing with homicidal grannies. He was about to say to hell with it and let his nonna take out the Frenchman when Regan spoke.

"'Get your stare-worthy, entitled ass over here now,'" Regan said.

Gabe looked up and Regan shrugged, holding up his cell as proof. "That's what the text said. The next one says, 'All the wine in the world can't make up for your crazy a—" She stopped, looking at everyone in the room *but* ChiChi. "Maybe I should skip ahead?"

"Scroll to the last two," Jordan said, picking at her cuticles.

"Um, okay, here it is. 'Your grandmother is about to assault a foreign diplomat with her handbag.'" Gabe grabbed ChiChi's purse, which was clutched in her angry little hands.

"I am a wine connoisseur," Frenchie argued.

"He's a criminal," ChiChi argued louder.

"He is the head of foreign investment for the country of France!" Jordan rebutted.

"See," Pricilla said, pulling out a petit four from her purse and taking a bite. "Politicians are all criminals."

"He was stealing Marco's crystal bird," ChiChi accused.

"I was not stealing anything, I was merely admiring the display when these three started beating me with their umbrellas, and then that feline scratched me." The Frenchman looked from his arm to the cat and then to Lucinda. "I hope it's had its shots."

Lucinda cuddled Mr. Puffins to her chest. "I'm going to shoot you if you don't give us back our Randolph!"

"Ah, hell," Gabe said, a headache forming behind his left eye.

"I have no idea who Randolph is, and as I tried to explain to these ladies earlier, I have nothing to do with his disappearance."

"I never forget a face and I have seen yours before. Probably on one of those police shows on television," Pricilla shot back, licking the icing off her pudgy little finger so she could point with it.

And Gabe's life just got a hell of a lot worse because this man wasn't a diplomat, and Pricilla *had* seen his face. It was plastered on every ad promoting this week's wine conference. Their criminal was none other than Simon Bonnet, one of the largest wine importers in France and this week's keynote speaker.

"And we found this near the town display, right next to Randolph's pedestal," ChiChi said, shoving an Eiffel Tower key ring in Gabe's face. He blinked. "As in, the scene of the crime."

"Oh, boy." Regan's face paled and Gabe would have bet good money she was shy one key ring.

"Can you read the last text?" Jordan asked, taking a petit four from Pricilla.

"Um, okay." Regan read the screen. "It says, 'I'm taking the rest of the week off. Paid.'"

"And to think I brought you one of my persimmon rolls," Jordan added.

Gabe cringed. He hated those persimmon rolls. They were almost as bad as ChiChi's fruitcakes. He still had the one from Thanksgiving in the back of his truck.

As if reading his mind, Jordan harrumphed and then headed for the door.

"Hang on." Gabe grabbed her arm. There was no way in hell he could lose Jordan the week before Christmas. Not this Christmas. As insane as she made him, she also made his life run smoothly. She was the gatekeeper for all of his family's crazy ideas and problems. If she left, he would be forced to go with her, because there was no way he could deal with his family alone.

Then the damnedest thing happened. The Frenchman laughed.

Simon and Regan sat, one in the chair, the other on the desk, and spoke in rapid French, giggling and sharing stories. Gabe watched with fascination—and, if he were being honest, pride—as the man literally transformed in front of his eyes. Under Regan's attention his brows lowered, his eyes lit with excitement, and his whole body relaxed.

She didn't flirt or use her beauty to charm him, which she easily could have. Instead, her magic was making him feel validated, taking the time to listen and to share.

With a final laugh and a firm shake of the hand, Regan led him out of the office. Simon patted Gabe on the shoulder and said something about grandbabies and holidays.

"You going to just let them walk away?" ChiChi barked.

A wise man would answer yes. Last he'd heard, though, the roles of all three wise men were already cast. And he wasn't one of them.

CHAPTER 8

This one," Holly said as she walked around the tree. It was full and lush and smelled like Christmas. It was also ten feet tall and wider than their kitchen.

"How about we find something a little more…quaint?" Regan suggested, gripping the ax handle tighter and steering her daughter toward the smaller trees.

Choosing the right tree was a lot more difficult that she'd anticipated, and, if the way the ax handle was already giving her blisters was a sign, cutting one down was going to be painful. Cutting it down in the middle of a race, when most of her competitors were dads, was going to be impossible. Which was why Regan and Holly came early, to scout out a good tree. Because when that whistle blew and people started scrambling for the available trees, it was bound to get messy.

First step was to get Holly to agree on one that was not fit for Rockefeller Center. It was the dreamer in Holly. She believed that if they had the perfect tree then they would have the perfect Christmas.

Telling herself that she did not fall under those same illusions, yet determined to make this Christmas everything Holly dreamed it would be, Regan put on her game face and contemplated just how big a tree they could get and still cut through the trunk in the allotted fifteen minutes. Because how many more years would Holly still believe in Santa? In Christmas miracles?

"How about that one?" Regan said, pointing to a beautiful tree toward the back of the row. Holly ran through the column of trees to stare up at it in awe. There was no way she could get it on top of her car, let alone in her house, but if Holly loved it then they could always have it delivered and put it on the back porch.

"Nope," Holly said dismissively. "Not *quaint* enough. Plus it's got a red tag." Which meant that it had already been sold.

Most people in St. Helena didn't have to wait for payday to buy a tree. They had come down weeks ago, picked out the best one, prepaid, and *still* came to the St. Helena Cut and Run.

The Cut and Run was an annual fund-raiser held by the Community Action Committee to fund the Christmas musical, and with a portion of this year's profits going toward the Safe Return of Randolph fund, nearly the entire town had turned out, which wasn't a surprise. Regan had begun to understand that St. Helenites loved their town, Christmas, and Randolph. And not necessarily in that order.

She had tried several times over the past week to return the stupid statue. But no matter what time she went, there were always mourners holding a silent vigil. Sometimes not so silent, she thought, remembering Mrs. Lambert of the

Grapevine Prune and Clip singing her version of "Ave Maria" while holding a clip-off to help raise funds for Randolph.

"Five minutes left until the Ninety-Third Annual Cut and Run. All contestants please make your way to the starting line." A voice came over the speaker, which was on loan from the school.

Regan followed Holly over to the next row, the fake snow crunching under her feet. She waved to Jordan, who was too busy draping Ava in her coat to wave back, and said hi to Mrs. Collette who, just as Holly described, smelled like saltines and sounded like she had a megaphone surgically attached to her vocal box.

The deeper they had gone into the Christmas tree patch, the thicker the crowd had grown and the more nervous she had become. There were more people than golden tags. And since only the golden-ticketed trees could be cut in the contest, someone was going home empty-handed.

"Mommy," Holly cried from two rows over. Regan could hear the excitement in her daughter's voice and *knew* she'd found her Christmas tree.

Cutting through the jolly forest, around a scantily clad Ava who, with red-streaked hair and diamond-pierced navel, had managed to lose her mother and the bottom half of her skirt, and sidestepping a woman with a blinking red walker, Regan finally found her daughter. She was staring up at the most beautiful tree on the lot.

It was a shiny hunter green with lots of lush branches and the perfect tip for her mother's star—a symmetrical goddess. Regan would have to have it delivered, which meant an extra charge, and the tree was a bit tall, but with some heavy maneuvering they could fit it through the door. Now all she had to figure out was how to get it, since the trunk was way more than a fifteen-minute chop.

"She's a pretty one," Isabel said, stepping out from the other side of the tree. She wasn't wearing a rainbow knit cap, a men's flannel, and holey jeans with gardening gloves dangling out the back pocket. No, Isabel, in fur and lumberjack boots, somehow managed to look runway ready. And in *her* back pocket was a tall, well-built man with hands the size of watermelons and an ax big enough to chop through Holly's tree in one whack.

"This is my brother, Paul. Paul, this is Holly's mom." Isabel placed a possessive hand on his arm. "He's home for the holidays and is sweet enough to be my swinging ax tonight."

"Regan," *Holly's mom* said. "Nice to meet you."

"It is very nice to meet you." Mr. Swinging Ax held Regan's hand until Isabel elbowed him.

"We saw a tree over there with your name on it," Regan said, placing a possessive hand on *her* tree. She had actually counted five Stark-ticketed trees thus far.

"Just seeing what else is out here. We could always use one for the front porch." Isabel gave the tree a swift kick. "This is nice, but I imagine it would take quite a while to chop down. Even for someone Paul's size. Too bad you don't have a man to help out. Well, happy hunting."

Regan almost shot her a happy greeting in return, but that finger would cost her a whole lot more than a quarter.

"Do we need a man to get a tree, Mommy?" Holly whispered, looking up at Regan as if her answer could forever change the course of her little five-year-old life.

"Are you kidding? Just look at these guns." She flexed her arms. When Holly didn't look so confident, Regan dropped to her knees and cupped her daughter's face with both hands. "No, baby. We just need each other."

Which was what Regan was still telling herself three minutes later when she gripped the handle of her ax and looked down the line at her competition. Tall, built, and swinging axes, these guys took their Cut-and-Run duties seriously. As Jordan had explained earlier, it wasn't so much about getting the tree.

The Cut and Run had become a way for the local families to compete on a scale outside of acres, vines, and *Wine Spectator* scores. For Regan, this was about proving to her daughter that Martin women could do anything they set their minds to. And a tiny bit of it was about sticking it to Isabel, who was standing directly behind her.

"I wanted to let you know that I told Paul not to chop down the tree you were looking at. Holly has been talking nonstop about her dream tree, and I would hate to think that we took something from her that obviously meant so much."

Regan wondered when Isabel was going to lay it on the line. Yesterday, the list of who was being considered for the musical had been posted. It had Holly and Lauren going head to head for the role of Christmas Kitty.

"You know, I can always lend you Paul after he chops down our tree," Isabel offered with about as much sincerity as a rabid Chihuahua.

Regan looked at Holly, seated next to the three Mrs. Clauses, and back in the direction of her tree. "Thanks for the offer, but I'll have to pass."

"That's a shame." Isabel toyed with the fluffy ball on the end of Regan's rainbow cap. "I really wanted Holly to have her tree come Christmas."

"Oh, she'll get her tree."

Regan had never had a father growing up, but her mother always had a Christmas tree. It may have been a different kind of childhood than the rest of the people here, but Regan had never gone hungry and she always felt loved. She was going to cut down that tree and Holly was going to have an incredible Christmas.

"Just remember," Isabel added, "you have fifteen minutes to cut it down *and* drag it across the finish line. Oh, and once you enter the forest there are no rules."

Regan's head whipped around just in time to watch her smirk and saunter away, but not before she whispered in Paul's ear.

Holy crap! She would need the entire fifteen minutes just to get to the tree and chop it down. Plus the thing was a whole three feet taller than she—and that was if she had on her stilettos.

Regan looked back at the stands and found Holly. Holding a thumbs-up and a bright smile plastered on her face, Holly let loose a "Go Mommy!" and the Mrs. Clauses started doing the geriatric version of raising the roof.

Axes ready for battle and feet planted firmly on the ground, the line prepared itself as Sheriff Bryant raised his gun. The shot exploded and Regan, even though she'd watched him pull the trigger, jumped, costing herself a good three seconds.

Chaos erupted, and good lord, Regan couldn't find a single other woman in the herd. It was all muscle and testosterone and ego-driven men fighting for the dominant position. Then she received a hard shove to the back and she sprang into action. Okay, it was more like a stumbling start, but it was a start.

"If you are going to represent," Frankie hollered, swinging the blunt end of her ax and taking out a man the size of Adonis at the kneecaps, "then do our sex proud."

Regan grunted and, shoving the fuzzy tassels from her hat out of her eyes, zeroed in on her tree. Boots slammed into the packed mud and the sound of metal on wood echoed through the man-made forest. People had already located their trees and were chopping away. Regan didn't care about the other men, or about Frankie taking out what looked to be the second to oldest DeLuca with a knee to the groin, or even about coming in first. All she cared about was that she made it across that finish line with a tree for her daughter.

Several fights erupted in the aisles, and after nearly taking an elbow to the head, Regan dropped to her knees and crawled along the middle row of trees, taking the most direct route to her target. Branches smacked her in the face and gravel cut into her hands and knees, but she pushed forward, dragging that damn ax with her.

When she got to the last row she understood why no one else was staking claim on Holly's tree. Because even if she managed to cut it down, she'd have to drag it back across the entire field.

"Shit."

Remembering her softball days, she choked up on the handle, pulled back, and swung. The blade hit at too much of an angle, reflected off the trunk, and curved right, taking Regan with it. She landed hard, hands and knees slamming into the ground and her butt sticking up in the air.

Dusting herself off, she swallowed back the pain and tried it again, with the same results. Only this time she flew into the tree, the handle of the ax shanking her in the side upon landing. By the seventh try, Regan had lost the gloves, but instead of a better grip like she had hoped, it only gave her splinters and a really big raw spot.

Jingle bells started rattling as well as the drummers drumming, signaling that the first person had already crossed the finish line and there was a declared winner. Panicked, Regan glanced around, her heart aching when she saw that a number of the men around her were already dragging their trees toward the finish line.

Thinking of Holly up there in the stands, she brushed the dirt from her face and took another swing. Instead of plowing into the tree headfirst, which was where the momentum had tossed her, a pair of strong arms caught her around the waist.

"Easy." The warm breath tickled her ear, and Regan didn't blame her nipples for expressing their yuletide spirit. Or her legs for turning to a quivering mess when a strong hand flattened against her stomach and brushed the underside of her breast. By the time Gabe had her righted and facing him, her whole body was reaching Defcon 1.

"You okay?" he asked, taking the ax so he could gently inspect her hands. They were red, chapped, and bleeding. And that one raw spot had multiplied to cover most of her palm and a good number of fingers.

Those intense eyes landed on hers, and it took everything she had not to give in. To be like those women she'd watched growing up who had allowed themselves to lean on a man when life got hard.

"I have to get Holly that tree," she said, stepping back and out of the safety of his body.

"Okay," he said, bringing the ax up. Regan was about to tell him that she didn't need a man when he flipped the ax around and held it out to her. "Then get her a tree."

Blinking back the tears, Regan gave a single nod and took the handle. She pulled the ax back and right as she was about to swing forward she felt Gabe surround her, his front to her back, his hand resting on the ax.

"Go in at a forty-five-degree angle, like this." He wrapped his arms around her and, placing his hands over hers on the handle, demonstrated how to swing. Then he stepped back and Regan immediately missed his warmth. "Now try."

She did. And it worked. A small piece of wood splintered.

"Oh, my God! Did you see that?" she screamed, and realized she was jumping up and down like Holly.

"I did. Impressive, Vixen," he said with a smile that warmed her, well, everywhere. "Now, this time hit it straight on and then repeat the angle."

Regan followed his instructions, and with every swing she took out another chunk of trunk. Finally the tree started leaning. She dropped the ax and went around to the other side and shoved it over with her foot. With a loud snap it fell to the ground.

She'd done it! She got Holly her tree!

"If there wasn't a timer ticking away I would kiss the hell out of you right now," she said.

Gabe kissed her anyway. Short and sweet, and when he pulled back, he gave her a smack on the bottom.

"Then I guess you'd better get that sweet ass of yours moving. You have a tree to win. And I have a kiss to claim."

Regan grabbed the top of the tree and started tugging, noticing that Gabe stayed behind, letting her have her moment. It was heavy and awkward and slow going, but she was making good time. She passed the first cluster of trees when she ran into a solid wall of "ax-hole."

"Whoops, I didn't see you," Paul said, looking sheepish.

"Get out of my way."

"Look, you seem like a nice lady. Actually, I considered asking you out earlier." He ran a hand down his face. "My sister's a little unstable when it comes to winning, and she really wants Lauren to have that part in the musical. Just tell your kid you're taking her away for Christmas so I can move out of your way and you can get your little girl her tree."

"Hey, Paul. What seems to be the problem?" Gabe said, appearing from the next row over. He placed a hand on Regan's shoulder.

"Hey, Gabe. No problem. Just seeing if the lady needed any help."

"She's doing just fine on her own."

Paul's mouth turned up as his eyes slid down Regan's body. "I can see that. Better get going, the whistle's going to blow any second now."

Shoving Paul aside, Regan dug her heels in the ground and pulled her tree. She came through the last clearing and saw the finish line. She also saw that she had less than forty seconds until time ran out. She pulled faster, ignoring the sap dripping down her hands and the way her lower back rebelled. It wasn't going to be enough.

Then, suddenly, the tree felt weightless. She looked back and saw that Gabe had picked up the trunk and was practically shoving her forward. She opened her mouth to tell him she didn't need his help, then closed it. Because if the goal was getting Holly her tree, she knew she couldn't make it alone. No matter how much that ticked her off.

Gabe pushed her right over the finish line, past the crowd of well-wishers, and around the back of the bleachers before he let her stop. Irritated and humbled and breathing heavy, Regan dropped the tree and snapped, "I could have done that on my own."

"I had no doubt." Gabe walked around the tree until they were only a breath apart. "But sometimes having someone in your corner can make everything easier. Life is about sharing, Regan. I wanted to share that with you."

His statement made her wish for things that she knew could never happen for a girl like her. It wasn't that she didn't want someone to share Holly and her life with. She had just learned over the years that when it came to forever not all women had that elusive quality that men were looking for.

Fiddling with the bottom of his shirt, she asked, "What was up with the tour of the bleachers?"

He looked up and grinned. She followed his gaze and saw a cluster of mistletoe hanging from the underside of the bleachers.

"How did you know that was here?"

He rested his hands on her hips, pulling her close.

"My grandfather started the tradition about sixty years ago. It was how he got ChiChi to give up her first kiss. It has been a tradition ever since." He lowered his head. "Now, can we stop talking? I'd like you to kiss the hell out of me."

Regan slid one hand behind his neck and pulled his mouth to hers. Then, for the first time since meeting Gabe DeLuca, she did as he asked.

Gabe's night went downhill from there. Holly had needed Regan to take her to the ladies' room and his family had wanted him to load up ChiChi's tree and get her home before it started raining. Family appeased for the moment, he'd gone off to find Regan, maybe grab another smoking-hot kiss, ask if she and Holly wanted to grab a bite of dinner, and offer to haul her tree home, when he discovered that she'd paid to have it delivered.

The woman who refused to leave town had finally cut and run. And he found himself frowning.

They hadn't arrived together, so he shouldn't have been disappointed, but he was. Disappointment turned to irritation when, after a hot shower, he walked out to find his brothers sitting in his front room, football on the plasma, feet on the coffee table, and enough takeout for ten.

"That had better not turn up on my charge." None of them responded. He took in the sticky counter, the chow mein noodle on the couch, and the beer ring on the side table. "Don't you have houses of your own to destroy?"

"Plates on the counter," Marc said, eyes glued to the game.

Gabe grabbed a plate, stole Trey's beer, and sat down.

"Hey," Trey whined.

"Did you buy it? No?" Gabe eyeballed him. "Then it's mine."

Trey helped himself to another beer from the fridge. "What crawled up your ass?"

Gabe had no idea. His brothers showed up unannounced and destroyed his house all the time. During football season it was an expected event. One that had been going on since he'd gotten his own place. So why was he so bent?

"Did our girl give up anything that could help us find Richard?" Marc asked.

"Nope."

"Nope, she hasn't told you anything, or nope you've been too busy trying to shake her tree to ask?" Marc said.

"I'm not trying to shake her tree," Gabe snapped. Okay, that was a lie. There was nothing he wanted more than to get in Regan's pants. But he wasn't going to do it to get information on Richard.

"Christ, maybe you should. Then you wouldn't be such a tight-ass all the time," said Nate, the tight-ass of the family, getting up for seconds.

Gabe was the easygoing one of the brothers. A difficult task since he was also the oldest and had to deal with his family's crap all the time. But he took a lot of pride in his ability to not let things rile him. This, though—invading a woman's life and lying to her on the off-chance that she had some kind of information on Richard—got him fired up. And not in a good way.

"As far as I know, she has had no contact with Richard. And there is no way she is sitting on a pile of cash. The woman doesn't have a damn bed for her kid."

Gabe shoved Trey's feet off the coffee table, went for another beer, and that's when he realized that no one was speaking. They were all staring at him like he'd grown another head. He dumped his plate in the sink, wiped down the counter, and inhaled three fortune cookies. Still, no one said a word.

Gabe sank back into the couch. "She's a single mom. I don't even date single moms. And somehow I have managed to screw up this one's life at every turn."

"She slept with our sister's husband," Nate said quietly.

"So did half of the women in this valley," Gabe said, feeling suddenly tired. "Why aren't we hounding them?" After Richard had disappeared, their investigator discovered that the bastard had conducted dozens of affairs. He loved them young, and he loved them often. But the only one he'd kept around for more than a few months was Regan. And now that Gabe had gotten to know her, he understood why. She wasn't the kind of woman you got casual with and walked away. She got under your skin and stuck there.

"He lived with her for a year," Trey said, as if Gabe didn't already know. As if he hadn't thought about that fact every time he saw her.

"And when he said he was going to Santa Barbara to make sure things were running smoothly, he went to Oregon instead. Three weeks later he and the money disappeared. He only made one call that day, Gabe. Only one. And it was to Regan," Marc said, stating nothing new. "For all we know she helped him take the money."

"What part of her kid sleeping on the floor didn't you guys hear?"

Nate's face turned serious. "Broke or not, those are the facts, Gabe."

"Regan didn't do it." That much he knew. But arguing with his brothers about it didn't feel right. Arguing with his family never felt right. It felt like a betrayal of his parents' memory.

"You're willing to bet Abby's future on that?" Marc challenged. "Half the people in this town still wonder if Abby was covering for her husband. A husband who she doesn't want and can't divorce. The other half are taking bets on how fast she'll tank Ryo. She's under enough pressure without running into Regan buying groceries or on her way to rehearsal for the musical."

"You were the ones who said we should keep Regan here, not me."

"Because you were supposed to be finding out what she knows," Nate reminded him. If his brother was going for the guilt angle, it was working. Gabe had stuck himself between a woman and his family. What the hell kind of mess had he gotten into?

"Maybe I should step in," Marc said. "She's working at the hotel. I could use the boss-employee angle. We already know she has a thing for her bosses."

Gabe glared at Marc out of the corner of his eye. It was a silent warning to shut his pie hole, but instead Marc kicked the footrest of the recliner down and leaned forward, his face going hard. "Maybe I'm a little young for her, though, seeing as she tends to have a thing for older guys."

Gabe jumped to his feet, his fists curled as he towered over Marc. "Maybe you should shut the hell up."

Marc stood, moving until they were chest to chest, shoving his kid-brother bullshit all up in Gabe's face. Marc was five years younger, but he outweighed Gabe by a good twenty pounds and at least two inches. Had ever since he'd turned sixteen.

As a kid, Marc had been a handful. His act-first, think-about-it-later personality intensified after their parents died, landing him in trouble with school and with girls. By the time Marc had graduated and gone off to college, Gabe felt like a middle-aged father. By the time Trey had left the nest, Gabe was done being a parent.

Which was why when Marc said, "Maybe you should start thinking about Abby instead of thinking with your dick," Gabe lost it.

He was done. Done being a parent. Done sacrificing everything on the chance that it could make his siblings' lives run a little smoother.

"Maybe Abby needs to grow the fuck up and get over it. And maybe, just maybe, Regan was as much of a victim as our sister." He grabbed the remote out of Marc's hand, punched the off button, and threw it across the room. It hit the wall and shattered. "You know what? I'm tired of wasting my time trying to fix this mess."

At that, all three of his brothers exchanged a look. Gabe didn't need to be a genius to figure out its meaning. They thought he was in over his head. And they were right.

"You slept with her," Marc accused.

"No. I did not."

"But you want to."

"What I want is to let this woman go on with her life. And for you guys to stay the hell out of my business."

Already grabbing his keys, Gabe headed for the door. If this was what it felt like to have a sibling meddle in his life, he was cured. ChiChi was right—it was like being smothered.

"My house better be clean and you guys gone when I get home."

By the time Gabe made it to Regan's apartment his temper had cooled some, but his guilt had kicked up a few dozen notches. The last time he and his siblings had had a blowout like that was the Christmas when Richard proposed to Abby. Gabe had been the only one not adamantly opposed to the union, and for three weeks leading up to the wedding, not one of his brothers had spoken to him.

"And look how that turned out, genius."

He'd assumed that it was his brothers being overprotective as usual, but maybe they had sensed what he'd been too blind to see. That Richard had had an agenda from the start.

He flipped his seat forward and leaned into the back of the truck's cab, pulling out several bags of ornaments and a box of tinfoil.

If he were smart, he would have gone to his office, cooled down while riffling through the piles of paperwork and endless e-mails that he'd been too busy following Regan to deal with, then called his brothers to apologize. But for the first time in a while, he didn't want to do the smart thing and he didn't want to babysit his siblings. He wanted to spend a nice evening making tissue-paper snowflakes and decorating a Christmas tree.

With his brother-in-law's former mistress.

Crap!

Shoving the bag back in the car and telling himself that this was as stupid an idea as kissing Regan had been, Gabe got behind the wheel. He shouldn't be here. And if she had wanted him there she wouldn't have cut and run.

Turning the key in the ignition, he flicked on his headlights and everything inside him stilled as he watched a shadow dart across the parking lot and duck behind a shrub manicured to look like a giant wine bottle. Through the thick fog that had settled on the ground, he couldn't see who was there or how big they were; all he knew was that they'd come from the general vicinity of Regan's car and had something slung over their back. And it wasn't a tote full of toys.

Reaching behind the seat, he blindly grabbed his ax and a Maglite. As he crept around the side of the building, he was acutely aware that no one was around and that Regan's new place, although right off the main drag of town, was extremely isolated. Back pressed against the cold concrete wall, he glanced down at Regan's car and noticed the trunk slightly ajar. Using his elbow, he cracked it open and peered inside. It was a disaster. Magazines, papers, flares, and CDs were scattered around. Her taillight was broken and the carpet had been ripped up.

He shifted back to the shrub he had seen the suspect disappear behind. Carefully, he made his way toward the giant wine bottle. Half of him hoped that the son of a bitch was there so that he could beat the crap out of him. The other half, the half that registered that he was a winemaker and not a PI, hoped the guy had fled. And yet a small part, a part he didn't want to acknowledge, was afraid that maybe it was Richard. And if it was, then what did that mean?

He could hear heavy breathing coming from the other side of the shrub, followed by a rustling of leaves. One hand on the Maglite, Gabe took a deep breath and, wondering why in the hell he didn't just call the cops, leaped out from behind the wine bottle, ax blazing.

"Don't move!" he yelled.

He heard a shriek and branches snapping, then a bright red light began flashing, followed closely by a cheery little, "Merry Christmas to one and all."

Dressed in black tennis shoes, black sweats, a black hoodie, and her hair pulled up in a messy knot on top of her head, Regan was stuck ass first in a shrub shaped like a corkscrew, clinging to Randolph and muttering some very choice words under her breath.

"God, Regan." He squatted in front of her. "Are you all right?"

"What in the hell are you doing?" she snapped. "And why are you holding a persimmon roll over your head?"

"Me?" He dropped his "ax" to the ground and shrugged. "Hostage negotiations. This in exchange for the deer." He pulled the Eiffel Tower key ring out of his pocket and dangled it in front of her.

"I have no idea what you're talking about." He shot a look, just one, at Randolph. She snatched the key chain and shoved it in the pocket of her hoodie. "You're trespassing and you should leave."

He started carefully untangling Regan from the branches. "Says the woman hiding ass-backward in the bushes with America's Most Wanted Deer in her clutches."

Even though she was only lit by the moon and his flashlight, he could see her cheeks heat as she fiddled with the strings of her hoodie. "I think I'm cursed."

"Cursed?" He laughed. She didn't. She was serious.

Setting Randolph on the concrete, he eased her out of the bush. She dusted herself off, and since the majority of the debris was on that sweet backside of hers, he helped with that too. When she realized he was doing more touching that dusting, she batted his hands away.

"Don't laugh." She paused dramatically, lowering her voice when she continued. "But I think I did something to piss off the Ghost of Christmas Past or something."

"Like obliterating the town Christmas display?"

"I'm being serious."

"So am I." He reached out and rested his hands on her hips. He couldn't help it. Whenever he was around Regan he had to touch her. Based on the way she shimmied closer, running her hands up his chest, she suffered from the same affliction.

"I swear, Gabe, I have tried five times to return this damn reindeer. Every time, someone shows up. Or there is a vigil going on. Or your grandmother calls me."

"Merry Christmas to one and all," the deer said.

Regan just stared at Gabe as if that was solid proof of a curse.

"Don't you think you're being a little paranoid?" He ran his hands up her sides, loving how her breasts pressed tightly against the snug black top she wore. He continued heading north, pulling her shirt as he went, exposing that little patch of skin above her belly button.

"No," she said, her eyes going heavy when he paused to remove a branch that was stuck to her sweats before pushing her shirt high enough to display a very pretty yellow bra—and not much else. "What are you doing?"

"Making sure you don't have any more branches stuck to you."

"Under my shirt? I landed ass-backward, remember?"

"We'll get there." Nudging the hoodie over her head, he pressed his mouth to the curve of her neck. Slowly made his way down her collarbone.

"We can't." She dropped her head back, giving him room to work. "We have a problem"—she gasped when he ran his tongue over the swell of her breast—"upstairs."

"I guarantee you"—he took her hand and placed it over the bulge in his pants—"that we have a much bigger problem downstairs."

"I told Holly I'd be back in five minutes. I let her watch *Miracle on 34th Street* on my laptop to keep her busy, but I don't like to leave her alone."

"I can deal with five minutes." He kissed her long and hard, taking his sweet time. He wasn't about to be rushed. Not now. Not when she was moaning into his mouth and had her fingers sliding over where he needed them most.

They couldn't have sex in five minutes, he thought, as his hand glided over her stomach to toy with the elastic on her sweats, but they could definitely round third.

"Five minutes ended five minutes ago," she whispered against his mouth, still tracing the outline of his erection through the denim. If she kept that up, they both might walk away feeling a whole hell of a lot more relaxed.

"Then we'd better get up there." He kissed her again, one hand coming up to cup her breasts. He could feel her nipple stiffen beneath her bra and had dipped his thumb inside to pull the lace aside when a bright light blinded them.

He blinked into the headlights, trying to make out who was driving the car, and then saw spinning hubcaps, a DELUCA1 license plate, and groaned.

"Shit, you really are cursed."

CHAPTER 9

I'll take him," Gabe said, grabbing for Randolph.
"No." Regan pulled her shirt back on and snatched the deer
by the antlers. "You buy me some time. I'll hide the deer."

"Why don't we just tell them the truth and then this
whole mess will be over?"

She jerked her head from side to side.

"Then why don't I say I had him?"

"I can't let you lie too," she said, feeling tears prick her
eyes. "And I can't tell them the truth because then they'll
know I deceived them. I am the webmaster for the Safe
Return of Randolph hotline, and ChiChi made me a junior
detective on the Where's Randolph campaign. If they find
out that *I* took Randolph *and* threw Santa through ChiChi's
rear window, the only three people in town who have been
nice to me from day one will hate me."

Gabe stroked her face and she leaned into his hand. "They
won't hate you."

"I'll take him back tomorrow. I promise. I can get Ava to watch Holly."

Gabe sighed. She could tell he didn't want to let her go. Or let this charade go on any longer. But she meant what she said. The Mrs. Clauses were the closest thing Regan had come to having a mother figure in a long time. She didn't want to lose that.

Hugging Randolph to her chest, she ran behind the corkscrew shrub and, making a mental note to join a gym immediately, made a wheezy lap around the building. Darting behind her car, she waited until Gabe approached the orange SUV, then slid Randolph in her trunk, closed the lid, and snuck up her steps.

She shut the front door, emptied her pockets into the Dirty Jar, gave Holly a kiss on the forehead, and hightailed it to the bedroom. Yanking off her hoodie, she pulled on the first shirt she could grab. She was just smoothing out her hair when she heard the doorbell.

"Mommy!" Holly leaped up off the carpet and scrambled to the window. "We have our first visitor." She peered out the window and started jumping. "It's Gabe and the Mrs. Clauses."

Whoops. Regan had started calling them that at home, but she never thought about Holly repeating it. Especially within hearing range.

Regan opened the door and barely had a chance to step back before the three Mrs. Clauses, each in a pink Santa hat, each holding a Christmas offering, and each with a pop-up chair slung over her shoulder, chimed in with a "Merry Christmas."

All three women stood on the stoop and blinked up innocently at her, and Regan got a bad feeling in her gut. She eased the door a little more closed than open and placed her body between the welcoming committee and the entrance to her house.

"Merry Christmas," Regan replied, tugging down the bottom of her shirt, which felt like it was creeping up, and hoped she looked halfway presentable. Her cheeks were still flushed and her breath was coming in low spurts. Partly from the jog and partly from Gabe's magical lips.

"Mommy." Holly nudged at her legs and gracefully squirmed her way around them to face their visitors. "It's not polite to leave guests standing on the front porch. You invite them inside and offer them a drink."

"And some would say it's not polite to drop in unannounced," Gabe murmured from behind.

"Says the man hiding in the bushes," ChiChi said, pushing her way inside. "Plus, we're here on official committee business."

Lucinda followed holding Mr. Puffins, looking dashing in a green Christmas tree dress with a star Velcroed to his head. Pricilla waddled through the door, but not before delivering a grandmotherly kiss, one to Holly and one to Regan, and digging through her crocheted handbag to offer both of them peppermint lollipops.

"Thank you." Holly beamed as she led them into the house.

Each granny set her plate on the counter and took her place in the family room in front of the tree. ChiChi set up her chair and the other ladies followed, even popping up a mini red and green one that was Holly-sized.

Which left Regan standing at the front door, staring up into the eyes of one sexy vintner. Not sure what to say or do with her hands, she settled on a lame smile. Then felt her cheeks heat when she thought of what they had almost done in the alley below.

Gabe leaned in, his eyes dropping to her shirt, and whispered, "My thoughts exactly."

She looked down and felt the embarrassment rise. In her panicked state she had grabbed one of Holly's shirts. It was tiny enough to smash her breasts, white enough to pass for wet T-shirt attire, and had PRRRRR scrawled across the chest in pink. And poking out, just above the top curve of the second and fifth *R*, was hard evidence that she was still turned on.

"Yeah, me too," Gabe said, his lips grazing her ear, before walking through the doorway.

"Here you go." Regan threaded gold yarn through the last tinfoil star and handed it to Gabe, a tingle shooting through her body when he purposefully ran a thumb along the underside of her wrist.

The Mrs. Clauses had arrived with cookies, cocoa, hot buttered wine—everything needed for a Christmas tree decorating party, including a few ornaments to add to their collection. And they had helped Holly find the perfect place for each one. The way they treated her daughter, went out of their way to hug her and make her feel special, touched Regan deeply. But what had melted her heart were the contents of the bag that Gabe dropped by the front door.

It wasn't filled with expensive presents or store-bought decorations. Gabe had brought tinfoil, yarn, tissue paper, popcorn—all the things needed to create a homemade Christmas tree. And Holly had been thrilled.

"One North Star, coming up." He pasted a piece of tape to the yarn and passed it up to Holly, who giggled and took the handmade decoration.

Holly tapped her tiny finger against her chin and scanned the ceiling before pointing to the corner on the far side of the room. "Over there."

"As the lady wishes." Gabe carefully stepped around to the other side of the tree.

And that was exactly how they'd spent the last hour. The Mrs. Clauses stringing popcorn and shouting strict directions from their thrones. Holly perched on Gabe's shoulder, sticking hundreds of tinfoil stars and tissue paper snowflakes to the ceiling to complete the illusion of a Winter Wonderland. And Regan wondering if her new friends understood just what a gift they had given her and her daughter.

"Not there," ChiChi said from her chair, shoving a handful of popcorn in her mouth and using a laser pointer to make a red *X* on the star in question. "It needs to be right above the tree." The laser flew to the spot on the ceiling that was just above the tree's point.

Lucinda reached over, grabbed a handful of popcorn for herself, and studied the room. Mr. Puffins opened one eye. It went wide and then narrowed in on the moving beam. "She's right. It's the biggest one we made, so it should be right over tree."

"Oh, I like that idea." Pricilla nodded eagerly.

"Nope," Holly said, reaching up to stick the tape to the ceiling in the place she had deemed perfect. "The biggest one was my nana's and it goes on top. Right, Mommy?"

"Right, angel."

Regan dug through their Christmas box and pulled out a clump of bubble wrap and tissue paper. Carefully she unrolled it, her chest constricting when she got to the heart of the packaging and saw the first golden edge of the blown glass. This had been her mother's favorite decoration, one of the only things Regan still had of hers.

"Would you look at that," ChiChi said, the awe clear in her voice. "Bring that over here."

Regan handed it to the older woman and watched, her heart in her throat, as one by one the Mrs. Clauses gingerly passed it around, inspecting it thoroughly. It was the most beautiful thing Regan owned and, silly or not, she wanted the ladies to think it beautiful too.

"Is this a family heirloom?" Lucinda asked, handing it back.

Regan took the star and ran her finger along the edges. They had gotten smoother over the years, just as the lead in the glass had weighted to the bottom, leaving irregular patterns and bubbling.

"It belonged to my grandmother. And it was one of the few things that my mother brought with her from Mexico."

"It's lovely, dear," Pricilla said, wiping at the corners of her eyes. "Just lovely."

"And Mommy always puts it on last," Holly explained, scrambling out of Gabe's arms the second he set her down and her feet hit the carpet. She took Regan's hand and all but tugged her to the tree. With a serious face, she looked up at Regan and informed her, "She's ready, Mom."

Regan felt her eyes sting. First, placing her mom's star on the tree always made her want to cry because it was a reminder, not only of what Regan had lost, but of what a great woman her mother had been.

Second, the minute that star went on the tree this wonderful evening would come to a close: Holly would go to bed, the Mrs. Clauses would head home, Gabe would escort them, and Regan would be left alone with the memory of the night but the knowledge that it was over.

Last, she would spend the evening staring at the makeshift decorations, the thought behind them, and wish for things that could never come true.

Holly kissed the star then Regan, who stretched to place it on the top branch. Normally it wasn't such an ordeal, since their trees tended to be about four feet. This one was at least eight feet tall, five feet wide, and being the mac-daddy of trees, even on her tiptoes she couldn't reach.

Gabe appeared in front of her. Without a word, he bent down, slid his arms around her butt, and smiled. After getting a good handful of her backside he pulled her to him and stood, bringing her within arm's length of the tree's top. She leaned over Gabe's head and, aware that she was shoving her PRRRRRR right in his face, carefully placed the star.

"It's perfect," Holly screamed, almost wiggling herself right off ChiChi's lap.

"I agree," Gabe said to her chest.

He lowered Regan to the ground, sliding her body down his at a painstaking pace, his hands still firmly on her ass, making sure that every single one of her good parts brushed over and against every single one of his. When her feet touched the floor, she was pressed thigh to chest against Gabe, his downstairs hard against her belly.

Oh God, she was going to lose it. Right there under her mom's star and in front of her daughter, a cat with pipe-cleaner branches, and three little old ladies, Regan was going to kiss Gabe. And the twinkle in his eyes said he was going to kiss her right back.

"It will never work," Pricilla said, breaking the spell. And stating what they both already knew.

Regan took a step back, but not before she saw the frustration in Gabe's eyes. He thought that they could make this thing between them work. And if Regan was capable of a short, casual fling he would be right. But she wasn't. And that made the whole situation wrong.

"Give it here," ChiChi squawked, grabbing the laser pointer and fiddling with the dial. "I'll make it work."

A fine beam danced around the room, catching Mr. Puffin's attention. The furry noble fir with claws ignored Lucinda's cry and leaped off her lap, racing across the room and chasing the light as it went from red to green to yellow. By the time it cycled to white, the poor cat had run into three walls, crawled up—and down—Gabe's leg, and knocked over the entire Crock-Pot of hot buttered wine.

"Nonna," Gabe hollered. Pricilla was already reaching for a towel, and Holly was chasing Mr. Puffins to avoid another disaster.

ChiChi looked up and, oblivious to the chaos, handed the laser pen to Gabe. "Be a dear, and place this inside of the star. I think it will add just the right amount of magic."

Gabe ran a hand down his face. "Nonna, I swear to—"

"I think that sounds lovely, ChiChi." Regan brushed her fingers lightly across Gabe's knuckles. "Don't you, Gabe?"

He shot her a look that said he thought quite the opposite but took the pen anyway. And ChiChi was right. Once placed inside the star, the whole room glowed with golden haloes, and it was pretty damn magical.

"Now, Gabe, make yourself useful and help Holly with her teeth. We have business to discuss with our marketing goddess."

Holly hugged each granny, pet Mr. Puffins, who, tail standing on end, was crouched behind the tree staring up at the golden twinkles on the ceiling, and took Gabe by the hand. Regan could barely breathe as she watched the two of them disappear into the bathroom.

"Yes, quite the sight," ChiChi said, placing a shaky hand on Regan's shoulder. "Brings a tear to my eye."

"Enough of the hallmark moment," Lucinda said. "We've got a problem and you, being our secret weapon, are going to help us fix it. Now sit."

Once again, Regan found herself seated in a tiny chair, staring up at a trio of grannies in Christmas garb—ChiChi's more couture than cliché. All in their glasses and all looking down at Regan in a way that made her nervous.

"We heard from Gail at the market that Suzanne asked her to take Monday morning off and babysit little Mariella," Lucinda said, snatching up Mr. Puffins and reshaping the pipe cleaners to look more like a cone than a square.

"I assume Mariella is her granddaughter," Regan ventured, when the ladies went quiet.

"Suzanne is Gail's daughter-in-law. And since she was born with a corkscrew lodged firmly up her hind quarters—"

"Suzanne never asks Gail to sit," ChiChi interrupted Lucinda, sending her a reprimanding glance over the top of her glasses. "But her own mother is in Hawaii. Usually she would just cancel whatever plans she had rather than ask her mother-in-law."

"So it got us thinking," Pricilla whispered, leaning down, Crock-Pot in hand, as if the information she was about to impart was a matter of national security. "What could be so important that she would ask a favor of Gail?"

"Then I saw Penny at the vet when I was picking up Mr. Puffins's insulin shots, and she said her granddaughter asked her to sit her two youngest on the same day and for the same amount of time."

"And this is evening news material, why?" Regan asked, noticing how all six eyes went wide in disbelief.

"Because they're a part of the yoga pants posse," all three ladies yelled at once.

"And they are having a mandatory PTA meeting Monday morning at nine," Gabe said from the doorway. When everyone stared at him mutely, he just shrugged. "Jordan is still on the board and needed the time off. I gave it to her. What?" he said, when ChiChi looked ready to spit.

"They knew that Mr. Puffins had an appointment at the Paws and Claws Day Spa," Lucinda snapped, gripping Mr. Puffins's costume and sending pipe cleaners everywhere.

"I have two hundred minicakes to make for a wedding, and ChiChi is supposed to be in San Francisco with Abby meeting with the new marketing company Gabe found." Pricilla patted Regan on the knee. "Sorry, dear, that was insensitive of me."

Regan shrugged. Hospitality may not be her dream industry, but it beat working with Abigail. *And* she was good at it.

In fact, today had marked the end of her first week at the Napa Grand, the end of the wine seller's convention, and the end of cleaning toilets. It had also been her first official day as the newly promoted Manager of Special Events and VIP Coordinator.

After convincing Mr. Bonnet that ChiChi was getting up in years and that the holidays were especially difficult because it reminded her that none of her grandchildren were married, he had laughed off the situation, explaining that his own wife had threatened to find his daughter-in-law a lover if their son didn't give her grandchildren soon.

Jordan, impressed with Regan's people skills, had immediately assigned her to handle any and all needs of "The Bonjour Group," as they had been deemed.

Before the Ms. Clauses could accuse another innocent Frenchman of crimes against the town, Regan had emptied out one of the dining halls, arranged the tables in intimate seatings for six, and provided all-you-can-guzzle complimentary beverage service and free Wi-Fi. She'd single-handedly turned what could have been a scheduling disaster into a successful networking luncheon. And Jordan had quickly promoted her from housekeeping to events coordinator.

"They are trying to pin the Randolph disaster on us, use it as a way to get us impeached so they can take over the musical. So we have to make a unified front. Prove to them that we are not a bunch of old biddies. That we still know what's best for this community," ChiChi said. "And I just know that once that board sees your ideas on the town's new image, their faith in us will be restored and that Isabel Stark will have to find herself a new committee to hijack."

Regan loved the idea of sabotaging Isabel's plans. But that these ladies were expecting her alone to sway the board was a lot of pressure. If she made a mistake, even a small one—like, say, getting caught replacing Randolph—and let her Mrs. Clauses down, she would feel horrible. Not that it mattered. There was no way she could make that meeting. She had work.

Regan opened her mouth to apologize when she found it suddenly full of popcorn. A heaping handful. Afraid that if she opened it again she might wind up with a mouthful of yarn since they were running low on snacks, she took her time chewing.

"I already talked to Marc and he said you can start late and make up whatever time you missed at the end of your shift," ChiChi said, her tone leaving no room for argument.

"And I'll bring Holly back to the bakery with me. It will give us a chance to talk about what kind of tea party she wants for her birthday," Pricilla added.

On special occasions, Pricilla's Patisserie doubled as a tearoom that had become the crème de la crème of birthday party locations for little girls in a three-county radius. Regan had looked into it as a solution to their short-on-space living situation.

Martha Stewart had listed Pricilla's Official Teas as one of the premiere places to host a child's party on the West Coast. It was all about decadence, elegance, and etiquette. It was everything that Holly could dream of. It also had a ridiculous wait list and would take Regan two months to pay for the two-hour party.

"Oh, Pricilla, thank you for the offer, but there is just no way—"

And in went a gingerbread man, his wife, and three children. Regan's mouth was so full that her eyes watered.

"Now, seeing as the arrangement was struck between your daughter and myself, as long as you feel safe having Holly with me is all that matters," Pricilla said, dusting the ginger crumbs from her cardigan sweater, which boasted beavers with antlers.

Holly came out of the bedroom in her footie pajamas and climbed on Regan's lap. "Grandma Pricilla and me made an arrangement. I promised to help with the cakes for that wedding, and she promised to host my party in her shop."

"You did?" Regan asked, finding it difficult to speak through the gingerbread and tears in her throat.

Holly nodded and snuggled against her chest. She held her daughter close, expressing with her eyes what she could never get across without bursting into tears. The women exchanged a knowing glance, and Gabe came behind her to rest a supportive hand on her shoulder.

"We thought the Saturday before Christmas would be best, since after Christmas people tend to get busy. All that's left to do is choose the menu and decorations. Oh, and you can pick up the invitations at my shop on your way to get your new couch Sunday."

"Couch? What couch?" Regan slapped her hands over her mouth when Pricilla pulled a chunk of white-chocolate peppermint bark out of her crocheted handbag. It was like the Mary Poppins bag of baked goods.

"Did you not tell her anything?" Lucinda slid a glance at the other two Mrs. Clauses.

"You've been here the whole time, Lucinda," ChiChi countered, waving her hands in a dramatic circle and scaring the cat. "If you didn't hear it, it wasn't said." She turned back to Regan. "Our friend Peggy is moving into one of those retirement homes in Calistoga. She has to get rid of her furniture and I mentioned that you were looking for a couch. She said that if you haul it away by Sunday you can have it, a kitchen table, and the guest bed for a hundred bucks."

"A hundred bucks?" Regan said through her fingers. She thought back to the envelope of cash Gabe had slid back into her pocket and smiled.

The couch would probably be yellow with mauve roses all over it and covered in plastic—but who cared. It was a couch. They had been sitting and sleeping on the floor for almost a week, and her back was killing her.

"I can load it up in my truck if you want some company," Gabe offered, his fingers gently squeezing her shoulder and doing all kinds of squeezing in her belly.

Regan nodded. It was all she could do. Everyone was being so nice.

"Okay, then, we will get out of your way so you can put Holly to bed and I will see you tomorrow," Gabe said, ushering the Mrs. Clauses to the door. After a round of hugs and good-byes, including an awkward moment with Gabe where she settled on a hug, Regan tucked Holly into bed and went to the kitchen.

Normally, she loved this time of night, when Holly was asleep and the house was quiet and she could relax. Well, that was, when she wasn't working or picking up Holly's things or surfing the net for inexpensive and simple patterns for cat and frog costumes. Tonight, though, all that peace and quiet was anything but calming.

She grabbed a spoon from the drawer and went for the fridge. It was a Rocky Road kind of night.

She didn't think of Gabe as she grabbed a mug. Or when she filled it full with some of the hot buttered wine that hadn't spilled. And she sure as hell didn't analyze how she had nearly had sex with him in a bush.

Not that it was all her fault. He had scared her, attacked her with a persimmon roll, and then kissed her—and man oh man, that mouth of his should be outlawed. One more second of those lips on her body and she would have wound up pantyless and panting with a bad case of shrub burn.

But the Mrs. Clauses had shown up. Again.

She hadn't been kidding when she told Gabe that she was cursed. Not that she would have changed anything. Getting busy with Gabe while Holly was alone upstairs was a bad-mommy move. One that she would be sure not to make again.

Getting involved with Gabe in general was also a bad-mommy move, and it was clear that making out with him had been a mistake. A big one. A big, hot, delectable, and totally insane mistake, which had been the direct result of too much adrenaline, too many hormones, and an unnatural amount of testosterone. If their past wasn't enough to smack some sense into her, their awkward parting was.

Awkward was putting it mildly. Not sure whether she should hug or kiss or merely thank him for a fun night, she'd become all arms and legs and uncertainty. Then ChiChi went for her purse and pulled out something that looked suspiciously like mistletoe and Regan panicked, giving him a friendly hug. Then she patted him. On the back.

Regan leaned against the fridge and banged her head on the door a few times. The man whose lips had kissed their way down her chest and brought her to near orgasmic levels while still clothed had gotten a send-off fit for Fido.

This was why she didn't date. Because she sucked at it.

She opened the freezer and was pulling out a carton of Rocky Road when a light tap sounded at the door. She jumped, smacking her head on the top of the fridge and sending a small avalanche of freezer burn into her hair. Grabbing the ice-cream tub before it rolled out onto the floor and taking the spoon for protection, she silently crept to the door, being sure to slow her already elevated breathing.

She looked through the peephole and had to stop herself from giving in to a happy dance. Gabe leaned against the rail with his thumbs tucked into his jean pockets, looking finger-licking good.

She opened the door and her heart caught. And not in a good way. Mr. Easygoing was looking anything but. In fact, his hair looked like he'd done a lot of raking his hands through it, and his expression was almost sad.

Then he took in her ice cream, the deadly spoon, and by the time he got to her hair a small smile was spreading across his face. He stepped close to her and ruffled her ponytail. Little bits of ice scattered to the ground.

"Holly wants a white Christmas. Still working out the details," she explained. She didn't know what was more embarrassing, the ice shard dripping down her right cheek or her Abominable Snowman slippers.

His smile widened. Then he said, "We need to talk."

And hers faded.

Gabe was thankful that Regan was still wearing her sweats and tee. It had taken him so long to get rid of the grannies, he was afraid he'd find her asleep—or worse, in her nightie. He was going to have a hard enough time sleeping without adding the image of what she slept in to the mix.

"Okay, what do you want to talk about?" Her words came out breathy and her eyes were sending him all kinds of mixed signals. Almost as mixed up as he felt at the moment.

He wanted nothing more than to pick up where they'd left off, but she had a sleeping kid fifteen feet away, and he had to ask her something he didn't want to. Because seeing her tonight, surrounded by his grandma and Holly, had reminded him that family, even if they were sometimes a gigantic pain in the ass, were important. And his family needed some answers.

Her face flushed. She stepped onto the stoop and quietly pulled the door closed. "Actually, you don't have to answer that. I know why you're here and you're right, we need to talk."

"Is that right?" He knew full well that she hadn't a rat's-ass clue why he was there, and he bet he knew exactly what she wanted to talk about. So he raised a brow and waited for her to talk herself in circles.

"Every time we're together, stuff gets out of hand."

"What stuff?"

"You know exactly what stuff I'm talking about."

Yeah, he did. But he wanted to hear her say it. When she pressed her lips tight and shook her head, sending melted ice drops splattering on his arm, he took a step closer. Close enough to hear her breath pick up and see her eyes go heavy.

He didn't kiss her or even touch her. He just invaded her space as much as possible without actually initiating contact.

"See, Vixen," he whispered, watching the pulse at the base of her neck skyrocket. "When you refer to *stuff*, I can only imagine you're talking about how whenever we're together we can't seem to keep our hands off each other. And when we do touch it's so damn combustive it's hard to breathe."

Her throat worked hard to swallow, but when she finally managed it her chin hitched up, her lips tightened into a thin line and her stubborn side took over. "Which is why I think we should avoid each other."

"Is that right?" He reached out and traced a finger over her mouth, loving how those lips relaxed and instantly went pliant under his touch. He knew he should be asking her about Richard, about her run-in with Abby, but she was ready to kick him to the curb and he needed to give her a reason to keep him around.

Not to mention, there was no way he was walking away now. Not before he got a chance to figure out what this insane chemistry was about.

"Most of your family hates me. My daughter is falling in love with you. And you're not looking for anything permanent. I could go on."

She had a point. A good one. But he still found himself stepping closer. Found his hand settling on her waist. Found that there was no way in hell he was going to be able to walk away.

She was quiet for a moment, her eyes studying him. "Why did you come here tonight?"

"Because my brothers were at my house, I wanted to help you set up your tree, and I needed to see you," he said, knowing the last part was the real reason he'd come.

"Then why did you come back?"

"For this." He cupped the back of her head and pulled her in for a kiss. It was hard and heated and over way too fast, because Regan stumbled backward, out of his arms and into the front door.

"We can't do this anymore." She shook her head, her hands fumbling to find the doorknob. "Because one day we won't be able to stop."

"Can you be more specific, because *this* will happen, Regan. And I'd like to know how many more cold showers I'm going to have to take."

"No. *This* can't happen, Gabe. Ever. Because there is nowhere for it to go that won't hurt the people that we love. Between our past, your family, my family..." She looked over her shoulder at the bedroom window as if just remembering that her daughter slept only a wall away.

"No," she repeated firmly, pushing open the door and stepping inside the apartment.

Gabe put his hand on the door before she could shut it. "It's going to happen, Vixen. You know it. I know it. Hell, every time we share space we practically tear off each other's clothes. Denying it is just going to make things worse."

She shot him a glare that was part irritation, part desire, and wholly hot. Then she shook her head. "Not if we don't let it. Good-bye, Gabe."

"That would be good *night*, Gabe, because I will see you Sunday, bright and—"

The door slammed in his face. He heard the metal tumble and lock engage and stepped back. He listened for her through the door but only found silence.

Regan was already gone. And sadly, he acknowledged, so was he.

CHAPTER 10

I told you that you didn't have to do this," Regan said from the passenger seat.

"And like I told you, it's no big deal. I have a truck, a free day, a good set of arms." She stared stiffly out the window. "Besides, why waste money on a rental when you don't need to?" he reasoned, feeling pretty stiff himself, but for a whole other reason.

A *Storage Wars* marathon, a couple of ice-cold beers, and an even colder shower hadn't helped him one bit. All he had to do was think of Regan in that yellow bra, panting in his ear, and he was as bad as a fifteen-year-old.

He'd called her a couple of times yesterday to confirm what time she wanted him to pick her up. He'd been sent to voice mail. Not that he blamed her. He'd shown up unannounced, crashed her tree-decorating party, and then mauled her in the parking lot. And on her front stoop.

Which was why, when he pulled up right around break-fast time with a box of doughnuts, two peppermint lattes, a packet of invitations courtesy of Pricilla, and the mind frame to wait in the truck until she came out of hiding, he wasn't shocked to see Regan already loading Holly in her Honda. She said she'd called Stan down at the service station, and he had a trailer he was willing to rent her.

Holly took one look at the doughnuts on his dashboard and said she would rather ride with him. Gabe had smiled. Regan had scowled. And Holly had polished off two doughnuts with pink sprinkles. End result, he currently had one of the sexiest ladies he'd ever met and one of the cutest girls he'd ever seen riding snug in his truck. And he couldn't be happier.

"Thank you," Regan said, so quietly he wasn't sure he heard it correctly. Actually, he was positive that was her thanking him, but he wanted to hear her say it again.

"What?" He made a big ordeal of turning down the stereo. When she didn't repeat herself, he reached out and touched her thigh, giving it a playful squeeze. "The radio was too loud."

"You heard me," she said to the windshield.

"Yeah, I did. I just wanted to make sure you said what I thought I heard. It sounded kind of like a compliment."

"I said thanks." It came out just as quiet, but this time her hand covered his. He slid her a sidelong glance, but she remained staring straight ahead.

"I can't wait to see my new bed. I hope it will be soft and fluffy and purple with kitties on it," Holly said from the back seat of the king cab.

"Well, I'm not sure about the kitty part. But I'm sure it will be soft and fluffy," Regan answered.

Holly's voice dropped in volume, a hint of sadness creeping in. "But I'm gonna miss our camping, Mommy. It was fun, just you and me under the stars."

Tightening her hand on Gabe's, Regan twisted in the front seat. "I had fun too. You're a pretty special kid, you know that?"

Holly shrugged, accepting the praise like a kid who knew she was loved and cherished. Gabe was once again surprised at what a great mom Regan was. Being a single parent was tough enough; he'd seen Jordan struggle daily. And yet here sat this woman, who hadn't been much more than a kid herself when she'd had Holly, but she'd figured it out. Even alone and struggling, she had managed to make sure that each and every decision made was in the best interest of her daughter, in turn making Holly's world magical.

"You're a pretty special mom," he said in a voice just meant for her, which finally had her looking his way. She opened her mouth but nothing came out. She looked flustered and surprised and adorable as hell. And that made what he was doing all the more shitty.

Oh, he wasn't there to please his brothers and see what he could find out about Richard. He was there because spending time with the two Martin women made him feel alive, as though all of the other bullshit in his life didn't matter. It also made him an asshole, because at the end of the day, this would lead nowhere good.

Gabe pulled into the driveway and put the truck in park. Regan was back to staring out the window. Only, instead of the wonder she'd had in her eyes a minute ago, he saw irritation—and a lot of it.

"Lauren!" Holly shrieked at the window, her hands waving excitedly at the blonde-haired girl who stood on the front porch at their final destination. "Lauren, Lauren. It's me, Holly," she yelled louder, right in his ear.

"Don't think she can hear you. Window's up," Gabe said, amused. Regan sent him an apologetic look, but he just smiled. Holly was one cute kid.

"Gabe! That's my friend Lauren!" Holly yanked at her seat belt. "She's in my class and we played together at recess. She and Chloe and Summer are my BFFs. But next week I'll be the *F* and Summer gets to be the *B* 'cuz we thought we should share. Can we play, Mommy? Can we?"

Regan looked at the impressive house and twisted her hands in her lap. Plastering a smile on her face she said, "Sure, angel. Now that I think about it, I bet it was her grandma that I talked to earlier. You two could play while we load up the truck."

"Yes!" Kicking open the door, Holly raced up the driveway singing Lauren's name the entire way. Lauren reciprocated the excitement and before long the two girls disappeared into the house.

"Cursed," Regan said, shaking her head.

Gabe didn't even question Regan's statement because the second Isabel appeared on the porch with a cordial wave, *cursed* was not the word he was thinking to describe his current situation.

Isabel was dressed in black yoga pants, a barely-there tank, and fake lashes. He watched her eyes widen as recognition bloomed and her wave took on a caffeinated tick as if she'd downed one too many skinny lattes. Her persona went from socialite to seductress.

Isabel's plans had just shifted, and by the way her walk took on a sexy sway, Gabe was now her target of interest.

Outside of mumbling something Holly would have nailed her for, Regan didn't move. She actually looked a little pale and completely ticked.

"You okay?"

"What?" She looked down at their intertwined hands and back to him as if remembering he was next to her. He tightened his grip. "Oh, I just expected a little old lady in a muumuu and rollers."

"Yeah, well, this isn't how I expected our date would start," Gabe said.

"Date?" Regan looked over at Gabe. His shirt was soft and relaxed and made his shoulders look like ones she could count on. Then he flashed that orgasm-inducing smile, the one which curled up slightly to one side, declaring all of the things he would like to do to her, and the air rushed out of her lungs.

She'd been battling hormone-induced suffocation since he'd stepped out of his truck earlier that morning in a pair of worn jeans that highlighted his butt perfectly, breakfast in hand and ball cap pulled low on his head. He looked like your basic super-stud mover to the rescue.

Then Holly had asked him to put her hair in a rubber band. Which he did. And it ended up more of a porcupine than a pony. But Regan noticed that where she saw a supersexy guy, Holly might begin to imagine a superspecial daddy.

Even if Regan were ready to risk a broken heart to give love a try again, she couldn't do that to Holly. Because ultimately Gabe would get bored, move on to the next woman, and that would crush her daughter.

"This isn't a date. *We* aren't dating."

He quirked a brow. "Then why am I here?"

"A good set of arms, remember?"

"Fair enough." Did he just flex? "But if this isn't a date, then why are you holding my hand?"

Regan jerked her hand back and crossed her arms over her chest. Partly to look tough but mostly to keep from touching him again. "You held my hand first."

"And you held back."

"*This* is not a date," she felt compelled to state again.

"If you say so, Vixen." Gabe crossed that good set of arms over his equally good set of pecs, and she had to squish her brows together to keep from looking down at his guns. She had never really been into arms before, but there was something about his that made her want to wrap them around her and beg him to never let go.

"You want to keep staring at my arms all day? Or are we going to go get you some furniture? Honestly, I'm up for either"—he smiled—"because even though floor sex or wall sex is hot, afterward a guy needs a place to lay and cuddle with his date."

"You are not staying the night. We are not having sex. And this is not a date!" Regan hopped out of the truck and slammed the door before he could scream, "Liar, liar." She also tied her sweatshirt around her waist just in case her pants were smoking.

Before she could shake off the post-Gabe-encounter buzz, which she told herself was caused from irritation, she was confronted with the second most annoying resident in St.

Helena. However, said resident seemed to have eyes only for Mr. DeLuca.

"Morning, Gabe," Isabel cooed, beckoning him onto the porch so she wouldn't have to step out into the light drizzle. Her hair looked smooth and coiffed while Regan's was frizzing by the sprinkle.

Isabel slid her hands around Gabe's neck in greeting, plastering her silicone to his chest. Gabe mumbled a "Nice to see you," and with a brief pat on her back, stepped away. Fast. So fast Isabel was still doing the air-kisses.

Then she glared at Regan through a pair of Gucci glasses, as if Regan had intruded on their moment; as if it wasn't raining; as if Gabe had come here to see her.

"Regan, I didn't expect to see you today," Isabel said, her welcome as plastic as her family's corks. "What a small world. Oh, wait, is this about the Costume Committee?"

Isabel knew exactly what she was doing there. Knew exactly who was buying her mom's hand-me-downs, and the way she kept her face pleasantly devoid of any real emotion told Regan that she'd not only come on purpose to witness the groveling, but now she wanted Regan to voice it. In front of Gabe.

There was a whole other conversation that Regan imagined she and Isabel were going to have someday soon, but for today Holly needed a bed, so Regan sucked up the ego and played nice. Which meant she would *not* bring up the secret town council meeting planned for tomorrow, and she would most definitely *not* poke Isabel in the eye.

She reached in her purse and pulled out a red glittery envelope. "Actually, Holly's birthday party is coming up and we wanted to drop off the invite."

Isabel blinked down at the invitation in Regan's hand but made no move to accept the offering. Then she looked up, a smile firmly in place, but her eyes turned mean. "Actually, I don't think Lauren can come."

Regan's confidence faltered a little. Women like Isabel always made her feel insignificant, but she would be damned if Isabel overlooked Holly as easily. So she practically shoved the card into Isabel's hand. "You haven't even seen what day it is."

Isabel took the card and flipped it open. "Ah, yes. Next weekend Lauren is at her dad's. His family is in town doing the whole Christmas festivities." She shoved it back at Regan. "Maybe next year."

She shouldn't be upset that they weren't coming. Spending the whole afternoon with Isabel watching and judging would have been exhausting. But Holly really wanted her best friend there and, in spite of her mother, Lauren was a sweet kid, one who had gone out of her way to make Holly feel welcome at her new school.

Regan stuffed the invitation, and her bad attitude, back in her purse. It didn't matter if Isabel and Regan didn't mesh—for the kids they should at least try. If Holly and Lauren continued playing together at school, Regan was going to be seeing a lot of Isabel, which meant that someone had to make the effort. She just hated that the someone had to be her.

"Maybe we could get the girls together sometime after school or over the break," she offered, thinking of how that would lessen the blow of Lauren not being there Saturday. "I could do a little mock party, just the two of them. Make cupcakes or something."

"That sounds great. I'll have to check the calendar. We're pretty busy this season." Dismissing Regan, Isabel turned to Gabe, all smiles. "Speaking of calendars, I must have used up one of my Christmas miracles."

"How's that?" Gabe asked, his eyes darting between the two women, trying to figure out how he'd just gotten pulled into the middle. But Regan noticed, giddily, that he slid closer, almost offering her his alliance if she needed it. She didn't, but the thought was sweet.

"I was just talking to Daddy about you. He's having a small soirée tonight and wanted me to bring you along." Isabel looked at Regan. "Please don't think I'm being rude, but it's an industry-people-only kind of event. *Wine* industry. I imagine you'd get bored anyway."

And that was when those rage issues Gabe was always warning Regan about kicked in. Being dismissed was one thing. Being treated like she was stupid was another.

She'd dealt with girls like Isabel her whole life. She knew how to turn the other cheek, how to smile while ducking when they were going for the jugular. When she was younger she'd had to suck it up because her mom cleaned houses for most of their families. But she wasn't that girl anymore.

"That's okay, I'm really not all that into plastic corks. Plus, we already have dinner plans tonight." She slid her arms through Gabe's. "Right, Gabe?"

Gabe smiled big and long, and Regan knew she'd just played into his hands. "Regan's right. Tonight she promised to feed me since we'll spend most of the night testing out that new couch of hers." She felt him flex and swallowed. "You know, to see where it fits best."

Isabel's hurt eyes flew from Gabe's to Regan's and narrowed into two scorned slits. Regan instantly regretted using him to get to Isabel. Sure, Lauren's mom could be nasty and rude, but that didn't mean Regan had to be nasty back. Isabel was still Lauren's mom and Regan was better than that.

Regan dropped Gabe's arm and took a step closer to Isabel. "Look, I think somehow we got off to an...awkward start. We have two wonderful daughters who obviously love spending time together. Why don't we start over?" She stuck out her hand. "Hi, I'm Regan, Holly's mom."

Isabel stared at her hand, then at the powerful DeLuca at her side, and Regan could almost hear her weighing all the possible outcomes. Taking on a single mom who worked at the local hotel would be fun for her. Taking on a DeLuca could be devastating to her family. *That* Regan knew firsthand, and the way Isabel's features softened, she did too.

But before anyone had a chance to speak further, Holly came running out of the house with Lauren right behind her, phone in hand.

"Mommy!" Holly screamed. "Lauren's coming to my party. She's the first one to RSVP." Holly pronounced the acronym as a single word, going heavy on the *S* and the *P*.

Regan looked at Isabel, silently begging her, from one mother to another, not to break her daughter's heart. But Isabel only smiled, walked over to stand behind Lauren, and rested her hands on her shoulder. The effect was creepy. It was almost as though Lauren was the puppet and Isabel was the ventriloquist.

"I'm sorry, Holly. But Lauren is at her dad's this weekend and we have to talk to him first—"

"I already did," Lauren said, stepping away and breaking the connection. She waved the phone wildly. "And he said that I could go cuz we don't have anything to do this weekend and Holly's my best friend."

With every word, Isabel's smile got brighter and brighter until Regan was convinced her forehead was going to break.

"Plus, it's an official Pricilla tea party." Holly bounced on the tips of her toes.

"Just like the one you wanted to throw me when *I* turn six," Lauren declared, clapping in unison with Holly's bouncing.

It may not have been Isabel's forehead that broke, but something inside the woman shattered, and all of the jagged edges were now aimed at Regan. "Pricilla's is booked years in advance. I know. I have been on the wait list since Lauren was born."

She paused, her focus flickering between Regan and Gabe. "You must have pulled some pretty *large* strings to get that party for this weekend."

Her eyes went wide and took on a sinister spark that hollowed Regan's stomach.

"It's just dinner," Regan repeated, standing in the dark and resting her cheek against a bag of frozen corn. No matter how many times she said it, it didn't stop her heart from hoping that it might turn into more. Which was silly because she'd only asked Gabe to dinner to stick it to Isabel. She'd tried to rescind the invitation, but Holly had reissued it. And then charged her a quarter for being rude.

Rude didn't even begin to describe what Isabel had been. And there weren't enough quarters in the world for Regan to get over the way she'd implied that A) Regan was the kind of woman who would use sex to get her daughter a freaking party at a teahouse, and B) sex was the only way a woman like Regan could catch a guy like Gabe's interest. Not that having sex with Gabe was totally out of the question, but they had more between them than just sheer chemistry.

Right?

Lightning crackled though the night sky, illuminating the kitchen a second before thunder shook the apartment. After another few seconds she shut the freezer door and went to the oven. Thank God for gas. She was not going to let Isabel ruin her night.

She opened the door, inhaled the smell of chilies and melting cheese and, flashlight in hand, checked on dinner. Her mom's enchiladas bubbled, a perfectly golden top layer forming.

The thunderstorm had blown in and subsequently blown a transformer on the far side of town, leaving most of St. Helena with no power. Gabe and Holly had gone to the store and bought a warehouse supply of candles and a few dozen flashlights.

Gabe had thankfully put together Holly's new bed before the power went out. Now he was moving it from wall to wall until Holly decided where she wanted it.

Not that Regan was any better. She'd moved the couch four times in their peanut-sized apartment, only to put it under the window—the place where Gabe had originally suggested, although, he'd said, they'd have to move it around some more later, just to be sure. That was when Regan took it upon herself to hide in the kitchen and scour her new table and chairs until they gleamed.

She had a house full of furniture, a happy daughter with a bed, and a sexy man staying for dinner. She was going for perfection tonight.

Holly scrambled across the linoleum, sliding to a stop next to the sink, a little breathless and a whole lot excited. She was practically vibrating. "Scissors and tape?"

"Tape's in the junk drawer. I'll get the scissors."

Holly jerked open the top drawer and yanked out tape, a pile of construction paper, the bottle of fast-drying, super-strength glue that was guaranteed to stick any two surfaces together, even if it were a child's hand to a head of hair, and looked up. "I've got adult supervision this time. And I like my bangs."

"You had adult supervision last time." Regan rolled up on her toes, stretching to reach the craft basket on the top of the fridge. No such luck. "What are you guys doing in there? It's pitch black."

"Gabe and me tied a bunch of flashlights together and then he hung them from the lamp. Upside down."

Regan placed one palm on the puckered finish of the freezer door and contorted her body to gain an extra half inch of reach, her fingertips barely brushing the woven basket. She tried again, this time managing to knock it back another inch.

"Damn it."

"That'll cost you a quarter," Gabe said, his voice a sexy rasp in her ear.

One strong hand slid around her waist, splaying across her midriff and creating all kinds of electricity. His calloused fingers pressed her back, until the curve of her bottom fit snug against his groin, and she had to brace herself against the freezer door since her body had turned to Jell-O.

The other hand trailed up her arm, over her elbow, her wrist, between her fingers, before palming the basket handle.

"It's a surprise." Gabe's lips grazed her lobe. Setting the basket on the counter, his thumb teased the skin that peeked out between the top of her jeans and the hem of her shirt.

Gabe excelled in multitasking. In fact, he was a multitasker extraordinaire. He explored every inch of her stomach while digging out the scissors and a ball of twine, reminding her that she was a woman. A woman who had wants and needs that went beyond what her double-A boyfriend could provide.

Gabe made her feel sexy and smart and wanted. And silly or not, she hadn't felt wanted in a really long time. Not in the way that Gabe was making clear, as he pressed his erection against her back. Plus her battery-operated boyfriend didn't like to cuddle.

Regan wanted someone to share her life with. Not the hard times—she was more than capable of handling whatever came at her on her own. But times like this, with Holly busting at the seams with laughter, a warm meal in the oven, and the table set for three. Someone to share her wonderful daughter with, and after she went to bed, someone to snuggle up close to.

Her head fell back, resting on the center of his chest, and she looked up into his eyes and felt her panties go wet. Even through the candlelight she could see exactly what he was thinking, and it involved the table, her naked, and maybe a tub of Rocky Road. Or maybe that was her thinking.

"Perfect," he breathed, setting a black Sharpie on the counter. Whether he was talking about how well they fit, or the Rocky Road sexcapade, or that he'd found the tools he needed, she didn't know.

A lazy smile crossed his lips and his finger, not so lazy, dipped slightly below her waistband, running along the edge of her panties. A quick tease, gone as fast as it came. But effective as hell.

"Just give us ten minutes."

Gabe's words hummed through her.

Ten minutes? That wouldn't even give the ice cream time to soften. He had her so wound, ten hours wouldn't even do it.

As if reading her mind, he chuckled. "I meant that Holly and I need a few more minutes and then we'll be done."

"Oh. Right. Ten minutes." She stepped away and, hoping that the dim candlelight hid her blaring red cheeks, busied herself with stirring the rice on the stovetop that didn't need stirring.

She could feel Gabe watching her, waiting for her to look up. When she did she forgot to breathe, because his gaze slid from her eyes to her lips, slowly over her breasts and hips, stopping when they got to her bare feet.

She felt her body heat and all she could think was, *Don't look at the table. Don't look at the table.* So, of course, she was so busy telling herself not to look at the table that she looked at the table. And Gabe saw. And understood. And slid her a smile so hot she still felt its burn even after he and Holly had left the kitchen. Even after she told herself that she was not going to have sex with Gabe—kitchen table or elsewhere.

Ten minutes later, she walked into the bedroom to gather the troops for dinner. Two feet from the threshold, she ducked into the shadows and watched from the doorway, careful not to intrude. Gabe and Holly had so much glitter on them they looked like a couple of Christmas ornaments.

Blinking though the limited light, and a little moisture if Regan were being honest, she watched as Gabe helped Holly sprinkle glitter on a piece of paper then carefully stick it to the wall.

"One, two, three," they said in unison, Holly holding up a little finger for each count. When finished, Gabe slowly peeled back the paper, and any hope that Regan would be able to walk away from today with her heart fully intact fell to the carpet with the construction paper.

She swallowed, so touched by the drawing on the wall that she didn't even question where all the extra glitter had come from, or how she'd ever manage to get it out of the carpet, let alone all of Holly's ringlets. Because the far wall, which earlier that evening had been white and bleak, now had the most beautiful display Regan had ever seen.

Brown construction paper hung in a grid, forming a mock window frame. Each of the four panes hosted part of a Sharpie sketch that, when viewed together, appeared to be a giant kitten peering in the window with a full moon in the background, all accented with glitter.

"Gabe and me made it," Holly said. Then she held up her hands, which were covered in glitter and fast-acting glue. "And he supervised. Did you know he's an artist?"

"No," Regan said, still staring at the detail he'd put into making a dismal room into a special place for Holly. She rested a soft hand on Holly's head. "Go wash up, dinner's ready."

"But it's dark." Holly looked down the small hallway, her eyes huge. Besides the candlelit kitchen and the makeshift flashlight lamp in the bedroom, the rest of the apartment was pitch black.

"Here." Gabe walked over and handed her a flashlight. "And make it speedy. I have to wash up too." He held up his sparkly hands. When Holly disappeared he turned to Regan. "Since we couldn't find kitty sheets, we figured a kitty wall was just as good. When you move out I can paint over the glitter and Sharpie. I also told Holly that next weekend I could come over and with more time—"

"It's perfect," Regan said, and she meant it.

Gabe stood at the counter, scrubbing the last of the dinner dishes, when he heard bare feet slapping the linoleum. Soap to his elbows, he turned with just enough time to brace himself and catch a freshly pink and mostly naked Holly as she launched herself into his arms. Wearing nothing but Hello Kitty underwear and bath water, she soaked through his shirt and crawled inside his heart in under three seconds flat.

"How was bath time, kiddo?" he asked.

"Shhhh," she sprayed. "I'm hiding from Mommy."

"Then we need to find a better hiding spot."

He looked around, knowing he didn't have a chance of fitting in Regan's pantry by himself, let alone with a squirming partner in crime. Then he spotted the table. Shifting Holly to his other hip, he crouched down and slid both of them underneath, careful to be quiet when scooting the chairs back in.

"Hey, Gabe, have you seen Holly?" Regan called out from the other room, her voice high and animated.

Holly smothered a giggle. Gabe put a finger to his lips and Holly went serious, into hide mode, giving him a firm nod. All day long he'd struggled to keep himself in check. Sleeping with a woman was one thing, but getting involved with her kid was something he wasn't ready for. Especially when that kid looked up at him with hero worship in her pretty little eyes. Yet there he was, hiding under the damn table, soaked from neck to thigh, wondering if he could be her champion. But if there was anything that the past six years had taught him, it was that being one person's champion meant breaking someone else's heart.

"Holly?" The hall closet opened and clicked shut. Then Regan's legs came into view, the same legs that Gabe had touched under the table all throughout dinner. Her knees, upper thigh, he'd covered every inch. Even clad in denim they drove him crazy. Not as crazy as her cute bare feet, which were small and feminine and tipped in red polish with little white snowmen on each big toe—and standing right in front of him, a bath towel dangling at their side.

Dramatically, Regan tapped her foot, giving the pretense of being stumped. Suddenly, she dropped to a squat and, eyes full of mischief, cried, "Gotcha!"

Holly squealed and tried to scramble out from under the table. Regan caught her and wrapped her in the towel, poking and tickling her sides, making the squeals erupt into fits of giggles.

It took Gabe a lot more than just scrambling to wedge his massive frame out from under the table. And the wet jeans plastered to his thighs weren't helping any. Neither was Regan laughing at him. Or the fact that he wasn't the only one who'd been drenched by the dripping nudist. Regan's tank was translucent, her bra was green, and Gabe was suddenly hard.

"Need any help?" Regan asked when he knocked his head against the table's corner.

"Nope, I got it."

"You sure? Wouldn't want you to break a hip."

"I'm sure." But it still took him another few seconds to navigate the chair.

"It's okay to ask for help if you need it, Gabe. ChiChi sometimes needs help getting up our steps," Holly offered.

He knew those steps, had walked them several times that day, each time with some piece of furniture strapped to his back. So Holly's attempt to make him feel better, although sweet in nature, only reminded him of every one of his thirty-five years.

"I'm big," he grumbled. "Not old."

But by the time he got out, Holly was dried and her nightgown was on. Both ladies stood with wide eyes, trying not to laugh at him. The image of them standing there, secret smiles on their faces, made his chest tighten and go a little panicky. Because they'd just had a moment, a family moment, and he was somehow a part of that.

"All right, Christmas angel. Lights-out time."

"Can Gabe put me to bed?"

Holly looked nervous, like he was going to say no and ruin her world. Regan looked terrified, like he was going to say no and ruin Holly's world. All Gabe wanted to do was burn rubber out the door, afraid that if he put Holly to bed he *would* someday ruin everything.

Any man would be lucky to be a part of their family. Just not him. He already had a family and they drove him batshit crazy. But how could a guy say no to those big blue eyes?

"If it's all right with your mom."

By the time he read *Kitty Goes to Washington* the third time by flashlight, Holly was passed out, Gabe's hands were sweating, a twitch had moved to encompass his left eye, and he was pretty sure he'd developed a severe allergic reaction to kitty talk. He'd also developed a serious weakness for the little girl sawing logs next to him. Pulling up her new purple sheets, he tucked her in tight and exhaled.

He didn't have to be her hero. Hell, he didn't even have to be responsible for her. He could just be her friend. A friend who spent time with her mom.

A friend who spent time with her mom and was totally full of shit.

Figuring his best bet would be to call it a night so he could think this through, he closed the door and made his way to the kitchen. Standing at the threshold, he quietly took in the view. And what a freaking incredible view it was.

Sponge in hand, Regan leaned over to wipe down the table, her jeans pulling tight while exposing her lower back. It was just about the sexiest thing he'd ever seen.

Gabe slowly walked up behind her and, spanning her waist, slid his fingers back until he could press his thumbs into the small of her back. Slowly he ran them up her spine, pushing up her shirt as he went.

"Feel good?"

Her only response was to let out a low, throaty moan. So, like any normal guy, his new goal was to get her to moan, over and over. When his thumbs worked circles at the knots in her lower back she dropped her head forward, giving him complete access.

He had just reached the sweet zone and was fiddling with the catch of her bra, Christmas green with little red dots today, when she straightened and turned around. He didn't back up, which left her wedged between the table and his body, and him with his palms just an inch shy of those breasts.

"About today," she said, her voice raspy. "I'm sorry for using you to get back at Isabel."

"You mean when you had your hands all over me?"

"They weren't all over you," she sighed. "I'm trying to say that I am sorry for using you."

"I like your hands all over me." He leaned in and whispered in her ear, making sure to graze the rim with his lips. "And you can use me all you want."

Regan rolled her eyes, but he could tell she was also feeling the heat because the second his thumbs moved up her rib cage, shaping the underside of her breasts, her nipples budded under the wet cotton of her T-shirt. He never made the conscious decision to slide his fingers over the bra to palm her breasts, it just happened. She inched forward, into him, and he stopped thinking about all of the reasons why this was a bad idea and focused on the only two that mattered.

She wanted him.

He wanted her.

Wrong or not, neither could deny that there was something between them. It was that same undeniable connection that he'd felt the first time he'd met her. Even though he'd been pissed and angry and knew he should hate her, all he could think about was how much he wanted her. Only that time, he'd had the good sense to walk away.

He was drawn to the only woman in the world he couldn't have, and yet as he watched her eyes darken and her pulse beat against her neck, he couldn't seem to find enough energy to care. Being with Regan, like this, felt right.

Deciding to deal with the fallout tomorrow, he pressed his lips to the hollow of her throat, running his tongue over her pulse. Slowly he worked his way down to the curve of her breast, tugging at the V of her top to pull it lower.

"Wait. Holly," Regan said, her body too alert and her voice too clear for his taste.

Without stopping, Gabe made his way to her ear and whispered, "Passed out. Door is shut. We'll be quiet. I promise," and then bit down gently.

"She once slept through a Seahawks game. She never wakes up," she replied huskily, her hands back on him. This time she trailed her fingers down to his wrists and pulled them securely around her, locking them at her lower back.

So Vixen liked to be held tight, fine by him. Hauling her up against him, he took her mouth in a kiss that left them both panting.

Then her phone rang and she pulled it out of her back pocket. "It's your grandma."

Slowly he pried it from her fingers, sent it to voice mail, and set it on the table.

"That could have been important. I have that council meeting tomorrow."

"You can call her back in the morning." He nipped her lower lip, getting them back on track. "I've been thinking about this all day."

"All week." She snuggled into him, her body rubbing against his. But it was her admission rather than the brush of her fingers above the hem of his low-rise jeans that shot straight to his groin.

"All week?"

"Actually, weeks," she corrected, looking up at him through her lashes. He felt her fingers beneath his shirt, cool and soft, sliding up his stomach to his chest. "Ever since the night at The Spigot."

"The Spigot?" He leaned back so he could look her in the eye. She had to be shitting him. "You didn't even like me."

"I like you now," she whispered, lifting his shirt and giving him an openmouthed kiss in the center of his chest.

"Yeah?" He fisted up the hem of her shirt, loving how her stomach muscles jumped as he pulled it higher. "Well, I *always* liked you. And I really like your shirt."

"You hated me." She tugged it back down. "And it's old."

"I never hated you. And it's wet." He pulled it down further, plastering it to her body, and smiled. "And extremely see-through. See." He dipped his head and sucked her through the thin cotton.

The phone rang again. This time it was his. With a frustrated growl, he reached for the off button, glanced at the screen, and hesitated.

"Let me guess, it's ChiChi," she teased, her hands sliding up his chest. When he didn't answer her, Regan went from turned on to tuned in, and it took every last ounce of control Gabe had not to throw the damn thing through the window.

"Gabe?" She looked at the screen and took a small step back, right into the table. "It's your sister. You should probably answer it. And then you should leave."

"I should." And he should probably take this as a sign from the universe to back the fuck up, walk out of her kitchen and out that front door, because the only thing he could offer Regan was surface—and what he wanted, what she deserved, went so much deeper.

"But the hell of it is"—he turned his phone off and tossed it on the table next to hers—"I don't want to."

"I don't either," she admitted quietly.

He cupped her face and kissed her hard, bringing the focus back to where it should be. Not on family, or history, or the crap ton of other things that they couldn't change, but on the one thing that they could—getting naked.

Regan briefly hesitated, then tangled her arms around him, kissing him back with enough force that they both stumbled against the table. Letting gravity, his new best friend, take over, he followed her down on the table, shoving the chair out of the way and doing his best not to crush her.

He looked at her wet shirt again. "And I don't care about my sister, or that this is going to blow up in our faces. Right now, all I care about is getting this off you before you change your mind." With a quick tug, her shirt went flying. "Or the phone rings again." Her bra was nice and sexy...and had to go. "Or you remember you have to make Holly's lunch." He flipped the catch and the lace fell loose, and she shrugged out of it, letting everything spill free. And hot damn—stacked didn't even begin to describe her.

"God, Vixen." He cupped her breasts, shaping and weighing them, taking his time. Breasts like these deserved to be treasured, and he intended to treasure the hell out of them.

"Yeah?"

Regan was resting back on her elbows, nipples jutting prettily, her silky hair spilling across the tabletop, looking like every guy's wet dream. And yet there was a shy uncertainty in her expression that tore at him. How could she not know how beautiful she was?

"Hell, yeah," he whispered, taking one peak in his mouth, giving it every ounce of attention it deserved. By the time he got to her other breast she was writhing beneath him.

This was exactly what they both needed. No more wondering. No more arguing. No more games. From now on, the only game they were going to play would have a strict no-clothes policy.

He cushioned one hand between her cold back and the even colder tabletop to give himself more leverage and considered asking her if she wanted to move to the couch. But he felt a little tug at his jeans, watched as Regan's fingers slid home, and realized that interrupting would be rude. So he kept his mouth shut and thought about adding a new rule: soft surfaces optional.

The button on his pants opened, her hands dove inside, and all thinking shut down immediately. He could only feel. Her soft hands curled around the base of him and with one stroke his big plans for taking his sweet time snapped. Fast now, finesse later.

He went for the button on her jeans, got the zipper down, and was nearing the promised land—

"Mommy?" Holly's voice came through the hallway, into the kitchen, and right between them.

Regan froze.

Gabe yanked his zipper up.

Holly called out again.

"What, honey?"

"I have to go potty and it's still dark." Gabe wanted to tell her that it was nighttime, it was always dark.

"I thought you said she sleeps through everything," he whispered, handing Regan's T-shirt to her and pulling his own over his head with hurried hands. Ms. Calm and Collected was nowhere to be seen.

"Be right there," she called out, then looked at Gabe with apologetic eyes. "Everything but liquid before bed."

He stopped, T-shirt midway over his head. "I gave her a glass of water." He closed his eyes. "Actually two."

"It's okay." Regan abandoned the bra and just slid on her shirt, covering up those perfect tens. "I shouldn't have...I mean, this is why I don't...Dating with a daughter in the house is—"

"Mommy? I really gotta go."

Regan sighed, but Gabe didn't fail to notice the embarrassment and regret already clouding those pretty eyes.

"I'm sorry," she whispered, skirting past him. He grabbed the back of her jeans, stopping her. The kid had to go— and by the agitation in her fourth call, he imagined pretty bad—but he didn't want it to end like this. Regan was more than embarrassed, she was mad at herself and Gabe didn't want that.

"Regan, it's okay. No harm."

"No, it's not okay." Her eyes went bright, and he was pretty sure she was about to cry. "I don't do this. I made myself one promise: Holly first. Always."

"And what about you?" he asked softly, tugging her fingers.

She gave a small, sad shrug. "I think I'm always stuck in mommy mode and when she—"

"Mom-my?"

Regan looked at the doorway and then back to their linked hands, and he could see that she was being pulled in two and it was killing her. So he let go first. "Go on. Take Holly to the bathroom and then snuggle in bed with her and be a mom. We can figure this out later."

She nodded and reluctantly headed for the hall. Midway she stopped and turned back to face him. "Gabe, what if being a mom is all I can be right now?"

"Then it will be enough."

CHAPTER 11

A nd by blending the traditions with the past and the tools and technology of today, St. Helena will remain a relevant community whose roots are deeply planted in the Founding Fathers' ideals of community," Regan said, staring into the rearview mirror and adopting her most confident expression.

Though no one in the town hall would be able to guess it by the amount of cover-up under her eyes and caffeinated energy pumping through her veins, Regan had achieved no more than one hour of sleep. She had stayed up most of the night preparing for today. And thinking about Gabe.

There was no way those yoga pants mommies were going to bulldoze over her Mrs. Clauses. Just like there was no way Regan was going to walk away from a chance at something incredible with Gabe.

The more she thought about it, the more she realized how silly she had been. Every day single moms dated and fell in love, and every day they still managed to raise healthy, wonderful children. Her mother hadn't been able to manage both, but that didn't mean Regan couldn't.

Then it will be enough.

Had he really said that? Regan felt her cheeks heat.

If she could handle raising Holly all by herself for the last...almost six years, then she could handle a relationship with a man. Especially when that man was sweet and thoughtful and honest. And went out of his way to make her feel special, as though she mattered.

With a final dab of lipstick, she gathered her purse and opened the car door, ready to dazzle. That city council was going to take one look at her PowerPoint presentation and realize just how important tradition was. How important the Mrs. Clauses were to this town. And how important this town could be to its people.

She stepped out, smoothed down her power skirt, and smiled. Breathing in the crisp air, she looked up, and it was as if the heavens themselves were shining down. She hoped it was a foreshadowing of just how great today was going to be.

She opened the truck, smiled down at Randolph, who was going to be returned to his rightful home today, pulled out her briefcase, and—

"There you are, dear."

—slammed the trunk, catching her blazer in the latch and tearing the shoulder out. She tugged the sleeve loose and turned, spying ChiChi wearing poinsettia-red-and-green bangle bracelets, shuffling across the parking lot toward her.

ChiChi looked frazzled, her eyes wide and darting right then left, as if she were afraid to be seen talking to Regan. That was when Regan noticed that the parking lot, given that the emergency meeting was supposed to begin in just ten minutes, was extremely sparse of townspeople and pitchforks.

"What's going on, ChiChi?" Regan glanced at her watch.

"What's going on," ChiChi repeated, her voice elevating with every syllable. "That backstabbing twit Isabel is going on. She's out to screw you."

"*What?*"

"Did you volunteer for the Costume Committee?" the old woman panted, her hand on her heaving chest.

Regan felt her own chest return to somewhere normal. By the way ChiChi was carrying on, she'd thought she'd missed the meeting or something had happened to Holly.

"*Isabel* was kind enough to put my name down to help out, so yes."

"Help out? Child, that woman put you down as costume chair, meaning you run the entire committee. And she's in there right now telling the council how you haven't made it to a single meeting, your committee has not been informed of what is going on, and that you haven't even decided on patterns or bought the fabric."

"Now?" Regan checked her watch for the tenth time in so many minutes. "The meeting doesn't start until nine."

"We're on the agenda at nine, she's been flapping her gums since eight fifteen."

Of course she has, Regan thought, her heart back to hyperspeed. "Wait, *I* have to buy the fabric?"

"The fabric, patterns, *and* all related materials. The council will pay you back, but you have to invoice them."

"ChiChi, I don't have that kind of money. Even if I did, I said I'd help out, not run the thing."

"Which is why that woman signed you up as chair. She wants you to fail. And if you walk in there with nothing to show, those members are going to crucify you."

"And let me guess." Regan closed her eyes, understanding what was really going on. "If that happens, it will discredit me and the council won't listen to our presentation."

"Oh, they'll listen. They just won't support your ideas. They already think I'm soft in the head for losing Randolph. I can't have them thinking you're a flake." ChiChi shook her head, her eyes going hard.

"Because you would be replaced by Isabel."

"And you'd lose your job." And Holly's scholarship. "Which is why you've got to open your trunk."

"My what?" Regan gasped.

"Lucinda went out and bought you a mess of fabric, and Pricilla is lending you her extra sewing machine. Your first committee meeting was last night and you all decided on a carnival theme. If they ask, say *Jesus Christ, Superstar* meets Cirque du Soleil. They love that kind of thing." ChiChi was already shuffling back across the parking lot. "Now open that trunk and make room. I'll be back in five minutes."

"I don't even have a committee," Regan hollered back, splaying herself across the back of her car.

"You do now. Lucinda is the fastest sewer in wine country. Seven years running."

Five minutes. There was no way in hell she was going to show the Mrs. Clauses her trunk. She had to do whatever it took to convince the council that her ideas were brilliant and keep Holly at St. Vincent's. And that did not include incriminating herself.

Turning around, she fished through her purse and pulled out a receipt, a pen, and a stick of gum. Blowing a bubble, she scribbled a note stating that she had to use the ladies' room and to start loading if she wasn't back in time. Then she scanned the parking lot for a place to hide Randolph. If ChiChi caught her with that deer...Regan didn't even want to go there.

Certain she was alone, she cracked the trunk, threw a plastic tablecloth she had bought for Holly's birthday over Randolph, and slapped the note to the back window with the hot wad of gum. Reindeer under her arm, she took off in a full sprint, heading toward a utility shed at the far end of the property. She was just rounding the side of the town hall when she saw Isabel in the window.

Their eyes locked. Isabel saw the bulge under Regan's arm. She gasped with understanding and a sinister smile passed her lips before she bolted for the door...and straight for Regan.

"Crap!" Regan doubled back and slipped in a side door. She shuffled down the hall as fast as her heels would allow, trying every door along the way.

Locked.

Locked.

And locked.

Damn.

Angry heels clicked on marble behind her, gaining in venom and speed. Regan turned to see Isabel come around the corner, her focus zeroing in.

"You!" she accused.

"Merry Christmas one and all," Randolph greeted.

"Shh," Regan snapped and, pretending she hadn't heard Isabel and that her tablecloth hadn't just spoken, spun back around to head down another hallway, past the water fountain and seven more locked doors, finally toppling into a woman wearing blue scrubs and pushing a cart with a mop and bucket.

"*Lo siento mucho, señora*," Regan said, gathering up the industrial-sized box of tampons and spare toilet paper, placing them back on the cart. She was dusting the powdered soap off the poor woman when she became aware of two things.

Randolph had decided to peek out from beneath his tablecloth to gift the janitor—who was rapidly making the sign of the cross, her eyes rapt on the stolen mascot—with a radiant smile and Christmas greeting. And, the designer clicking had stopped.

"*Es el diablo*," the woman whispered, her eyes staring at something over Regan's head. "*Corre!*"

Regan didn't have to ask who was behind her; the description and look of sheer terror on the woman's face was enough. She shoved Randolph into Regan's arms and Regan in the direction of a janitor's closet.

Once inside, Regan slammed the door, flicked on the light, and screamed.

Dozens of lifeless eyes stared down at her. Men, women, children, infants. All of them silent, their mouths gaped opened as if ready to speak. And all of them naked.

One hand over her mouth, the other over Randolph's eyes, she backed up, right into a rack. Blue backpacks decorated with red crosses crashed to her feet with enough force to alert the entire building. CPR training pamphlets and supplies scattered across the floor.

Keeping her focus on the ground, she shoved all of the backpacks into a corner and tried to come up with a plan. One that didn't include Isabel finding her with Randolph.

"Merry Christmas one and all," Randolph greeted.

"They're dummies. They aren't real, so shush before someone hears you," Regan hissed at the ceramic-and-plastic statue with the glittery red nose. She could swear that his smile grew a little wider.

Setting Randolph in the far corner of the closet, Regan piled all of the CPR dolls against him, careful not to damage his sheen. Once he was securely hidden, she reminded him to be quiet, clicked off the light, and left the room—only to come face to face with a very winded, very wet, and very pissed Isabel Stark.

The janitor was apologizing profusely about how she was just mopping up the south hall, doing her job, didn't see Isabel in time, and hoped that the mop handle wouldn't leave a bruise on her beautiful forehead.

Isabel, however, didn't miss the look passing between Regan and the woman, nor did she miss Regan coming out of the closet. The closet which Regan plastered her body against.

"Stop touching me," Isabel harped, batting away the other woman's hands. She marched over to Regan, took in the business suit, and glared. "It's too late, you know. The board already hates you. So it doesn't matter that Holly got the lead."

"Holly got the lead?" Regan whispered, and no matter how hard she tried to be angry, her heart warmed and a smile broke across her face.

Her baby had done it. Set her mind on something, practiced hard, and got her dream part. No matter what happened in that meeting, how bad Isabel tried to make Regan look, Holly was going to play Christmas Kitty.

"Not for long. Every parent has to volunteer, as stated in the bylaws. And you"—Isabel poked her in the chest—"didn't do your fair share. I am sure the council will see it that way and then Lauren, who is the understudy, will get to play Christmas Kitty."

"Actually, Isabel," Regan began, trying to remember what ChiChi had told her, "I have met with my committee and the costumes are coming along wonderfully. In fact, we decided to take a *Jesus Christ, Superstar*–meets–Cirque Du Soleil approach to their design. I'm sure the council will just love our ideas. It's very New Age meets traditional."

Isabel's mouth fell open and Regan patted herself on the back for that last part. The costumes, just like the direction she hoped the council would embrace, merged the new with the traditional.

Isabel didn't have a snarky comeback. In fact, she stood so silent that Regan was about to leave. Convinced Isabel would need time to strategize on how best to next screw with the Martin women, and remembering that ChiChi was waiting in the parking lot, she eased off the door. She had taken only three steps when Isabel pounced.

Shoving Regan aside, Isabel yanked open the door, flicked on the light, and didn't even let out so much as a gasp.

"*Es el diablo,*" the janitor whispered, jerking a chin toward Isabel.

"What are you hiding?" Isabel said, her eyes scanning the room. "You came in here with a big box and now you only have your purse."

"Tampons," the heavy accent cut through the air.

Isabel looked from one to the other. The janitor folded her arms in front of her and glared as if daring Isabel to call her a liar.

With a huff and one final scan, Isabel slammed the door. A very muffled "Merry Christmas one and all" sounded through the wood.

Regan closed her eyes and banged her head against the wall as Isabel yanked open the door again and riffled through all of the bodies to come up with the only one that mattered. The one with the bright red nose and big smile. And the one that was going to ruin everything.

"I knew it!" Isabel cheered. "I knew you had to have something to do with ChiChi's car and the Christmas display. Wait until the board hears about this. Those old biddies' savior is none other than the person who single-handedly tried to steal Christmas."

Regan grabbed Randolph. "I will tell them."

"Tell us what, dear?"

Regan couldn't answer, because when she turned around about thirty sets of eyes, all alive and all members of the town council, greeted her with strained smiles. Then they saw Randolph and the smiles fled, leaving only strain.

"Yeah, tell them, Regan," Isabel prodded.

"You found Randolph!" ChiChi screeched, waddling up to lay a loving pat on the reindeer's head.

"Is that true?" a thin man with thin limbs and an even thinner head of hair asked. Benson was not only head of the town council, he was also the former high school principal and known for sniffing out BS. Which probably explained why his nostrils started flaring the second Regan opened her mouth.

"I was waiting at my car for ChiChi," Regan said, the woman in question beaming up at her with all the faith in the world. Regan swallowed. "We were supposed to go over the costumes and material choices for the Christmas musical before the meeting, and I spotted a building out in the field—"

"The utility closet by the old oak tree?" Jordan said, stepping forward and making Regan relax a little. Jordan stood beside Regan, placing one hand on Randolph and the other on Regan's shoulder. It was a silent declaration of alliance. One that wasn't missed by anyone in the crowd, especially Isabel, whose upper lip twitched.

"Is that where you found Randolph?" Selma, one of the councilwomen, asked.

"Uh, he was wrapped in this tablecloth," Regan went on, neither admitting nor denying that she had indeed *found* Randolph.

"Clearly whoever took him wanted to make sure he didn't get damaged," Regan reasoned. "I mean, why else would they wrap him up so carefully? In fact, I bet it was all some ridiculous mistake, and even though they wanted to return him, it went public so fast they probably were too scared."

"You know what, you're right," Mrs. Moberly, the council secretary and town librarian, said, pushing her glasses farther back on her nose and coming forward to pet Randolph's tail. "I bet they read about the Randolph sanctuary clause on the website you built. They probably thought they could return him anonymously and avoid criminal charges."

"Ingenious idea," Benson said, smiling down at the deer.

"Actually," Regan said, gesturing to her Mrs. Clauses, "it was these ladies here who rallied together, brought in the sheriff's department, and got the news of Randolph out to the public. It was done with the same hard work and passion as they devote to the Community Action Committee."

"Are you all actually buying this?" Isabel spat.

Regan had almost forgotten she was there. By the way a few council members jumped at her shrill voice, she wasn't the only one. Maybe it was because as nearly every council member had made their way forward to pet Randolph, Isabel had been shoved to the back.

"You all really believe that someone *stole* Randolph, then returned him, wrapped in a blanket—"

"Tablecloth," ChiChi corrected.

"Whatever," Isabel snapped, her forehead growing with every heated breath she took. "The point is, there is no way that someone could have hidden him in broad daylight and not a single one of us saw him."

"But Regan saw him," Mrs. Moberly corrected, annoyance fogging up her glasses.

"Are you all really this blind?" Isabel flung her hands against her thighs.

All of town hall stood silent—the uncomfortable kind of silence with everyone staring back and forth between Regan and Isabel. Regan held her breath. Isabel crossed her arms. No one spoke. Not even the janitor, who was polishing Randolph's hooves.

Should she just come clean, tell the council the entire story and hope that they didn't punish Holly for Regan's mistake?

God, maybe Gabe was right. Maybe she had some deep-seated anger issues left over from Richard and they made her act like a crazy woman. Because who would throw eight innocent reindeer through the window of an SUV and then abscond with their leader?

"Can't you all see what this is?" Isabel's tone implied that anyone who didn't was a fool.

"Of course, we see," ChiChi said, wagging her head as if greatly disappointed...in Isabel. "It's a Christmas miracle, dear."

And on cue, Randolph blinked his nose and said, "Merry Christmas, one and all."

Because it was a day ending in *Y*, Gabe had rolled out of bed at dawn. He'd taken a cold shower, eaten leftover chow mein out of the box—also cold—and headed to the office. Before he could even address the Everest-size pile of paper-work, his phone had started ringing, then his in-box lit up, and by the time he remembered Jordan was coming in late, he'd accomplished jackshit.

Unless he counted dispatching all of the Safe Return of Randolph calls. Apparently, ChiChi had put his number and e-mail address on all the posters.

Was this what Jordan dealt with every morning? He needed to either get his family to handle their own shit or give Jordan a raise.

The phone rang.

Maybe both.

Needing some fresh air and space that didn't give him a migraine, Gabe took a walk through DeLuca Manor. The for-mer carriage house, originally built by his great-grandfather in the late eighteen hundreds, had been renovated into a modern masterpiece of architecture and finishing. Situated on the back of a vast expanse of lawn and surrounded by heritage oaks, the stone-and-mortar-faced building, with its domed cathedral ceilings and pair of antique six-hundred-lamp chandeliers, had become one of the most photographed and recognized buildings in the Valley. It also contained one of the last memories Gabe had of his father before he passed.

Gabe walked through the massive wooden doors, and even the addition of the hundred dressed tables and thousands of lilies for tonight's event couldn't overpower the scent of redwood floors and oak barrels. Even the smell reminded him of his old man; of the way his father had tried to appear supportive when Gabe had confessed that he wanted to go to art school instead of run the winery.

His shoes echoed off the walls as he made his way through the main hall and to the small set of stairs hidden behind rows of oak barrels. He took the stairs two at a time and breathed in the crisp morning air as he gazed out over the rolling acres of vines.

His father used to bring him up here to talk about the day and slip him a little scotch from the flask he kept hidden in his breast pocket. The one he'd kept a secret from his wife, which she had dutifully washed and refilled weekly.

His father had shown his love for his wife in everything that he did. His mother had put up with all of his father's crazy ideas about cross-pollination and cross-breeding different species of grapes, loving the way he would lose himself for hours in the field. And in turn they had both loved their children fiercely. Right up until the day they died.

Too bad his dad hadn't left detailed instructions about how he wanted Gabe to raise his siblings as he had with the business. Or how to successfully blend two families who were both too bold and too stubborn on their own. Not that Gabe was thinking of blending two families anytime soon, but if these last few weeks were an indicator of how the rest of his life would go, he needed to figure out a way to untangle his own happiness from being dependent on his siblings'.

His cell rang. It was Marc. Again. All of his brothers had called at least once, and it wasn't even lunchtime. Gabe sent the call to voice mail. He didn't want to talk about Regan or Richard or what he had or hadn't found out.

Which was pretty much nothing.

A drop of water landed on his arm. He looked up at the darkening sky and watched as the storm rolled in. Rather than fight it, only to get back to a life that was smothering him, he decided to wait it out.

He moved away from the rail and walked under the overhang of the balcony. Feeling suddenly weary, he dusted off his dad's seat, leaned back, and closed his eyes. The rain tapped against the ceramic tiles of the roof, picking up in speed and volume.

He was tired and worn out, and he really should have stayed in bed.

It took him several minutes and multiple shifts to get comfortable. He tried legs pulled in, ankle over knee, crossed, uncrossed, finally settling on stretched out and leaning back. When he couldn't relax he laughed. Even after all these years, the leather cushion still hadn't molded out of his dad's shape and into his.

"What's so funny?" The sexy voice shot straight through his body.

Gabe opened his eyes, but didn't move. He just watched. Watched as Regan slowly made her way toward him. She was wearing tall, sleek black boots, a tight skirt, and a snug red top that looked soft and hugged every curve to perfection. And she was exactly what he needed right now.

Just looking into those baby blues, at those full lips, made his world spin back to right. He didn't even realize how far he'd shifted off axis until she walked out on that balcony and filled his mind with nothing but her. A strange reaction to have for the woman who confused him more than any other person on the planet.

"I was thinking how, no matter how hard I try, my dad's seat will never feel right." If he was surprised at his admission, he was even more shocked at how good it felt to finally say it aloud. To Regan.

She shrugged, sending her top slipping down one shoulder and exposing a lacy red strip. And sending him from stressed to rock hard in two seconds. "I suspect your dad would want you to make your own rather than try to get comfortable in his."

Gabe shifted and finally gave up. No matter what chair he was sitting in, comfort was damn near impossible with her standing only a few feet away and looking like sex in heels. "How come you're not at work?"

"They double-booked my shift, said I could have the day off."

"And you came here?"

She nodded. "Your grandma told me that if you weren't in your office you'd be fixing your family's problems up here. She asked me to bring you this. Said it was time-sensitive."

She held up an envelope and squinted as if trying to see through it. "But I'm pretty sure it's empty."

"Empty, huh? Then why did you come?"

With a smile that was 100 percent trouble, she walked straight toward him. He had to pull his legs back in to make room for her as she skirted right between his widespread knees. "What if I told you Holly's going to Pricilla's after school, and for one day I want to feel like something other than a mommy?"

"I'd say we're going to need a hell of a lot longer than a day to get through every fantasy I've cooked up over the past few weeks." Gabe set the envelope on the side table—definitely empty—and moved to the end of the chair, which brought her breasts right where he wanted them, at eye level. She was so close he could smell the rain on her skin, see the droplets that clung to her lashes, and see the hunger in her eyes.

He skimmed his hands over her boots, the backs of her knees, the backs of her thighs, not stopping until he got to her very bare, very sweet ass. He groaned. "And not one of them included you sans the silk, Vixen."

"I figured you already had one pair of mine, I didn't want to lose another," she teased, her hands coming to rest on his shoulders for support.

"You have to earn those back." Nudging the V of her top lower, he placed an open-mouthed kiss in the valley between her cleavage. Catching a drop of rain with his tongue.

"Well, you get one day. Then I go back to being a mom, and you go back to being a DeLuca. So make it count."

"Did I ever mention that I am an excellent negotiator?"

"One day, Gabe."

She looked stubborn and set on her ridiculous plan. It didn't matter, he had all day to convince her otherwise. Might as well start now.

"I also like a challenge," he said, raising his head to look up at her. But he didn't get the chance, because Regan got things started on her own.

"Then your challenge is to make this"—she slid her hands up his chest and into his hair, and he felt what *this* was all the way down to his dick—"go away in one day."

Then she was on him. Kissing him.

Vixen was kissing him.

Her skin was slick with rain, her mouth hot with need, her hands were everywhere and he loved it.

Gabe knew the attraction was mutual, but he had always been the one to instigate. Not today. Today, Vixen was open and aggressive and taking the lead. Hell, if this is what she was like when she was running things, he'd follow her just about anywhere.

His hands tightened on her ass, hauling her up against him and damn near exploding when she moaned against his mouth and bit his lower lip. There was nothing sexier than a woman who knew what she wanted and went after it, especially if that something happened to be him.

Her scent was nearly as intoxicating as her taste, because she tasted like sex and sugar cookies, a combination that was insanely hot. So when her tongue slid against his, he snapped. He could barely string together two thoughts when she was dressed. Now that he knew what she had on under her skirt—abso-fucking-lutely nothing—he was a goner.

He wanted her right now, right here. His hands slid down the globes of her ass and his fingers found their way back under her skirt and between her legs, gently gliding over her center.

She jerked at his touch and pulled back enough to whisper, "Not here," against his mouth, but her legs widened, giving him better access.

"Okay." With one hand he pushed up her top, baring her breasts, and sucked her nipple right through the red lace. It budded against his tongue.

"How about here?" His tongue traced the edging of her bra, over her breast, down into the valley between and over to the other side, gently nipping at the peak with his teeth. "Or here?"

"No, I meant—" But her hands were all over him, clawing at his chest, fisting in his hair, anything she could grab on to. Hot damn, the woman was sexy.

"Oh," he mumbled against her skin as his other hand cupped her heat and gently squeezed. "Here." This time it wasn't a question but a statement. Instead of only her going mindless, all the blood left his brain and rushed south. "Christ, Regan. You're soaked."

"There. Right there." Just the need in her voice was enough to make him embarrass himself. Then she moved against his hand, a sexy little sound coming up from the back of her throat. She did it again, pressing harder. The next was more frantic, almost desperate. "Gabe, I think I might—"

She had to be kidding. He had barely touched her. Hadn't even slid inside yet and she was breathing like she was about to—

"Oh, God," she panted, her head dropping back as she rolled her hips forward, grinding against his palm, bringing her skirt up to where he could almost see what he was cupping.

He didn't know what was more erotic, the knowledge that she was about to get off on his hand, or how he could see his hand disappear underneath her skirt but not see *her*.

"I need more."

Damn right.

Gabe slid his other hand down the back of her thigh, hooking it around her knee, and gently brought her foot up and set it on his chair, the heel of her boot straddling the armrest. There went her skirt, up and over her ass, and he froze.

"Gabe, now. I'm almost there." He could see it in the way her pupils were fully dilated and hear it in the need thickening her words. So was he and he was still fully clothed. Vixen, on the other hand...

"God, you are so damn beautiful," he breathed, taking in the sight of her. Her hair was wet from the rain and tumbling down her back, her shirt was shoved up to her armpit, her skirt was bunched around her waist. And there, right on the inside of her hipbone, was that sexy tattoo. Only it wasn't a bundle of holly, it was fucking mistletoe.

CHAPTER 12

Regan watched as Gabe's mouth kissed its way down her hip, getting closer to the impact zone. With agonizing slowness, and a gentleness that stole the air from her lungs, he sucked and licked and kissed until her whole body tensed in anticipation, nerve endings stretching out to meet him.

Regan didn't move, didn't breathe, didn't even beg him to hurry up. She couldn't. Just like she couldn't look away when he smiled up at her right before he ran his tongue in one long, thorough swipe straight up her center.

"Oh, God!" Heat shot though her, warming her entire body and making her stomach clinch. She'd known that he would be amazing—just the way he kissed was enough to tell her that. But amazing didn't even begin to explain what he did to her body as he explored, sucking and teasing, until her legs were shaking so bad she thought they were going to buckle.

Gripping his shoulders for support, she moved restlessly against his mouth, wanting to get there. But Gabe seemed in no hurry. His hands tightened, holding her still as he worked his magic. And that mouth of his had enough magic to be considered a Christmas miracle all on its own.

Then his fingers joined the festivities, and Regan thought she would die from the pleasure. Tension built, making her back arch and hips push forward, striving toward an invisible finish line that she could feel was right there. Just out of reach.

Gabe finally picked up the pace, sliding a second finger inside her and bringing her so close all she had to do was press down and—

Her breath stopped, right there in her throat, making her vision blur and her mind turn to mush. Making her forget that she had a slew of costumes to stitch, that Holly wanted tacos for dinner, that she was out of milk, that she was naked on the balcony of a winery with a man buried between her legs where anyone could walk by and see.

None of that mattered, because in the moment of forgetting, she remembered that she was a woman. And nothing had felt this right in a long time.

And then her mind emptied as Gabe gave a final swirl and gently bit at her bundle of nerves. She heard herself scream and she felt as if she was falling, fast and hard, without a care in the world.

Thunder cracked overhead and the rain came down, pounding the tile floor. When she finally opened her eyes and came back to herself, she was straddling Gabe's lap, the heels of her boots digging into her bare ass, her face smashed into the curve of his neck.

"That was about the sexiest damn thing I have ever seen," he whispered gruffly, his hand under her hair kneading the back of her neck with such tenderness that it made her throat close. "Are you okay?"

No. She wasn't. He was holding her as though, to him, she were precious and special. Which made her feel precious and special. Made her feel as though in that moment maybe she could be the kind of woman a man like Gabe would want to spend the rest of his life with. Would want to call his family.

He isn't looking for permanent.

She knew that. She also understood that if he was, she wouldn't be the kind of woman to inspire that kind of commitment. So she stared out at the sky and watched the rain cast a glassy shine over the vineyard below, listened as it danced across the roof overhead.

"Hey." He dipped down and looked into her eyes. "Are you thinking again?"

"Not anymore." She kissed his neck, his chin, working her way to his mouth, where she kissed him long and slow. She could feel his erection pressing against her and she pulled back—on so many levels. "But I think you need to catch up."

She slid her hands under his shirt, loving how his muscles bunched and tightened under her touch. Needing to see him, she pulled his shirt off and threw it on the chaise longue next to them.

His eyes turned dark and hot when she lifted her arms over her head, asking him without words to help. Which he was more than happy to do. He helped her right out of her shirt, skirt, and bra, stopping when he came to the boots, saying he wanted those left on. Then he went to work on himself, quickly dispensing of his clothes, until he was gorgeously naked and—holy moly—impressive package indeed.

He must have seen the mix of fascination and, if she were being honest, a little fear in her features, because he flashed her a cocky smile. She rolled her eyes and took his hand.

Not only had it been a while for her. A six-year while. But she was also vanilla when it came to sex. So getting wild on a chair in the middle of a vineyard was too much. They could start on the chaise longue and maybe work their way up to the armchair cha-cha. Plus the cold winter air bit at her skin, causing her to shiver. Why be cold *and* bare-ass naked in public when there was a snug-looking blanket draped over the back of the chaise?

She led him toward the chaise, but Gabe obviously wasn't thinking vanilla, because two steps from the sofa she found herself pinned against a stack of oak barrels by a mass of muscles with magical hands.

"The chaise," she said, his mouth already on her neck, his hands going for Christmas miracle number two. Not that she didn't want a second *feliz navidad*. She did. A lot. More now than she had two seconds ago, before his head dipped to kiss her breast, before his thumbs circled her navel, and even more than before his erection slid against her stomach.

"Chaise," she repeated.

Gabe looked up, his eyes firm. "No. You said I have one day. Which means I need to get you to stop thinking about groceries and PTA shit if I want a shot at a second day. And a third."

"One day, Gabe. That's it. I don't think that—"

He kissed her silent. When he pulled back she studied his face, trying to figure out what he was feeling. If he was asking for more sex, or just more. More her, more him, more them. At the thought, her heart fluttered a little. Okay, a lot. She was already treading dangerously close to falling and didn't know if she could handle more.

"There you go with the thinking again."

"I'm just trying to read your face, figure out—"

Before she could blink, Regan found herself facing the wine barrel with Gabe's hard-on pressing into her lower back. His hands came around her waist and when he spoke his breath tickled her ear, making her shiver again—but for a whole different reason. "Don't read, don't think, don't figure, Regan. Just feel."

His hands slid up to cup her breasts and feel she did.

His skin felt hot, telling her just how cold it must be, but she didn't move away; if anything, she leaned into his touch. Giving herself over to the experience—and to Gabe—she dropped her head back against his shoulder and blocked out everything but his touch.

His mouth worked hot open-mouthed kisses along her neck and spine while his hands worked her into a frenzy. He bent a little at the knees, and when he stood back up his erection slid between her legs from behind. He eased across her, pulled back, and eased across her swollen flesh again, releasing a low "Ohhhh" from her lips. He kept up the pace until she was helplessly panting and her body felt like it was too small to hold in all of the pressure.

"You. Inside me," she whispered, reaching around with both hands and digging her nails into his ass. "Right now."

"Best idea you've ever had." He tightened his grip on her hips and, in one fluid motion, Regan found herself turned around and seated on an oak barrel, Gabe nudging his way between her thighs.

He tore open the condom packet that appeared out of nowhere, which meant she was getting an A+ in the "no thinking" department. He slid it on and Regan attempted to help. *Attempted* being the operative word, since she spent most of her time teasing and kissing. But he gave her a resounding A+ in that department too. He also gave her a kiss that almost knocked her right off the barrel.

He slid her forward, placed her feet on the edge of the barrel beneath, and in one smooth, gentle slide, seated himself fully inside of her. Shocked at how perfect he felt inside of her, Regan let out a sigh of contentment. Even began to wonder if they had been building toward this moment their entire lives. It sounded ridiculous since they hardly even knew each other, but something about this moment felt so right.

"God, you feel"—he pulled out slightly and rolled back in—"so fucking incredible." He filled her again, picking up the pace until the world shifted beneath her. Literally.

"Gabe, the barrels," she moaned, not really caring if they came tumbling down, as long as he didn't stop until she came tumbling down.

"Shit," he said. "Wrap your legs around me."

She did and found herself pressed against the cold stone of the wall, Gabe never breaking the connection. He felt so good, Regan didn't even mind the freezing wall or the stones pressing into her back. Her hand roved everywhere, and her legs squeezed with everything that she had. All she could do was feel Gabe's lips on her neck, his body slam in and out of her until everything went black and she couldn't feel anything.

She heard Gabe moan her name and he followed her into a floating oblivion. When she came back to herself, he looked up at her and smiled. "Now the chaise."

She thought he meant for another round, maybe two. Instead he walked them over to the chaise and placed her on the cushion, only to crawl in next to her, hold her close. He pulled her hair off of her shoulder and placed little kisses on her spine.

"I've been dreaming about that for years." He pulled the fuzzy blanket over them.

"Years?" She turned over to face him so she could smack his chest. Which she did. All six of his packs. "You mean weeks."

"Years." He trapped her hand against his chest with his, the expression on his face serious. "Now, you want to argue some more or can we take a nap?"

"Did you hear that?" Regan whispered. And if she was talking about all those sexy little noises she was making a little while ago, his answer was yes. But he was too spent to talk, so he shifted closer, smelled gingerbread, and tightened his arms.

"Gabe, I'm serious." She elbowed him.

"So am I," he said, eyes firmly shut but still managing to find all her curvy spots with his hands. He pulled her to him, loving how she gasped when she discovered he was already hard. "I take this problem very seriously. And think it is our duty to solve it."

At that she smacked his chest. "Someone is coming. And I have to get my clothes."

"Then get your clothes," he said, nibbling on her earlobe.

"I can't," she hissed. "You're practically laying on top of me."

Yeah, he'd noticed. Liked it, even. And though he too could hear movement coming from down below, he was fairly confident that whoever it was would go away. Fairly. Not many people knew about this place, but he didn't need to let her know that.

"Better?" He rolled all the way on top of her, since the "practically" seemed to irritate her.

"No." She glared up at him. He smiled back down at her. Then he kissed her, taking his own sweet time about it and waiting until she was as hot and bothered as he was before pulling back.

"How about now?" When she just stared up at him with dazed eyes he knew his job, for the moment, was complete. So he rolled off of her, giving her that space she was so adamant about.

It took a moment for her brain to unscramble, a condition he sympathized with, and then she stumbled to her feet. She gathered up most of her clothes, frantically searching for her bra, which he had tucked under the blanket. He, on the other hand, put his arms behind his head, leaned back, and watched the show. And what a show. Regan Martin had one hell of a smoking hot body. She was lean in all the right places, soft where she needed to be. And he didn't even want to talk about how sweet she tasted.

Prickly and stubborn and so damn sweet she made his heart do stupid shit. Like feel.

"What are you doing?" She threw his shirt at his head.

"Thinking up how we're going to spend our next rainy day."

"Yeah, well, if you don't help me find my bra, you might not see the next rainy day."

She was about to get all worked up. Which made them even, because watching her prance around in a skirt and no bra had him all worked up too.

He pulled her bra out and dangled it from his fingers. She reached for it, and he yanked it just out of reach. Meaning she had to reach across him and he got another up close and personal of those perfect tens.

"Gabe," she said, crossing her arms and only managing to make him hotter. But then he saw the look in her eyes. She wasn't having fun.

"Hey." He stood up and helped her get in her bra, which went against every man rule, helped her into her sweater and then pulled her into his chest. "I'm sorry, I was just screwing around. I didn't mean to upset you."

"I'm not mad. I just don't want someone to catch us up here and for everyone to think that I got my job by..."

Ah, hell. She didn't say "banging the boss's brother," but it was what she was thinking. And it was what the gossip mill would say if Isabel and her PTA buddies found out. He kissed the top of her head and then helped her into her jacket.

"First off, you got that job on your own merit." And because his brothers wanted to make sure she stuck around. Shit. "The stairs are hard to find and very few people know about them."

"I found them," she said, looking up through her lashes at him and damn near slaying him on the spot.

"And I used to sneak up here and have sex when I was in high school," Jordan said from the doorway. "Never saw a naked ass like that, though. Impressive, boss."

"Shit." Gabe grabbed the blanket and draped it over his body, careful to cover Regan in the process. Clothed or not, she was feeling exposed and embarrassed. He could see it in every detail of her face.

"I hope you have a damn good reason for coming up here," Gabe said, harsher than intended.

Jordan's eyes went wide a moment before narrowing into two slits of pure attitude. "Although not as fun as yours, I do have one. Want to hear it, or are you going to yell at me some more?"

"Sorry," Gabe said, guilt weighing hard. He never snapped. But hell, he could feel Jordan's disapproval all the way in his conscience. The problem was, even though she was aiming it at Gabe, he could tell Regan was taking it personally.

"Apology accepted, although I think it is chivalrous of you to get surly on your woman's behalf." Jordan offered "his woman" a warm and supportive smile, making it clear that it was just Gabe who was the disappointment.

"Sorry. I was coming up to...how did ChiChi put it in her threatening call? Ah, yes. That I was to come up here and tell Regan that I would be thrilled to join the Costume Committee. And that since it happens to fall under my new job description as committee grommet, it is my task to find a location for Thursday's sewfest, which I think will also double as a bitchfest." Jordan's smile told him just who they would be bitching about. "And since Regan's place smells like decomposing fur, I was wondering if we could use yours?"

"My pla—"

"Yes? Great. Thanks, boss. You're a stand-up guy." With a final glance at Regan, one that women shared when bonding over castrating the opposite sex, Jordan turned and left. And with her she took all of the ease and comfort that Gabe and Regan had accomplished that afternoon.

"Explain to me how I ended up here, sewing glitter and shit on a costume for some kid that I don't even know," Frankie said, peeling dry, hot glue off her fingers. "Especially when I was supposed to be one of six committee members."

"Pricilla and Lucinda are finishing up the last-minute details on the cupcakes for Holly's party tomorrow. And ChiChi had a headache," Regan explained, and didn't believe the excuses any more than when the Mrs. Clauses had explained them to her.

"They didn't know I had agreed to actually show up and help," Jordan said, finishing the last stitch on the frog's body and knotting it off. She cut the thread with her teeth and went on, confirming Regan's suspicion. "Effectively ruining their matchmaking plan."

"That still doesn't explain why I got sucked into this."

"Because scaredy-pants Regan didn't want to do this alone," Jordan said, jerking an obvious chin at Gabe, who sat on the couch with Holly watching *Puss in Boots*. "I figured since I had to be here, between the two of us we could pry out of her what's going on between her and Gabe."

Regan's foot froze on the pedal, running the needle right up the crotch of the pantaloons and almost sewing her finger to the fabric. The Band-Aid, already firmly in place from her last needle run-in, saved her. She grabbed the seam ripper and angrily tore out each stitch.

"Nothing." And that was the God's honest truth.

Since Monday, absolutely nothing had happened. He hadn't called or e-mailed or done more than send her a friendly smile when he'd come to visit Marc at the hotel. It should have made Regan happy. It was exactly what they had agreed upon. It didn't. It actually made her feel a little foolish and a whole lot confused. And every time she thought she'd gotten a hold on her emotions, Gabe would show up and remind her that casual was a hard concept for her to grasp.

Tuesday she'd gone to Pricilla's to pick up Holly after school, something that was quickly becoming the norm, and found Gabe building a throne out of plywood and PVC piping, the three Mrs. Clauses sipping peppermint lattes and acting as backseat builders from the comfort of their chairs. Gabe had been sweaty and manly, and the second she'd walked in the Mrs. Clauses had made a sudden and obvious exodus, leaving them all alone. Then Gabe said he had to go, tearing out the door and leaving Regan with the PVC and not a clue as to what she'd done wrong.

Wednesday she'd been at Stan's Soup and Service Station, eating a bowl of chipotle tomato bisque while Stan ran a diagnostic on her car, when Gabe walked in to buy a part for one of the work trucks and to grab lunch. With a sexy smile he'd walked over, and Regan, determined to bring things back to seminormal, had asked him if he'd like to have a bowl of soup with her. He'd just taken a seat and inquired about Holly's play rehearsals when Trey walked in. The youngest

DeLuca shot one look at them and Gabe had immediately asked Stan to make his order to go.

By Thursday, Regan had accepted that whatever she'd felt had been one-sided. Even worse, she accepted that Gabe not only regretted their day together, but it had been such a bad experience that he was going out of his way to avoid her. Whether he was afraid she would get clingy or he was embarrassed to be seen with her, either way it hurt. A lot.

She told herself that it was for the best. Even convinced herself during the day, but at night when Holly was asleep and Regan was left alone with her thoughts, she would try to figure out what had gone wrong. And how to fix it. Leaving her tired and miserable and without a clue as to what to do—other than cry.

She'd been reminding herself that this was why she didn't date—not that they had even gone out on a date, as *date* usually implied a meal or some kind of public statement—when she walked inside Picker's Produce, Meats and More to get something of the *more* variety. Specifically, Rocky Road.

She had just dumped the second gallon in her cart and was on her tiptoes reaching for a third when a really nice pair of arms stretched around her and grabbed the last carton from the back of the refrigerated case. When she turned, she found Gabe looking stressed and uncomfortable.

So she was shocked when he apologized for not calling and asked if maybe she could stay after the sewfest so they could talk. Which ruined her day even more, because it reminded her that the sewfest was still planned for his house.

Instead of shoving the ice cream down his pants and calling him a jerk—or shoving her hands down his pants when he pressed her up against the frozen peas and said he'd missed her—she had agreed to give him ten minutes and then proceeded to buy her ice cream like any sophisticated woman who dabbled in casual sex would do.

Too bad her heart wasn't up for casual. Which was why sitting in his kitchen, watching him pad around barefoot with Holly tossed over his shoulder like a sack of flour and acting as if the last week hadn't happened made her want to scream—at him for making her feel not enough, at herself for believing he was different. Which was why when he came in to grab a beer from the fridge she glared at him.

He glared back.

Jordan was right. This session was going to double as a bitchfest.

"Absolutely nothing," Regan confirmed, after Gabe had taken a seat on the couch, far away from the women and right next to a sleeping Holly.

"Really? Because you both looked to be doing a whole lot of something when I saw you Monday," Jordan said, hand-stitching the gold piping on the frog prince's cape.

"Can you say it louder? I don't think he heard you," Regan whispered, glancing toward the front room.

"He was there," Frankie mumbled around a bag of green glitter beads hanging from her teeth. She didn't sew, but she was proving lethal with a glue gun. "It isn't like she's telling him something he doesn't already know."

"Oh, my God." Regan slapped her hands over her mouth and looked at Frankie. Her voice dropped to a horrified whisper. "Do you know?"

"That you and Gabe had sex? Duh."

"You were supposed to keep it a secret," Regan snapped.

"We actually never had a conversation about keeping anything a secret. Maybe because we haven't talked about it at all!" Jordan snapped back. "Every time I call I get your voice mail, and when I stop by work you're busy. Some might even say you're avoiding me."

Which she was. But not because she didn't want to talk about it. She did. She just didn't want to put Jordan or Frankie in a position where they felt they had to choose sides. Because Regan would lose.

"I wasn't sure what to say," she admitted.

"Well, no one had to say anything to me." Frankie's tongue peeked out the side of her mouth as she put a dab of hot glue on the frog's head and secured another plastic gem. "I figured it out. I mean, the look he shot you a second ago made the Kama Sutra look missionary."

Really? She thought he'd looked mad. "Do you think anyone else knows?"

"How could they not?" Frankie snorted, confirming Regan's biggest fear. St. Helena was a small town that loved to gossip. She'd spent her life being the subject of speculation. She didn't want to go through that again. Didn't want that for Holly.

"The way you guys are avoiding each other around town, it's obvious you did the dirty and now you're trying to play it cool," Frankie added.

That was the problem. *He* was playing it cool. Regan, on the other hand, didn't have a cool bone in her body. Not when it came to him.

"Hey," Gabe said from directly behind her and Regan jumped. When she turned, her heart did more than jump. There he stood in jeans and a sweatshirt, his hair sticking up in the back, and a sleeping Holly snuggled against his chest. "I was thinking that maybe I should put Sleeping Beauty down in one of the guest rooms."

No, there was nothing cool about her feelings for Gabe.

Regan nodded. It was all she could do. If she opened her mouth, she was sure something close to "I love you" would escape. And to a guy who'd made it clear he wasn't looking for serious, those three words would for sure send him burning rubber out of her and Holly's life.

Gabe blew so hot and cold she never knew where he stood. But she was pretty sure where she stood—right on the edge of heartbreak. And watching him tuck Holly in bed would send her over. So after Gabe disappeared down the hall, Regan turned back to the table and knew she had to tell her friends.

She needed a fresh perspective—one that would remind her that, Christmas wish or not, Gabe would not be under her tree come Christmas morning.

She took a deep breath and leaned in to whisper. "I think I blew it. I wanted to feel like something other than a stressed-out single mom for a day, and like a sex-deprived idiot, I threw myself at him."

"You say it like he suffered some kind of hardship." Jordan laughed. "I was there—well, for the post-nookie clothes scramble—and trust me when I say, it didn't look like you had to throw yourself too hard. The man couldn't keep his eyes—or his hands—off you."

"That doesn't mean he likes me, though," she admitted, humiliation making it hard to see. Or maybe that was the tears.

"Of course he likes you," Jordan said, placing her hand on Regan's. Gabe had said the same thing. Then again, he'd been trying to get into her pants. Sex did stupid things to men—apparently women too.

"Then why has he been avoiding me all week? I show up, he leaves skid marks out the door. I didn't expect him to ask me to be his girlfriend or anything. I just didn't think he'd be ashamed of me."

Both women exchanged a look, one that Regan didn't fully comprehend. But there was enough eyebrow quirking and pointed stares to send her stomach into a nervous nosedive.

"What?" Regan asked. "What are you not telling me?"

But she already knew. This was where her friends would tell her that Gabe was way out of her league, and wishing for anything more was dangerous. So when Frankie folded her arms over her chest and leaned back in her chair and Jordan sighed, Regan's stomach reappeared in her throat.

"Fine. I had a talk with Gabe."

"What?" That was so not what she expected Jordan would say. And, oh, so much worse. "About what?"

"About screwing around with single moms. About how the rules are different. About how he needed to really know what he was doing before someone got hurt." Jordan lowered her voice, continuing before Regan could reply—well, scream. Regan had been on her own since she was eighteen; she didn't need someone fixing her business. "I get it. I'm a single mom too. I know what it's like to feel alone and how easy it is to forget you're a woman. Then some good-looking guy with a great package comes along reminding you what you're missing, and you drop your pants for a quick scratch."

Regan felt her face heat with anger. "You had no right to talk to Gabe or anyone else about my itches! Quickly scratched or otherwise. I'm not Ava. I'm not part of your purity-for-eternity campaign."

Lines of concern cut through Jordan's forehead. "No, you're not. But you're also not the kind of person to take something like sleeping with a man lightly."

"You don't even know me," Regan accused.

"Yes, I do," Jordan said, and Regan realized it was true. They may have only met a few weeks ago, but the women in front of her had quickly become two of the closest friends she'd ever had. And Jordan was hitting painfully close to home with her assessment. "I also see the way you look at him, Regan."

"We…love…you and don't want you to get hurt." Frankie forced the words out as if such an admission were painful.

Not nearly as painful as Regan's next words. "Why? Because a man like Gabe could never love a woman like me?"

"God, no." Jordan stared Regan down, not continuing until she knew Regan was listening. "Self-loathing is not and never will be the new black. At least not one that you could pull off attractively. You are smart and beautiful and a wonderful pain in the ass."

"Is this where you tell me 'It's not you, it's him'?" Regan smiled, a little.

"No, this is where I tell you that Gabe is not ready for a woman like you. He already raised a family and he's convinced himself that he doesn't want another one."

The realization that Jordan was right knocked the wind out of her. Gabe had told her the same thing. And until this moment she hadn't understood that deep in her heart she had been clinging to the hope that maybe he'd change his mind.

"Do I think he will always be a familyphobe? No." Jordan took Christmas Kitty's mittens out of Regan's hands.

They were wrinkled and the fur on the thumb was worried into small tufts. "But I don't want you and Holly to be the experiment to see if he's ready. Especially when, for a DeLuca, family always comes first."

Even his home spoke volumes for how much he loved his family. Sure it was a bachelor pad with lots of dark furniture, stainless steel, and a television bigger than her Christmas tree. But on nearly every wall and surface were family photos, mementos, signs that Gabe DeLuca was a family man—and he already had a family.

"Maybe Jordan was wrong about talking to Gabe," Frankie said, gathering up the leftover sequins and plastic stones and leveling Jordan with a look. "I know if she did that to me, I'd kick her ass. No question." She looked back to Regan. "If you want me to, just say the word. But I think what she's saying about the DeLucas is spot on. Do I think he could fall for a girl like you? Totally. You're all girly and maternal and shit. Do I think he would someday screw you over if his family asked him to? In a heartbeat. So before you go bringing him home for dinner, remember that having someone you love walk out sucks golf balls. But when you're a kid...you never get over wondering what you did wrong."

With that, Frankie stood, shoving the fabric scraps and beads in a bag, and grabbed her keys. "I'll finish the frog's head on my own. I'm practically OD-ing on all the estrogen in the air." She got to the door and stopped, her shoulders slumping. Without turning around she said, in a none-too-nice tone, "I would like nothing more than to hop on my bike and breathe concrete for the next two hours. But since Jordan refused to let me drive the hog in the rain, she's my ride home."

Jordan folded the cape and frog's body. She was reaching for the broom when Regan grabbed her hand. "I'll get it. You take Frankie home and I'll clean up. Thank you… for everything."

Jordan threw her arms around her and hugged her tight. "I never meant to make things harder on you. I just don't want to see you hurt."

"I know." Regan tightened her arms around her friend.

"You don't hate me?"

"No." Regan laughed even though she felt like crying. Gabe had been put on notice, and Jordan's intent was heartwarming. But the result was quite the opposite. Regan had worried all week about what she had done wrong. Now she realized that the answer was nothing. She was a single mom, struggling to balance career and family and toting around a lifetime of baggage.

Her problem didn't lie in the fact that she wasn't enough—she was too much.

She gave Jordan one last squeeze and pulled back. It was better this way. She knew the score, and Holly wouldn't be hurt later on down the road.

"Good." Jordan took her shoulders. "You gonna be okay?"

Regan nodded. What was she supposed to say? She'd already admitted to attacking Gabe. There was no way she was saying aloud that she might have been stupid enough to actually fall in love with the guy, and that her heart was breaking because she knew he would never love her back.

CHAPTER 13

Gabe heard the front door shut and walked out into the front of the house to find Regan. He wanted to talk to her about the last week. He wanted to apologize.

After she'd scurried off Monday, Jordan had cornered him. Told him that he'd better have his intentions clear with regard to Regan because if he so much as hurt her, Jordan would have his nuts. Gabe had called his brothers. Explained in no uncertain terms that Regan was off-limits in the pursuit of finding Richard. Not that he was giving up on the search, because that was never an option, but he was done using a woman who he knew wasn't involved.

The talk hadn't gone well. In fact, Marc accused him of picking a piece of ass over his family. Which wasn't true. Gabe just couldn't justify hurting one family in order to heal his own. And if Regan ever found out that using her to get to Richard was the reason they'd first decided to let her stay, hurt wouldn't even begin to describe what she'd feel.

He paused for a moment, just watching her sew. Elbow-deep in gold glittery fabric, her forehead scrunched as she moved to the end of the pant leg, securing metallic purple trim to the seam. Her hair slid over her shoulder as she reached for the scissors and snipped the loose thread.

Without lifting her head, she said, "I'm almost done. Let me just clean up, and then I'll grab Holly and get out of your hair."

She was hurt. More accurately, he had hurt her. It was there in the way she held her head, the way her body went unnaturally still.

"No rush," Gabe said, feeling like an idiot. He knew something had changed between them. He even knew he'd blown it. Hell, he'd stalked her, ruined her career, made love to her on a wine barrel, then ignored her into regret.

She turned off the sewing machine and started gathering up her things. "I'll take these out to the car and come back in for Holly."

"Regan, about this week—"

"It's okay," she said brightly. Too brightly. Everything about her seemed amped up and all for his benefit. "Jordan told me. I get it."

She looked up and everything inside him stilled. There in her big baby blues, hiding under all the professionalism and distance she was creating, was sadness and confusion and shame all wrapped up in one gut-wrenching look.

Panic pushed at his chest. He'd gone out of his way to make sure neither he nor his brothers were ever overheard talking about their plan to find Richard. But Monday he'd been frustrated at how the date ended, pissed that Jordan was all in his business, and might have yelled a few choice words at Marc on the phone in his office.

"Actually, you know what?" Regan's eyes went from hurt to pissed. "It's not okay. I get that my life can be a lot to take and that dating someone with a kid has its challenges. And even though it was hard, I never lied to you about where I was at." She shoved at his chest, her thimble digging into his pec. "But you should have just grown a pair and told me, instead of avoiding me in town and making me feel like you're ashamed to be seen with me." Dig. Dig.

Ashamed? Ah, hell, he'd screwed this one royally. "I'm not ashamed of you." He took her hand in his and set the offending thimble on the table. Small or not, the thing had punch. "And I wasn't avoiding you."

She raised a brow.

"Okay, I was avoiding you, but not because I was ashamed." He slid his arms around her waist and inched her closer. How could anyone ever be ashamed of a woman like Regan?

That he'd made her feel that way tore at him. That she hadn't discovered his brothers' plan relieved him. That he knew he'd eventually have to tell her scared the shit out of him.

"I spent the first twenty-four years of my life being responsible for my younger siblings, and the last twelve being everyone's hero. It's an honor and something I take seriously, and sometimes it's suffocating as hell." He paused, remembering how it felt to wake up with her in his arms, and inched her even closer, until he could see the gray flecks sparkle in her eyes and the pulse thundering in her throat. "The other day with you was incredible and intense and I got spooked. Then I saw Holly at Pricilla's and she was telling me about her party and I wanted it to be perfect so I started building her a damn throne and—"

Regan pressed three fingers to his mouth. "I don't need you to be my hero. Holly and I manage just fine."

"More than fine." He kissed each one of her fingers, most of them tipped with Band-Aids. "You are an amazing mother who's managed to raise an amazing daughter all on your own, which is what I figured out sometime between having my ass handed to me by Jordan and seeing you in the freezer section."

"I don't need to be rescued, but I do need honesty from the man I'm sleeping with." She tugged at the hem of his shirt. When she looked back up her expression was one of uncertainty. "I mean, if you're still...if we're still..."

"Oh, we're still." Not one to miss an opportunity, Gabe covered her mouth with his. Her arms slid around his neck, and she melted into him. The taste of her lips filled his head, and it would have been so easy to set her on the counter or try out a new table, but he remembered Holly, just two rooms over. And even though he had been adamant on the no-juice-before-bedtime rule, he didn't want to mess this up.

He wanted Regan in his bed. And Regan was a single mom. Which meant that he would have to work on his patience and get used to cold showers. With one last kiss he pulled back.

"Why don't you clean up and crawl into bed?" He tightened his arms around her. She snuggled deeper. "It's late and you have work in the morning."

Her body sagged against his and she shook her head, bumping it against his chin. "About that. I don't want Holly to wake up with a man in the house or catch us in bed or another close call like the other night. I think it would be confusing."

He smiled as she rambled on, and when she finally paused he said, "Agreed."

"So if this sounds too complicated..." She looked up. "What?"

"I said I agree." He tucked a strand of hair behind her ear. "I meant, it's late, why don't you take my bed and I'll crash on the couch?"

"No, I can't make you sleep on the couch. You'd have a horrible night's sleep. You could barely get out from under the table. Sleeping on a couch will cripple you for a week at least. I'll just pack up and head home."

"I'll sleep even worse if I'm up all night worrying about you making it home safe. Feeling like crap that you woke Holly up on a school night. And that you have work early in the morning."

Those full lips of hers quirked and all he could think about was kissing her again. "God, you really do have a hero complex." Then she took a deep breath, making her chest rise and fall, and a hero complex was the least of his worries.

"I don't have work tomorrow. I took a Sunday shift so that I could finish those." She glared at the costumes on the table. "But, you're right, waking up Holly would make for a miserable morning for all involved. So, if you can point me to the linens, I'll take the couch."

"ChiChi would kill me if she knew I let you sleep on the couch." And the couch would kill her. It was comfortable enough for watching the game and napping on Sundays, but it was hell on the back.

"See." He dropped on the sofa, stretched his legs out, and then tugged her down with him. Right on his lap. She made a big deal out of bouncing up and down, testing him out like she was Goldilocks until he was as hard as the couch.

"A little lumpy for my taste."

"Little, my ass," he grumbled, grabbing *her* ass and flipping her around so she was straddling him and she could feel for herself how wrong she was.

"I thought I was going to bed." She leaned back, resting her hands behind her on his knees and rolling her hips forward, bringing all their good parts in perfect contact.

"Maybe we should test out the couch for a few minutes first." His hands settled right below the dimples on her lower back and worked their way up, under her shirt and around the front searching out her other good parts.

"Clothes stay on. Then I go to sleep with Holly and you sleep in your bed. Couch stays empty."

He dipped down and kissed her stomach. "Afraid you'll be tempted?"

"I'm just glad you only have one couch."

"Actually, I have one in my office too."

Before Gabe even opened his eyes he knew three things: he'd fallen asleep on the couch, Regan was not with him, and someone was staring him down.

That someone was a little taller than a fencepost, stood next to the couch wearing one of his old T-shirts, a mess of brown ringlets, and a scrunched face that said she'd nearly used up all her superkid patience. The curtains were open, but no light was filtering through, meaning it was either storming again or way too early to be awake.

"What time is it?" Gabe said, his voice struggling to wake up.

Holly plopped on the floor, pulled the too-long tee over her bent knees and picked up his phone. "Five thirty-seven."

Gabe groaned. "Want me to walk you back to bed?"

Holly shook her head, curls bouncing everywhere.

"Want me to get your mom?"

Again with the hair. Only this time she fidgeted with the hem of her tee.

Something was up. He could sense it in his gut. Could see it in her expression, in the way she was worrying that adorable lower lip just like her mom did.

Adorable or not, it was too freaking early. Because her eyes were also batting and innocent-looking, reminding him of ChiChi when she set her mind to something. Something that was sure to complicate his already complicated life.

He raised his brow in a silent last chance. Holly smiled bigger.

"Suit yourself." Gabe rolled over, grabbing a pillow and smothering it over his face.

He stayed like that, back to Holly, face wedged between the couch and the pillow, sucking in the leather, waiting to hear the pitter patter of feet back to the guest room. It didn't happen. She just kept silently willing him awake—he could feel it. He could also feel her little breath on the back of his neck. She was almost as bad as Marc, just cuter.

Which meant she'd wear him down.

Resigned to the few hours of sleep he'd managed to get, Gabe threw back the blanket and sat up. "You want some breakfast?"

"Pancakes with chocolate chips and bananas and a glass of milk?" She blinked. Three times.

He wiped a hand down his face, the stubble scratching his palm. His groggy mind tried to catch up, making a mental rundown of what he had in the kitchen. "No pancake mix. No bananas. But I do have milk and some chocolate chips." They were left over from one of ChiChi's failed fruitcake attempts.

Holly took his hand and walked with him to the kitchen, eyes batting the entire way. After starting the coffee—he had a feeling he was going to need it this morning—he plopped her on one of the bar stools at the counter, poured her a glass of milk, and scavenged the pantry for something other than beer, chips, and a half-empty jar of maraschino cherries.

In the eight years he'd owned the house he couldn't remember anyone ever using the breakfast bar. People usually sat at the table, or more often on the couch. *People* being his siblings, Jordan, Ava, and his grandmother. Gabe didn't entertain. Didn't like people in his space. It made him feel like he had to put on the DeLuca hat. He was beginning to hate the DeLuca hat.

He looked at Holly, milkstache above her lip, hem hanging past her ankles, and realized that somewhere along the way he'd lost the façade and, with the Martin women, he was comfortable just being himself. Not a side many people experienced.

He opened the fridge and rummaged through the shelves. "Okay, I've got bread, eggs, onion, and cheese. How about an omelet and toast? Scratch that." He studied the cheese. It was looking a little fuzzy, so he tossed it in the garbage. "Scrambled eggs with onions and toast?"

Holly's nose scrunched up. Either the kid was going to sneeze or she wasn't a big onion fan.

"You got any cereal?" she asked, her feet swinging back and forth.

"Yup, cornflakes."

"With chocolate chips?" Holly asked, her eyes darting back toward where Regan was sleeping.

So, Mom didn't feed the kid junk. Good to know. "One bowl of *plain* cornflakes coming right up."

Holly dropped her chin to the counter and blew out air. Smiling, Gabe grabbed two bowls, a couple spoons, and joined her. Holly poured the cereal, and Gabe polished off each bowl with the milk. He even opened a can of pineapple, also ChiChi's, pleased that he had covered three of the five food groups.

He helped himself to a cup of coffee, patiently waiting for Holly to spill. She was so amped her entire body was humming with the need to talk. So he'd do exactly what he did when Abby or ChiChi had a secret. He'd get busy, because the second he got invested in something the women in his life decided to talk.

Gabe lifted his mug, took a big sniff of hazelnut and caffeine, and could almost taste the first sip. He brought the cup to his mouth—

"Gabe?"

"Uh huh," he mumbled, watching her over the rim of his cup. When she didn't continue, he tilted the cup back and the liquid touched his tongue—

"I know it's not polite to *ask* someone for a present, but..."

The clank of ceramic on granite sounded as he set the mug down and turned his attention fully on Holly. Women tended to like that. And he could tell by the way she clasped her hands in front of her chin and smiled that, five years old or not, so did Holly.

"But?"

Holly took a big breath and exhaled so slowly Gabe was afraid she was never going to get on with it. Once she opened her mouth, he was suddenly afraid the only way she would stop talking was when she ran out of oxygen.

"Lauren's got a single mom just like me. Only Ms. Isabel is divorced from all three of Lauren's daddies, which is kind of neat because she gets to have four kitties of her very own, one at each house, and I don't even have one kitty of my very own. Well, not yet because we had to move and Ms. Jordan isn't our landlord anymore and Mr. Chester doesn't allow any kind of pets, not even goldfish. He says his wife's allergic and she would smell it all the way to her house and then where would he be?"

She gave a dramatic pause, her hands out to her side in a dramatic question.

Gabe swallowed, hard. So that was what Regan had been talking about the night of the Christmas party when he pretty much fired her and kicked her to the curb. If the kid wanted a cat for her birthday, he would figure out a way. Even if it meant paying Chester an insane pet deposit.

"I can talk to Chester about letting you have a cat." Hell, if Regan was on board he'd even buy Holly the cat. Let her pick out one of those expensive white ones with the flat face.

"No, then Mrs. Chester would divorce him and he'd come live at the apartment, and then we'd have to move again. And I just got my own bed."

And his day got shittier and shittier as the story went on. Every Christmas Gabe dressed up like Santa for his little cousins and his employees' kids. This year he was feeling more like the Grinch.

"Lauren was telling me that all three of her daddies want to go to the Christmas musical. But every kid only gets two tickets and I only have one parent."

Gabe saw where this was going and his heart ached for the little girl in front of him who wanted to make her friend happy, but desperately wanted more than one person in the crowd clapping for her.

Holly mushed a soggy flake against the side of her bowl with the spoon, then her hand stilled. "Ms. Isabel asked me if my daddy was coming."

Everything inside of Gabe stilled. He'd already decided not to even tread there about Richard. Now the opportunity his brothers had been hounding him for was being handed to him. Only it meant using a little girl's sadness about missing her daddy.

"Is he?" Gabe asked with a forced a casualness that he sure as hell didn't feel. The last thing he needed was for Holly to pick up on his tension and mention this conversation to her mom.

Eyes firmly on her cereal, she shrugged her little shoulders. "I don't think so. He's not around much. So Ms. Isabel said it isn't nice to waste and that I should give my extra ticket to Lauren so all her daddies could go."

Gabe rested his elbows on the counter and resisted the urge to hang his head in his hands. He would do anything to find Richard if it meant putting an end to this entirely screwed-up situation. Unless that anything included hurting Holly. Or Regan.

"Were you saving it for your dad, hoping he would come?"

Holly looked up at him. Her eyes vulnerable and uncertain. "I was hoping you would come."

Strong hands massaged Regan's back, easing her from a dead sleep. Feeling like a content cat, she rolled over and stretched. She opened her eyes and blinked twice, trying to get her bearing, but all she could see was the most gorgeous set of brown eyes staring back at her.

Regan was flat on her back in Gabe's guest bed, his hands were up her shirt, and, when she shifted her hips, she wasn't wearing any underwear. And she might have been purring.

"Morning." His voice was gravely and soft and sexy as hell. He nipped at her lip and then delivered a toe-curling kiss. Yup, she was definitely purring.

Morning?

Regan stopped midkiss. Her lids snapped open, the blinding light from the sun pierced her eyes and instantly cleared her mind from the sex-fog that was Gabe DeLuca. She took stock and, realizing just what she was doing, shoved him off and pulled the sheets to her chin. "What are you doing in my bed?"

"It's my bed, but I'm more than willing to share." He grinned, tugging on the blanket.

"What?" She frowned, then said, "Oh, my God! What time is it?"

"Eight fifteen." He rested back against the headboard, calm as could be.

"I'm late. And it's Holly's last day of school before break. She has her party. Her cookies—" Regan scrambled out of bed, felt a cold draft on her bottom, and leaped back under the covers, wrapping them securely around her. "Her cookies and our clothes are at home. You have to leave so I can get dressed."

"I'd rather you stay naked." He ripped the blankets back and she squeaked. "As for Holly, ChiChi picked her up ten minutes ago. Showed up with a change of clothes, a bag lunch and enough of Pricilla's special Christmas cookies to get twenty-four kids hopped up on sugar and food coloring."

Regan felt herself relax and, after covering herself in a cocoon of pillows, actually flopped back on the bed and closed her eyes. Then they snapped open only to find herself staring up into Gabe's eyes—again. Gabe, who was now missing a shirt.

"How did she know I was here?"

"She makes it her business to know, and before you start freaking out…" He smoothed the stress lines out of her forehead and the pillows off her legs. "I think last night was a setup. Actually, I think she has been setting us up from the beginning."

"Really?" Regan didn't know why that made her feel all warm and fuzzy inside, but it did.

"She sent you the job offer from Ryo."

"She did?"

"Then made me bring you that cake. And she's been doing everything in her power to get us in the same room.

Alone and often. In fact, she gave me explicit instructions to go back to bed when she left."

"Gabe, are you trying to tell me your grandma wants you to sleep with me?" Suddenly she didn't mind the lack of clothes.

"Sweetheart, I've been waiting forever to get you in my bed. Sleep is the last thing I had in mind." He rolled on top of Regan, and she realized he wasn't wearing any pants either. He was blessedly naked and, as he slid between her legs and pressed against her, ready to go.

"This isn't *your* bed, exactly." Not that she cared. When he held himself over her like that, his arms did the most amazing thing: they got even bigger and bulged and she couldn't help but slide her hands up them.

"We'll get there." He kissed her languidly, taking his time to build the heat, until her whole body was shaking with need. "We've got a couple couches to try out first. Oh, and I have this swing on the back porch that I went out and bought cushions for."

"You bought new cushions? Why?" Regan choked out as he nibbled at the sweet spot right behind her ear.

"Because watching you sleep naked, outside on that chaise with your hair all wet and your body slick, was about the sexiest thing I've seen." He rested his weight on one elbow, freeing up his other hand. Grabbing her shirt right below her breasts, he slowly tugged it up, baring her stomach, her nipples, and over her head, his eyes taking in every exposed inch. "Been thinking about it for days. Wondering what it would have been like to splay you out so I could lick every inch of you."

Regan slid her legs around the back of his thighs and, arching her hips, slid right over his length. "Want to move to the porch?"

"First, I want you here, in this bed, so I can touch every inch of you with my hands until you explode." His hands already roaming over her chest, belly button, hips, everywhere. He trailed a single finger down her stomach and right over the center.

"Then where?" she whispered.

"Where am I going to touch you next, or where am I going to take you next?" His finger made the same mind-blowing pass; this time, though, he lingered, making slow, mind-blowing little circles.

"Both," she gasped.

Gabe kissed his way across her jaw to her ear and proceeded to tell her in explicit detail where, why, and for how long he was going to take her.

Which was how she ended up in his bed four hours later, exhausted and ready for a nap. Gabe had given her the full and complete tour of his house, not excluding the laundry room or shower. But her favorite, by far, was his bed. It was big and soft and smelled like him. It was also because in his bed, he had pulled her close, holding her tightly as though he didn't want any space between. And afterward he had hugged her with those strong arms of his and fell asleep with his face buried in her neck.

Regan had never been in love. Sure she had loved Richard, but that was a young love, one that was born out of loneliness and insecurity and the need to be loved back.

She tightened her arms around his middle and closed her eyes, just taking him in. This felt different. It didn't make her feel anxious or hollow. With Gabe, all she felt was a sense of rightness.

Which was why her heart pinched painfully when he looked up, his face nowhere near right. In fact, he looked confused and angry—at her.

"Do you still see Richard?"

"What? No. Why?"

"Holly said she doesn't see *much* of him."

Holly? What the hell?

"You were talking to Holly about Richard?" Only moments ago his body pressed into her had felt safe, now it made her feel vulnerable. She tried to move, but he didn't budge.

"No, *she* was talking to *me*. About him. And I just want to make sure if he decides to come and visit you two, that Abby is prepared."

Of course. This was about Abby. Regan placed her hands on his chest and shoved. He didn't budge, but he begrudgingly rolled off of her and leaned against the headboard.

Regan sat up and pulled the blanket up and around her chest. Just when she thought they had gotten past—well, their past—there it was again. Only this time it was like the past six years were in the bed with them. And the only shot they had to get rid of it once and for all was honesty.

"Holly saw him once. She was just a baby and doesn't even remember." Although Regan remembered every second of the visit. Richard had apologized, saying that even though he was working things out with his wife, he wanted to do right by his kid. Regan had wanted to kick his ass for being a liar and a cheat, but she'd thought of her daughter, of how it felt to grow up without a dad, and decided to try and be civil. Richard had agreed to pay child support, Regan snapped a picture of him holding Holly, and then he left.

"She has a picture of that day. Sometimes she pulls it out and looks at it or asks questions about him. Like if she has his nose or if he was a good speller. One time she brought it to school, and her teacher told me she was showing it to all of her friends because they didn't believe she had a daddy."

That had happened right before they had moved to St. Helena. Regan had no idea she was being teased, and Holly had never said a word.

"What do you tell her? When she asks about her dad?" Gabe said softly. He didn't look mad anymore; he looked miserable.

"The truth. That her daddy loves her very much, but just because you love someone doesn't always mean you're ready to be a parent."

"So you don't see him?"

Now it was Regan's turn to get mad. She was answering a lot of questions, but none of her answers seemed good enough. "I already said no. Why don't you just ask what you really want to know, Gabe?"

"Did you love him?"

And all of the anger faded. Was he jealous? Of her and Richard? Or maybe trying to gauge where her heart was at?

She reached out and placed a gentle hand on his arm. "Gabe, I'm a third-generation single mom. I never knew anything about my dad except that he was a French businessman and he didn't want me. So when my mom died I had literally no one. Until Richard showed up, mature and handsome with his Italian roots and accent. He charmed me into believing I was special and wanted, and then charmed me right into bed."

Gabe rested a hand on top of hers, and she melted at the look in his eyes. The look of a guy who wanted to make everyone's world safe, but with her and their past, wasn't sure how. "Do you still love him?"

"No. After Richard left I was crushed, but then Holly came along and I was too scared to be anything else. That last time he came to see me I realized that I was more in love with the idea of having a family than I ever was with him."

"Thank God." Gabe kissed her long and hard, his fingers fisting in her hair, holding her to him. It was as though with that one statement he had given himself permission to love her. He might not be in love with her, but she could tell in the way his body shook and how fiercely he collected her to him that he was feeling every bit of this intense bond that she was.

When they came up for air, Regan was straddling him, legs locked around his back, and Gabe was holding her as though he would never let go. As though she was his.

He kissed her nose, her cheeks, her forehead, and then buried his face against her neck. "It would have been difficult to go after someone that you loved."

Everything inside Regan stilled. She didn't let go of him; didn't open her eyes; didn't even breathe. "What do you mean?"

"After that night..." Gabe pulled back, cupping her face between his big, strong hands and staring into her eyes. "After I confronted you and Richard, he went to Abby, told her about the affair and begged for a second chance. Really, he needed time for the last round of funding for their new winery to close." Oh. My. God. This could not be happening.

Regan knew exactly how much money Richard had raised. And the exact date it had closed. It had gone in and out of Holly's fund in under thirty minutes. Unable to reach Richard, she'd called an old college buddy who was a lawyer, asking hypothetical questions about liability and possible ramifications. Hypothetically, if the account had been in her daughter's name with Regan listed as one of the signers, she could be charged with aiding and abetting.

She'd never discovered whose money he'd stolen. Until now.

"We all thought he was serious about changing, about making it work with Abby. Hell, they were the couple of the hour. Six months later funding closed and the next day Richard and twelve million dollars disappeared. The bastard left Abby alone to face the investors and to take the blame, which is why she moved to Santa Barbara. She was too embarrassed to come home. And the cops started sniffing around, convinced that she had conspired with Richard, and made her life a living hell for two years."

They'd sniffed Regan too—asking about the account, the missing money, treating her like she was guilty. As soon as they realized she was broke and going nowhere fast, they left her alone with the direct instructions to contact them if she heard from Richard. Which she hadn't. Nor did she think she ever would.

Regan looked up at Gabe, all protective and fierce and incredibly handsome. And he was looking at her, for the first time, like part of that fierce protectiveness was for her.

It would be so easy to tell him the truth. Tell him that she wanted so badly for Holly to have something that proved her daddy loved her, she had naively helped Richard open that account.

She searched his face, looking for some clue that he would believe her. That what they had just shared trumped the past. He had believed her before, but it had taken six years and eleven jobs before he came around. Would he believe her again? And if not, what would that mean for her and Holly and their new hometown?

CHAPTER 14

R egan hurried out of Party to Go Go holding a bag full of
favors for Holly's tea. There were enough for fifteen kids,
one for every classmate coming. Each kitty bag had a kitty
pencil, kitty eraser, kitty candy, and sheet of kitty stickers.

An errand that without Holly at her side should have
taken five minutes became a thirty-minute ordeal when
Delores, the store's owner, felt the need to give hands-on
instruction on how to properly dress a gift bag. Only to
finish them herself when Regan came up lacking in the bow-
making department.

Thank God Gabe had taken Holly this morning. Holly
had promised to help Pricilla with the last-minute details
of the party, and Regan still had to get Holly's present. So
Gabe, who had been drafted to hang the banner and handle
all the heavy lifting, had offered to take Holly with him.
Which should have made the morning a breeze.

But it hadn't. Because all the kid-free time while buying
Holly's present led to too much I'm-not-just-a-mommy time

to think: about him and his lips and the way he touched her, looked at her, made love to her.

And the way she still hadn't told him about the investors' money. It didn't matter that she had not a clue as to where Richard or the millions went. Once Gabe knew about the account, the way he looked at her would change. Having Gabe in her corner would change. And she didn't know if she could handle that. Especially if he decided to retaliate and it somehow affected Holly.

Telling herself that it was an omission and not a lie, Regan clutched the gift bags and hurried down the street toward her car. She did not feel one ounce of guilt when she waved at Mrs. Moberly, who was placing all of the Christmas-themed books in the library's front window. Did not give in to the guilt when she thanked Stan after he mentioned that her new car battery was in and he could install it Monday. She knew that the universe understood her reasons for keeping a ginormous secret from the man whose bed she sometimes shared. But then she set the gift bags on the top of her car, opened her trunk—and immediately slammed it shut.

"No way," she whispered, cracking the trunk again. This time slamming it so hard that half the kitty-themed bags toppled to the ground. "No freaking way."

She closed her eyes, said a little prayer to ward off evil spirits and curses, and opened the trunk.

"Merry Christmas one and all," Randolph said, smiling up at her from behind the green and red box containing one kitty pillow pet that Holly had all but begged for. All but, because begging would be considered rude.

Well, there was nothing "all but" about the way Regan reacted. Rude or not, she dropped enough four-letter words to send Holly to Europe for the summer. Either this was the universe's form of a Dirty Jar and she was being punished for transgressions against the DeLucas, this town, and Christmas as a whole, or someone had a sick sense of humor. Or—Regan stood still, her back straight, head forward, only her eyes moving around the street, looking for clues—someone was setting her up.

Problem was, that someone could be anyone on the ever-growing list of people Regan Martin had crossed, intentionally or not. When Regan was satisfied that she was, for the most part, alone, she crouched low, getting in Big Red's face.

"You don't scare me," she whispered in her most intimidating voice. It was the same one her mom had used when Regan got caught beheading the neighbor girl's Barbie for making fun of her mom's accent. "In fact, you should be scared. It appears I suffer from anger issues—just ask your hooved brethren. And for your safety and my sanity, after Holly's party you are going back on that pedestal of yours, where you will stay. Forever." She grabbed Holly's present. "Let that penetrate through that thick, plastic head of yours." And, needing to get in the last word, she quickly slammed the trunk shut with a resounding thud, grabbed the party bags, and walked across the street.

Based on the outside alone, Pricilla and the Mrs. Clauses had gone all out. The dancing elves in the windows had been replaced with kitties in tiaras, and two miniature Christmas trees, covered in candy canes and glittery bulbs, framed either side of the glass door. What caught Regan's eye, though, was nothing shy of an early Christmas gift and made all of the Randolph rage fade into the background.

A small white sign hung in the doorway, surrounded by red twinkling lights and attached with a golden bow read, "Private party for Holly's 6th Birthday Tea."

As promised, Holly had assisted with every aspect of planning her party. She picked the menu, helped decorate, cut the sandwiches into little stars, and even dusted the tearoom from top to bottom. The Mrs. Clauses supervising and guiding and encouraging her at every step had made this so much more than just a party. It had been a warm welcome to the town and to their group.

Regan hopped over the curb and pushed through the shop's door. Inside it smelled like chocolate and cinnamon and looked like Christmas gone drag.

Red-feathered ornaments hung from every nook and cranny, while disco-themed snowflakes covered the ceiling. The tables had been shoved together and covered in green sequined tablecloths and kitties in Christmas garb. The only thing missing, besides the kitchen sink, were the Mrs. Clauses and the birthday girl.

Whistling along with Nat King Cole, Regan set the party bags in the basket by the door and was taking Holly's present to the counter when she stopped.

Standing under Holly's birthday banner and beside a life-size cutout of David Hasselhoff—complete with red swim trunks, a Santa hat, and a sign that read "Hoff Yourself a Merry Little Christmas"—stood Isabel. She looked manicured and regal and way too pleased with herself for Regan to feel anything but nervous. Especially since she was sans one adorable child.

First Randolph. Then "El Diablo." The Christmas curse was growing stronger.

Isabel gave the golden bell next to the cash register a little ding and then turned back to Regan. "Well, it looks like Holly's big day is finally here."

"Yeah. She's really excited." Regan looked around, hating that they were all alone, because with no witnesses it was hard not to grab Mr. Hasselhoff by the biceps and beat the crap out of Isabel. "So, where's Lauren? Is she in the back with Holly and the Mrs. Clauses?"

Isabel raised her forehead. "Mrs. Clauses? How quaint. And no, Lauren's dad and I switched weekends and she decided to have a little get-together with her friends instead."

Regan swallowed. Holly was going to be crushed. "Why would you do that?"

"Oh, well, because I remembered where I knew you from." Isabel looked her up and down. "You interned with the National Vintner's Historical Society, right?"

One sentence and Regan felt her whole world start to unravel.

"My ex-husband worked on that project. He headed up the fund-raising here in the Valley. He worked a lot with the other teams."

"Which one?" Regan asked.

"All of them, but mainly the Oregon team."

"No, I meant, which husband." Okay so it was a lame dig, but she was mad and it was all she had. When Isabel didn't even take the bait, Regan knew whatever the woman had was going to be epic.

"Oh, my first one. The same one who talked about this pretty little Hispanic girl who worked very closely with Richard. Imagine my surprise when I looked up the press release the other day after the council meeting and saw you.

Even more surprising is how incredibly similar Richard and Holly look. I can't believe I never noticed it. I mean, side by side one might even think they were related."

"Isabel, please don't hurt Holly to get back at me. She's had a hard enough time being one of the only kids in school without a dad."

"Don't worry," Isabel said, laying a hand on Regan's arm. "I would never tell people that Holly is Richard's."

"Thank you," Regan whispered.

She would never want Holly to be ashamed of Richard. But to have people talking about their relationship in a sordid way, meaning that their kids would eventually overhear and repeat every detail to Holly, would break Regan's heart. She didn't want Holly to go through the kind of childhood Regan had.

"However," Isabel said, "I know you can understand why I felt the need to warn some of my friends, whose husbands might be going through a difficult time right now. They have the right to choose whether their children spend time with someone they would never want their husbands to meet."

Regan felt her face drain. She actually had to grip the counter to keep from sliding to the floor. "Is this all because Holly got the lead in the play?"

"No, this is because women like you don't belong here, Regan. And it's time people in this town understood that." She rang the bell again, and when no one appeared, she walked behind the counter, pulled down a pink box with her name on it and walked to the door. Isabel looked over her shoulder. "Tell Pricilla to put it on my tab. Oh, and tell Holly happy birthday from me."

Regan waited until she heard the bell on the door jingle closed before she collapsed into the nearest chair. This could not be happening. Not once when she had considered moving to St. Helena did she ever imagine the conversation that had just transpired. When she'd come here, she knew there would be a few hurdles, but the job at Ryo and the chance to give Holly the kind of life Regan had dreamed of for her had outweighed all of the downsides.

"Hey, there you are. I wanted to talk to you before Holly—" Gabe took one look at her face and came to stand in front of her. He squatted down to eye level. She dropped her head to the table. "Regan, what's wrong?"

"No one's coming," she mumbled into the green sequins, a feather sticking to her lip. No one was coming to her daughter's sixth birthday party. The party that Holly had worked so hard on and was so excited about.

"Hey." He slid his fingers through her hair. "It's still early."

She shook her head, her forehead bunching the tablecloth. "I just saw Isabel and everyone knows about Richard. And they don't want their kids around someone who—" She couldn't even say it. Not to him. Not when he used to look at her like that, but now he looked at her like she mattered. "Oh, God, Gabe. What I have I done? I should have never come here."

"Mommy! Look!" Holly came bounding out of the kitchen in a white tea-length dress with a green sash and white collar. She gave a dramatic spin and the skirt belled out, reminding Regan of a snowflake princess. And the three Mrs. Clauses stood behind, looking proud as punch. "Lucinda made me the dress and Pricilla sewed on the apron and ChiChi lent me her crown."

Holly pointed to the small tiara on her head. It was plastic and gaudy and when Regan squinted she could have sworn it said Cheetah's Strip and Sip.

"I got it at Ruth's bachelorette party," ChiChi said proudly. Pricilla and Lucinda exchanged confused looks. "Her third one. When she married that podiatrist."

"Ah." Both ladies nodded with understanding.

"You look beautiful, angel," Regan said, hugging her daughter and placing a kiss on top of her head. She licked her finger and stealthily tried to rub off the strip-club logo. No such luck.

"It was Lucinda's idea. She said every little girl should get to be a princess for at least one day." That surprised Regan, since Lucinda didn't seem to have a feminine bone in her body. "So, Pricilla put it in the invitation that everyone should dress like a princess."

Regan looked at Gabe, who was pinching the bridge of his nose. Gathering Holly close, setting her on her lap, she said, "Oh, honey, I just saw Lauren's mom and—"

"She's sick," Gabe broke in, looking almost as surprised by his lie as Regan did.

Silently asking Regan to give him a minute, he squatted down on his haunches. "So your mom thought we should save her a cupcake."

"I'm sad she won't be here. She is the *F* to my *B*."

Regan choked on that, having a whole other *F* and *B* phrase to describe Lauren's mom, but let it go. She shouldn't punish Lauren for Isabel being a psycho parent.

Gabe rested a hand on Holly's head, careful, Regan noticed, not to mess with the crown. "Why don't you and the grannies go in the kitchen and pack one or two up, and I can bring them to Lauren later."

The grannies all looked at Regan, who was near tears, then at Gabe and nodded. They didn't know what was going on, but they knew something was off. Problem was, so did Holly.

"Maybe we could send her home with a few of my peppermint wafers," Pricilla said, placing her hand on Holly's back and shuffling her through the swinging kitchen doors. Before the door shut, Regan saw Holly's little face, perplexed and concerned, staring back at her.

She waited until she heard rattling coming from the kitchen. The last thing she wanted was for Holly to overhear them. "Gabe, that was sweet, but in a few minutes she'll figure it out."

"This is what I do. I solve problems. Let me solve this one." He smiled, pulling her up to standing.

"I don't lie to my daughter. I never have and I won't start now just because some stuck-up—"

Gabe leaned forward and gently pressed his lips to hers, delivering a sweet kiss. When he pulled back his face was serious. "I wouldn't ask you to. Ever." He kissed her again, this time lingering a little longer. "But I am going to ask you to trust me."

He was asking a lot, because she didn't do trust all that well. Maybe because it hadn't worked out for her well in the past. Or maybe because she knew he was talking about a whole lot more than saving a little girl's tea party. Either way, Regan closed her eyes and whispered, "Okay."

If Gabe thought corralling a group of investors in a down-turned economy was difficult, it was because he had never spent the afternoon with a group of sugar-streaming, six-year-old girls.

"How did you—"

Gabe didn't hear the rest of Regan's question because a three-foot-tall girl with blonde curls, a pink crown, and enough attitude to take on the entire PTA screeched by, cupcake in hand, wand over her head, and giving "bat out of hell" a whole new meaning.

When she collided with another princess—this one covered in cupcake—fingers started pointing, tears started flowing, and normally Gabe would have found himself walking...right out that door. Instead he walked over, righted both kids, wiped off the cake and tears and, after making sure Holly was having a good time, sat down with Regan to share a cupcake.

And that was when Gabe realized that Regan was asking the wrong question. It wasn't about *how* he'd done it but *why*. And for the past hour, watching a bunch of sugarcoated kids tear apart Pricilla's teahouse, he'd been asking himself that same question over and over.

The answer was easy. He wanted to be her hero. He wanted to be that person who made Regan happy, who she counted on. And he wanted to be that for Holly. Somewhere between trying to chase Regan out of town and then into his bed, Gabe had fallen for her. Hard.

"Seriously," Regan asked, breaking the cupcake in two and offering up half to Gabe. "How did you get them all here? Isabel runs the Mommy Mafia."

He took the cupcake, set it on a napkin, and sucked the frosting off her fingers. She moaned, then her eyes flickered around to make sure no one had seen them. That was his fault, one he meant to fix. Right now.

"I called a few of the dads I know and said I was looking forward to seeing them at the tea party. When they asked why I was going I explained that the birthday girl was my girlfriend's daughter."

Regan bit her lower lip and a pretty blush covered her cheeks. "What about when Abigail—"

"She'll get over it?" Gabe leaned over the table, the cupcake, and a stuffed cat with some kind of damn antlers on its head and kissed Regan. He kissed her in front of just about every gossip in town, knowing that his brothers were going to chew him a new one, that Abby was going to blow something, and that ChiChi was already picking out wedding dates.

And he didn't care.

By the time Christmas Eve rolled around, Regan had a Band-Aid on every fingertip, glitter permanently stuck to her forearms, and enough sewing experience to moonlight as a seamstress. She'd finished all the costumes, helped Holly run her lines, and still managed to see Gabe twice. Sunday she'd met him at The Cannery with Holly for breakfast. Monday she met him on his couch, in nothing but mistletoe. Holly had been at her final rehearsal.

Now Holly was backstage, covered in fur, red lamé knickers and vest, waiting for the play to start. Regan unrolled and rolled the program in her hands and looked over her shoulder, past the garland-lined rows of packed seats, past the thirty antlered glee club kids gathered in the back waiting for their cue, to the theater's entrance.

She hadn't expected the painful flitter that fisted against her rib cage as the lights dimmed and the doorway remained empty. Just like the chair to her left.

Holly would be devastated if she stepped out on that stage and saw her second seat empty. Then again, Gabe wasn't the kind of person to stand up a six-year-old. She looked at the entrance again.

"Will you stop? Every time you turn you smack me with the ball on your hat," Jordan said from the chair to her right.

"Plus, I think it's blocking everyone behind us from seeing"—Ava took in her hat—"anything."

"Oh, sorry." Regan took off her macaroni-trimmed elf hat, something Holly made for her in class, and set it under her seat. Muttering an apology to the woman behind her, she slyly took another peek at the door.

Jordan took Regan by the shoulders, turning her toward the stage, the clanking of metal on metal sounding. Jordan was wearing a red fluffy handcuff on her right hand. Ava had a matching cuff on her left. Regan raised a brow.

"Last night, Mr. Sex with Wheels decided to play Romeo and climb the trellis."

"He was dropping off my homework," Ava fumed, crossing her arms and jerking Jordan's hand to the side.

"In the bathtub?" Jordan jerked back. Ava rolled her eyes so hard, Regan was surprised they didn't fall out.

"I felt the testosterone all the way downstairs. By the time I busted through the bathroom door"—Jordan leaned closer to Regan and lowered her voice—"Mr. Sex was about to become Mr. Bubbles."

"Did you call the cops?" Regan was *not* looking forward to the teen years.

"Barney Fife? Are you kidding? That boy has five inches on the sheriff. I grabbed the plunger and started swinging at crotch level, yelling about my knife collection and castration. Then I called Gabe. He and the DeLuca men paid the kid and his father a visit. Mr. Sex on Wheels is now missing his wheels. But just in case he decides to bust out the Huffy"— Jordan held up their linked hands—"we're conjoined until she turns eighteen."

Regan wondered if maybe she should be cuffed to Jordan's other hand. She and Gabe didn't sound all that different from the horny teen couple. Making out in alleyways, meeting on lunch breaks for a little snack that had nothing to do with food, deflowering his new swing cushion.

The St. Vincent's high school band took their seats and the lights went black. Regan looked over her shoulder one last time.

"He'll be here," Jordan whispered over the swelling music. "When I was leaving the office, I ran into Marc and Nate in the parking lot. They both looked constipated and asked if Gabe was still there. So I imagine he's trying to solve another one of their self-made problems."

Regan didn't hear anything else because the curtain opened and standing middle stage was Holly. She was curled up in a ball on an enormous cat bed surrounded by giant candy canes and sugarplums. Balls of yarn the size of truck tires hung from the ceiling, each one with a swinging Saints cheerleader in a metallic space suit. It was like the Nutcracker fell down Alice's hole and wound up in a club in Vegas. And the crowd went wild.

Christmas Kitty opened her eyes and stretched and, sitting up, let out the perfect purr. It was sleepy and adorable and flawlessly executed. Unable to contain herself, Regan clapped and Holly's eyes flew to hers and paused...for only a second. Long enough to let Regan know that Holly knew she was there. And that the seat to her left was still painfully empty.

Regan smiled brighter, clapped twice as hard, trying to make up for the empty seat—something she had done Holly's entire life. Suddenly, Christmas Kitty smiled and, eyes on the back of the theater, started making muffins on the bed.

Regan turned around and saw Gabe, looking sexy in a pair of slacks and a dark blue button-down. He stared at the stage, a big smile on his face as he winked at Holly. Regan waved him over. His smile faded and he continued to stare at the stage, past her.

She waved again, thinking he'd somehow missed her in the crowded theater. He didn't wave back. In fact, he walked to the opposite side of the room and took a seat against the far wall next to one of his brothers. She wasn't sure which one; they all looked the same to her. Big, bad, Italian, and mean.

Regan dug through her purse, pulled out her phone, and dialed Gabe. She watched as he checked the screen, sent her to voice mail, and pocketed his phone. He whispered something to his brother.

Big and Bad nodded, whispered back, and then looked over at Regan. She would have to revise her earlier assessment. Mean didn't even begin to cover the look he shot her before jerking his chin in her direction.

Gabe looked up.

Regan smiled, once again trying to make up for whatever she was lacking. Gabe looked at her and then back at the stage, whispering to his brother again. And just like the chair, something inside Regan went painfully empty.

She fought to keep her smile in place, to keep the panic deep inside where it wasn't visible. Her face heated and her body felt awkward. It was as if every person in the room was staring at her. She looked back at the stage, her reason for being there, and blinked back the tears.

Gabe had purposefully dismissed her—in front of the whole town.

She tried to convince herself that it was nothing; that it was her own guilt getting the best of her; that he had shown up as promised. But an hour later, when the curtain closed and the final bow was had, Regan felt as if her body was going to snap from the tension.

Gabe's seat next to his brother was empty and he was nowhere to be found.

Nothing made sense. He had seen her. He had ignored her. Then, without a word, he had left her. She grabbed her hat and mumbled a hurried good-bye to Jordan and Ava, ducking out before the houselights came up.

Earlier that morning, Gabe had brought over a big pink box with an even bigger red bow filled with a dozen doughnuts with pink sprinkles for Holly's birthday breakfast. When he left he'd stolen a kiss and they'd made plans to take Holly to dinner after the musical.

Regan didn't know what had transpired in the past ten hours, but it wasn't good. She felt it in her gut. In the way his eyes had been cool and empty when he'd looked at her.

It was like she had been beamed back to six years ago when Gabe had found her with Richard.

Whatever was going on would have to wait. Tonight was about Holly, her amazing performance, and her birthday.

Regan squared her shoulders and hurried down the hallway toward the dressing rooms. She was going to hug her little thespian and take her out for the best birthday dinner a newly turned six-year-old could imagine. Then tomorrow, after Christmas presents were opened, she would confront Gabe.

Regan turned the corner and slammed into a tiny brunette with big brown eyes.

"Abigail," Regan blurted out. No introductions were needed. Even though the two had never met, the connection was immediate, intense, and might explode at one spark.

"I was going to call you after Christmas," Regan admitted. Abigail only crossed her arms. "To talk to you about..." Regan looked at the dressing room door, only ten feet away, and knew that now wasn't the time. Holly would come bounding out of the room, ready to celebrate her performance, and instead find her mom and teacher in a screaming match.

"Holly will be here any minute," Abigail said, by way of calling a temporary truce.

"Yes," Regan said, her chest relaxing a little. Abigail wasn't hiding the fact that she hated Regan, but at least she was thinking of Holly. "Thank you. And thank you for tonight. Holly was so excited about this play, and with you being the music director, this whole event could have turned out a completely different experience for her."

Instead of the tension easing, Abigail took Regan's thanks as a direct insult. "I am not in the habit of ruining families."

Okay, so maybe the implied truce wasn't as strong as Regan had first thought. She needed to defuse the situation and get Holly out of there, pronto.

"Why don't I call you Friday on my break and we can clear the air?"

"I don't see the point. We will never be friends and this town will never be your home. So let's cut through the niceties. I have an after-party to host and you have a daughter to collect."

"And I have a question," Gabe said. The chill in his voice was nothing compared to the pure disgust in his expression when Regan turned around.

Gabe stood, bouquet of pink flowers in one hand, stack of papers in the other, and stared down at Regan like she was a complete disappointment and waste of space.

Behind him was an army of DeLucas, one more intimidating than the next. With their chests puffed out and shoulders back, they took up so much space that there didn't seem to be enough left for Regan.

She wanted to run. Grab Holly, get in her car, and drive until the pressure building in her heart stopped.

She breathed in slowly and tipped up her chin. Letting them know that they scared her wasn't an option. So she took a step forward, knowing that if she could get Gabe alone things would be okay. She would be okay.

"Don't." He held up his hand, the one that was strangling the bouquet, to keep her away. And if that wasn't painful enough, he looked at Abigail, his face soft and concerned. "Are you okay?"

Regan felt as if he'd slapped her with the trunk of a Christmas tree, the star lodging in her chest and puncturing her heart. She never expected him to put her above his family. Had hoped maybe one day to be on equal footing with them. But never in a million years would she have imagined him to be purposefully cruel about reminding her where exactly she stood in his life.

Message read loud and clear.

"If you'll excuse me," she said, stepping around the precious family discussion. She got two steps before Gabe was in front of her, shoving a stack of papers at her.

"Mind explaining this first?"

CHAPTER 15

"What is this?" Regan asked, cautiously eyeing him and the papers.

Gabe didn't answer. Couldn't answer. The pain in his gut made it impossible to breathe, let alone speak.

The last thing he wanted to do was stand there with his family as witnesses and hurt the one person in the room who wasn't expecting anything from him. But he was out of options. And Regan was going to need one hell of a story to get herself out of this one.

Still, seeing her body tremble, her eyes dart toward the dressing room door, no doubt worried that Holly would come out, tore at him.

"She's with ChiChi."

Her face lost all color. Shit. Gabe hadn't meant to make it sound like this was some big DeLuca plot, where they were going to gang up on her when she was alone and scare her into leaving town. Then again, that's what this was. But ChiChi wasn't in on it.

"I see." Her voice cracked.

Nobody else could tell how close Regan was to tears, or how scared she was, but Gabe could. It was the way she refused to blink those big eyes, which had turned a cloudy blue, and how her hands had all but disappeared under the cuffs of her sweater. Regan was doing what she'd done her whole life, holding it together.

A part of him, the part that felt alive for the first time since his parents died, wanted to forget the whole thing and go back to two hours ago, when all he could think about was her naked in his bed, sleeping in his arms. The other part of him that was the head of his family, the protector of his siblings, the fucking hero of the day, pushed the bank statement into her hand.

Regan looked down and froze. "I don't understand. How did you get this?"

Not: What is this?

Or even: I'm sorry.

But: How did you get this?

Gabe took a step back, away from Regan, away from his family, away from the pain rushing at him.

"Does it matter?" Frustration tightened his fists, so he rubbed at the back of his neck to keep from punching the told-you-so smirk off Marc's face. When that didn't work, he turned his back to his family and faced the woman who had just ripped out his chest. "I believed you. Believed that you weren't responsible for any of this. I defended you to my family. And you lied."

"It's not what you think." Her voice barely filled the space.

"Really? Because it looks like you opened an account in Holly's name, transferred all of my sister's money there, only to reroute it somewhere else. Jesus, Regan, you put it in Holly's name. What kind of mother does that?"

"Don't you *ever* discount me as a mother. Everything I have ever done has been for Holly. Everything." She looked at the papers and back to him. "You want to know what this is?" She slapped the papers against his chest. And suddenly he didn't want to know.

Her eyes told him everything. He'd messed up. Big time.

His brothers had come at him, proof of betrayal in hand, emotions on high. He'd listened and then reacted. Not because he thought she was guilty—deep down he knew Regan would never take money she didn't earn—but because she scared the shit out of him. He didn't know what to do with a woman who didn't need him, didn't want him fixing her life.

So he did what any moron would do: he created a problem. Only this time he wasn't so sure he could fix his way out of it.

"*This* is what happens when a nineteen-year-old is pregnant and alone. I had no way to take care of Holly. No one would hire me. Then Richard showed up saying he wanted to do the right thing. So when he opened an account in Holly's name to help pay for diapers and formula, I didn't ask questions."

"It was a Swiss account," Marc accused. "Who the hell opens a Swiss account?"

"It had less than a thousand dollars in it. And he's Italian," she defended. "I had no idea what he was doing until I got a call from the bank asking why I had closed out the account. I assumed Abby had finally kicked him out and he'd taken back the money. But when I got the statement showing that twelve million dollars had been deposited and withdrawn only minutes apart, I knew that Richard had played me."

"Then why didn't you tell anyone?" Abby accused.

"When the police showed up asking questions about him, I told them everything. At first they saw exactly what Richard had hoped for: the daughter of an illegal immigrant and a teen mother with no job. Thankfully *they* were smart enough to actually check with Interpol and verify that I hadn't made the transaction." She shot a look at Gabe.

"They cut us out of the investigation. I only knew that the money was gone and Abby was a suspect. I had no idea who they had talked to or who they cleared," Gabe said.

"Yeah, well, neither did I. I didn't know whose money it was until recently."

"Why didn't you tell me the other day..." *In my bed, when I was holding you and spilling my guts about how I'd let down my family.*

"You mean confide in the guy who ruined six years of my life for *accidently* sleeping with his brother-in-law?" She laughed mercilessly.

"Finding this account has changed the entire direction of our investigation," Gabe said, needing her to understand just what this meant to his family. "It actually led us to another account Richard had set up for Holly in the Cayman Islands. Now we have a lead, a real chance at catching the bastard."

"You people really can't see past your family, can you?" Regan choked out. "All I want is to keep my daughter safe."

He took a step forward, needing to touch her, make this right. "Regan, I wouldn't have—"

This time she stopped him. "Don't go there, Gabe. You already did and you'd do it again. You would do anything to protect your family." Her eyes went wide and her lips parted on a breath. "Oh, my God."

She took a step back.

Then another.

"You were asking Holly about Richard." Her hand covered her mouth and his chest hollowed out as he saw her put everything together. "You came to my house to ask me about Richard, not to help me move. From day one you've been asking about Richard. Even when we were..."

She glanced around, as if suddenly remembering that his entire family and a few PTA parents were in the hall, listening to everything. Her face flushed with humiliation.

She dropped her head, and Gabe for the first time saw a glimmer of that little girl who had been teased and discarded and forced to stand on her own—apart from everyone else. Except that when she looked up, he realized that she no longer had a floor to stand on, he'd ripped it out from under her.

"I'm such an idiot," she said heartbreakingly soft. "You slept with me because..." She pressed a hand to her stomach. "I let you in my house, around Holly, trusted you with my heart, and the whole time..."

Now it was his turn to explain. Only this time he was guilty of everything she had accused him of.

"It started out that way." He took a step closer, and she backed farther away. "But then I got to know you, and in the end—"

"In the end"—her big blue eyes darkened with sorrow— "you were a jerk just like everyone else. And you want to know the worst part?"

No, he didn't want to know anything else.

"I really thought this year"—her breath caught—"that this year was going to be a perfect Christmas."

"Regan, wait." He grabbed her arm when she turned to leave. "I'm sorry. I am so fucking sorry."

She looked at him for a long time, the tears finally spilling over her pretty lashes. She opened her mouth and took a thorough inventory of his family. Holly came out of the dressing room then, dragging an apologetic ChiChi with her.

Regan looked back at Gabe and shook her head, sad and slow. "It's not enough this time."

With an angry swipe at her cheeks, she pulled herself together for Holly, her strength amazing to witness. Then she met her daughter halfway, hugging her tightly and congratulating her on her part in the musical before clasping her hand and heading toward the exit.

At the doorway Holly paused and turned, looking at him with confusion. Forcing himself to stand there and let them walk around the corner and out of sight was the hardest thing he'd ever had to do.

ChiChi rushed over, demanding to know what was going on. Nate and Trey were trying to explain the events. Marc was apologizing for not digging deeper to get the whole story. And Abby was tugging on his sleeve, asking him if he was okay. None of it mattered.

All he heard was the slamming of the metal theater doors in the distance. Gabe couldn't remember a time in his life when he hadn't acted in the best interest of his family. Even when it was the hard choice, he always chose family. So then why did his chest feel like it had been gutted?

Oh, shit. He looked from his family and then to the empty hallway.

Oh, shit. His breath came in fast, panicked bursts. The reality of what he had just done crashed in on him. Sure, part of his family was standing next to him, loud and bickering and trying to figure out what had just happened. But the other part, the part of his family that he didn't even know he possessed, had just walked out the door.

"I love her." When no one stopped yelling, he looked his family square in the eye. "I. Love. Her."

The hall fell uncomfortably silent. All five sets of eyes that were the exact image of his father's looked back at him. The only set that was smiling was ChiChi's.

"I love her," he said again, this time just to hear how it sounded. It sounded right.

"There are a lot of emotions going on right now. Let's take a step back and think this through," practical, level-headed Nate said, making Gabe want to shove him through the wall.

"Listen." Gabe waited for silence. He was only going to say this once. "I love Regan and Holly with everything that I am, and I will do whatever I have to do to win her back." He turned to Abby and took her hands in his. "I love you and I am sorry I allowed that bastard in our lives. But I can't keep punishing myself or Regan. So if it will be too hard on you to see us together, tell me now."

Abby blinked, sending tears down her cheeks. "You'd still ask her to leave?"

"No, I'd go with her. I'm not willing to give up Regan, but I also don't want Holly growing up in a place where Regan is an outcast. Understand?" Abby nodded, her mouth quivering. "So if you can't let this go, tell me now and I'll leave."

"Who the hell would run the business?" Marc asked, his kid brother not looking so cocky anymore.

He looked at his family. "I guess one of you would have to figure it out. But wherever my girls go, I'm going. So if you want me around, then we'd better figure out a way to make Regan stay."

"Mommy, wake up."

Regan felt little hands poke her shoulder. Careful not to move for fear that her head would explode, she opened her eyes and immediately slammed them shut. They were puffy and irritated, and the blinking lights overhead felt like lasers piercing her retinas.

Regan opened her eyes again, pushed through the pain and gasped. Her butt was asleep, her right hand was attached to her cheek with what she hoped was sap and not superglue, and something hard and pokey was sticking her in the kidney.

On second glance, she realized that she was lying under the Christmas tree next to an empty tub of Rocky Road, covered in popcorn garland, and spooning Randolph.

She had a piece of popcorn husk stuck between her teeth. Even sadder was that she hadn't even had a sip of alcohol. Regan had accomplished all of this awesomeness by her sober lonesome.

She remembered putting Holly to bed, remembered stuffing the stockings, and remembered getting the presents out of the trunk.

She also remembered taking one look at Randolph, alone on Christmas Eve, hiding under the plastic tablecloths with little Santas, and completely lost it. Then, to really put the guilt on, he had flipped his switch and wished her a merry

Christmas. Outside of Holly's, it would likely be the only Christmas wish she would get this year. And how pathetic was that?

Almost as pathetic as carrying Randolph in, sharing a tub of ice cream with him and telling him all about her Christmas curse. Even using his flank to cry on.

"Holy cow, Santa brought you Randolph. You must have been a really good girl this year," Holly said, scooting closer so she could pet Randolph's head.

Regan thought back to all that she had lost last night and wanted to disagree, but she kept her mouth shut.

Then she stared at her daughter, sitting under an enormous Christmas tree, and her heart melted, moving somewhere closer to right. Holly's face was flush with sleep and her hair was sticking up in the back. Dressed in red footie pajamas and clutching her kitty Pillow Pet—who she had named Gold Fish—Regan, for the first time in weeks, saw things clearly, and agreed.

She must have been a good girl, because she had Holly. And nobody else in the world could say that.

Scooping her daughter up, Regan settled Holly in her lap and held her close. She breathed in little girl scent and slowly exhaled while holding her tighter. "I love you, angel."

"I love you too, Mommy, but you're all sticky."

Regan didn't let go. And Holly, getting stickier by the second, didn't move. Regan looked around their dinky little apartment and a warm sense of belonging passed through her. It didn't matter where they lived or what kind of job she had, or that she'd have to look for new ones the next day. All that mattered was that, in her arms and together, she and Holly were enough. They always had been.

"Why don't we do presents first and then breakfast?" she said, tugging one of Holly's ringlets.

Holly shook her head and looked up at Regan with excited eyes. "We have to wait until my last present comes."

"How do you know it isn't already under the tree?" Regan had been keeping track of things that caught Holly's attention. She couldn't afford them all, but with her promotion had come a raise and Regan had been able to buy a few things she knew Holly wanted.

"Nope, it doesn't fit under a tree," Holly said, sending Regan's heart plummeting to her toes.

Not wanting to shatter her kid's Christmas wish but refusing to lie to her, Regan went for honest. "I did something that I'm not proud of."

"Did you pay the Dirty Jar?" Holly asked, as cool as if this was a daily occurrence. For Regan, as of late, it was.

"I did. Remember that letter you gave me to mail to Santa?" Holly nodded. "Well, I opened it and read it without your permission, even though it wasn't mine to open. And"—another deep breath—"I know you asked Santa for a forever home. And I know that one year we'll get that home, just not this year."

"I know," Holly said with a *duh* tacked on to the tone. "At first I wanted a forever home where I could have a kitty of my own, then I realized a daddy was better." If Regan's heart had been in her toes, now it was lodged painfully in her throat. "So Lauren and I sent him a second letter and Santa brought me Gabe." Holly's smile fell flat and her lip quivered. "Why are you crying, Mommy?"

Regan touched her cheeks, surprised to find that she was. She never cried in front of Holly. Then again, ever since

Richard, she'd avoided decisions that had the potential to break her baby's heart.

"Honey, Gabe isn't coming."

Holly's eyes went wide and bright. "Why?"

Because he's a jerk. Because he lied. Because you got stuck with a mommy who is missing something that makes her lovable.

Regan swallowed. "Because he is spending it with his family."

"But we're his family." The confusion in Holly's voice burned through Regan's chest.

She wrapped Holly tightly to her, hugging her fiercely and hoping to convey just how special she was, how loved she was, and most importantly, that just being herself was enough. "We are our own family, Holly. You, me, and Gold Fish."

"And Randolph?" Holly whispered, too much understanding in her six-year-old little voice.

Regan pulled back. "No, we have to return Randolph."

"Good, cuz the Dirty Jar's already full."

"They're all staring at us," Holly whispered, tightening her mittened grip on Regan's left hand. Regan's right hand was pulling a wagon.

The red wagon was heavier than she had expected, and even though a Christmas-morning storm sent frigid winds rushing though the main part of town, sweat beaded on her skin. Because the wagon, borrowed from Perkins' toolshed, held one very wanted, fresh-from-his-bath and smiling-out-at-his-adoring-public Randolph.

The adoring public, however, was not smiling back. They were scowling. At Regan, not Randolph.

Regan tightened her grip on Holly, giving her hand three little squeezes. When Holly didn't give her usual squeezes back, she stopped and looked down at her daughter, who looked back—terrified.

Dropping to her knee, Regan smoothed Holly's silky hair. "*You* did nothing wrong. I made a mistake and I have to fix it, but I can bring you to Pricilla's and pick you up after this is over."

Holly took in the crowd, the not-so-welcoming glares, and shook her head. "Nope. You and me is family. A mistake is only wrong if you don't right it." With her me-too squeezes, Holly tugged her forward toward the town Christmas display.

Already packed with spectators wearing their mourning best, a gilded podium, and the mayor at the mic, it looked more like a funeral procession than a Christmas celebration. Reminding herself that there was nothing left to lose, Regan threw her shoulders back and kept on moving through the crowd, around St. Vincent's upper-class glee club singing, "Randolph the Red-Nosed Reindeer," past an overjoyed Isabel, only stopping after she had squeezed her way up to the podium.

"Then one foggy Christmas Eve, Santa came to say," the glee club belted out.

The mayor took one look at the stolen goods in the wagon and stepped back. Regan walked up to the mic and tapped it. The muffled thump echoed throughout the street, instantly silencing the crowd and cutting off the glee club right as the altos sang an ominous, "Ho Ho Ho."

"Um, hello, everyone," Regan began, with her best the-funniest-thing-happened-on-the-way-over smile. No one smiled back. "Merry Christmas?"

Silence.

Holly looked around. Sensing that her mom was a total bust, she held up a finger and whispered something to Randolph, whose smile oddly appeared to grow bigger. Then Holly wheeled him in front of the podium and pushed his nose.

"Merry Christmas, one and all."

When the greeting wasn't returned, Holly ran up on stage and pulled Regan close. "Like a Band-Aid, Mommy." And then she ran back to the front row and gave her a double thumbs-up.

Quick and painless. Right. "I know you all have a busy schedule this morning, so I'll just come out and say it—"

"I stole Randolph." A voice came from behind. The crowd parted, all three hundred heads turned in unison to stare back.

Frankie stood on the curb in front of Stan's Soup and Service Station, covered in dirt and grape stains. Her hair was a disaster and she was holding Randolph. Well, not Randolph, since Regan had the stolen Randolph in her stolen wagon. But it was a close match.

The crowd looked back and forth between the two statues, trying to determine who had the real Randolph and who was the big fat liar.

She had no idea where her friend had bought the reindeer or why she was doing this, but Regan was touched. That Frankie was trying to take the fall made the lump in her throat that much tighter.

Sweet or not, though, she couldn't allow it. Holly was in the crowd, and Martin women didn't hide from their mistakes. No matter how bad it sucked to fess up. "Frankie, that is so incredibly wonderful of you, but—"

"We stole Randolph," the three Mrs. Clauses chimed in while marching across the street, each one carrying a Randolph look-alike.

"Impossible," Mrs. Lambert said, coming from the general direction of the Grapevine Prune and Clip, a Randolph in her clutches. "I've had him all along. See?" She pushed his nose. "Merry Christmas, one and all."

From the back row, Regan could see a bundle of auburn curls rise. Abigail DeLuca stood on her chair, and the entire audience gasped at what was most likely going to be the best throw-down in St. Helena Christmas history.

Regan stood frozen, her palms sweating and her heart thundering in her chest. Last night had been one of the hardest moments of her life, which was saying a lot because she'd weathered more than her share of heartache. But this was something she refused to weather, not in front of Holly.

She stepped down from the podium and took her daughter's hand. Before she could speak, Holly gave three squeezes and said, "Mrs. Dee, are you also going to fib and say you had Randolph?"

Abby looked down at Holly and then to Regan. The woman didn't say a word, but then she didn't need to. Regret was in her very expression. "No, honey, but give me a little while to get used to this." She looked back at Regan and shrugged. "By next year, who knows."

"Well, I'll tell you what I know." Sheriff Bryant stood in the back row, reading from his department-issued notepad. "That at precisely three thirty-seven this morning an unidentified white male wearing dark clothing and a Stanford ball cap, approximately six foot one in height and weighing one hundred and ninety pounds, was caught on video surveillance depositing one Randolph the Reindeer on the south side of the sheriff's station, next to the mail depository."

He picked up the statue and pushed the button.

"Feliz navidad, todos y cada uno."

Sheriff Bryant looked baffled. "Well, now someone mind explaining how that happened?"

"You have the wrong deer, Sheriff," a low and sexy voice called from the back.

The crowd parted and there, standing at a good six one and wearing a Stanford cap, looking ever-so-handsome in his jeans and dark shirt, stood Gabe, with a Randolph in hand. It had a big bow on its head and a matching pink nose.

"No one here could have had Randolph because I did," he said, making his way forward, his eyes never leaving Regan's.

"That's not even a real Randolph," Isabel snapped. "His nose is the wrong color."

"Oh, it's real, all right." Gabe set Randolph the Seventh at Regan's feet and tangled his fingers with hers. "I met this sexy, smart woman and tried to woo her. Only instead of impressing her, I ended up making a fool out of myself and accidentally ran ChiChi's car into the town Christmas display. And in a panic, I took Randolph. Only she was too classy to turn me in." He brought her hand to his lips and kissed it. "I only hope she can forgive me for being such an ass."

"Is that the truth?" Holly said, her hall monitor hand snapping to her hips.

Gabe dropped to his knees, getting eye to eye with Holly. "Yes, ma'am, and I've got three rolls of quarters to back Regan's up." Her little hand came out, and Gabe handed over the Dirty Jar money.

Their voices dropped to a hushed murmur as their heads leaned closer together. They were making some kind of deal, and by the look on Holly's face when they pulled back, Regan's daughter had somehow come out ahead on the negotiations.

"Question is…" Gabe looked over Holly's head to Regan. "Do you think your mom will believe me?"

"What part do you want me to believe?"

Gabe rose and, resting his hands on Regan's hips, nudged her closer. His voice dropped low when he spoke, and his hands dropped lower the closer she got. "The part where I said I was an ass and that you are the most beautiful and classy woman I have ever met. And the part where I tell you that I love you."

"That's a lot of parts," she whispered, her heart swelling in her chest until she was afraid that she would run out of room. "But I think I like that last one the best."

"Even if I admit that I put Randolph in your trunk?" Gabe whispered, wrapping those strong arms around her waist and giving her a slow, easy smile.

"You did? Why?"

They were both talking so hushed, Regan could see people sway closer, straining to listen. So Gabe dropped his voice even more. "I found him in the PTA room and thought Isabel was setting you up." Regan had assumed the same thing. "I considered just returning it to the town display, but you had been so adamant—"

"You mean stubborn?"

"*Determined* to do it yourself that I wanted to give you the time you needed."

"I had already given it back to your grandmother...in front of half the town."

"I figured that out last night. Right around the time I realized that you would also come here this morning to make things right."

"So you planned all of this?"

He nodded. "To say I'm sorry. Truly sorry for everything."

She looked around at her friends holding reindeers, a public statement that they had her back, and couldn't believe that Gabe had gone through all that trouble just to cover for her.

"You're forgiven. For the Randolph part," she clarified.

He pulled her even closer, their hips and thighs brushing. "Well, before you make up your mind on the rest of it, please let me show you the *best* part."

"Oh, she's seen his part," Jordan yelled. The crowd nodded.

Gabe winked at Holly, then looked down at Regan. "Ready?"

No, Regan wasn't ready. She was still stuck on the "I love you."

Holly pushed the pink nose on the Randolph imposter. But instead of a robotic voice wishing one and all a Merry Christmas, it was Gabe's voice that came out.

"Marry me, Regan."

Regan looked down and there around girly Randolph's neck was a diamond ring attached to a big red bow. It was old and aged with memories, and she recognized it immediately.

Holly handed the ring to Gabe. He held it for a silent moment, his face vulnerable and unsure. He must have misread her face, because his went slack. "If you don't want this one because of Richard, I can get you another one. It's just that it was my mom's and—"

"The ring is perfect." She slid her arms around his waist, resting her head on his chest. No matter how much she loved him, how much she wanted to say yes, she couldn't.

She felt Gabe tense, then he buried his face in her neck and whispered, "I sense a 'but' coming, Vixen."

"I can't." Gabe froze at her confession. She loosened her hold, unwilling to let him see the emotion in her eyes, stared at his arms that were so strong she wanted to crawl right back into them. "I love you so much, but I just can't. Your family—"

He cupped her cheeks and tilted her face up, and what she saw staring back made her breath catch. Gabe was looking down at her with so much intensity and love and heat that some of her doubts that stemmed from their past began to fade and give way to a few hopes for their future.

"You are my family," he said fiercely. "You and Holly."

Regan opened her mouth to point out that he also had a big bad Italian family who hated her, but before she could get a word out he leaned down and gently kissed her. "Last night you said it wasn't enough," he whispered against her lips. "You're right. It wasn't. Anything that doesn't include dinner with you and Holly and waking up with you in my arms, every day, will never be enough. I love you, Regan. I don't care where we live or who shows up to Christmas dinner, as long as I have you. You two are home to me, you're my family. Please say you'll let me be yours."

Regan had received a Christmas miracle six years ago and promised herself that she would never forget what it felt like. So when the warmth spread through her body, surrounding her heart and filling her with joy, she closed her eyes and for the second time since she was seven she thanked Santa.

"Was that a yes?" ChiChi shouted from the back.

"I can't hear a thing back here," Pricilla harped.

"It's cuz she stepped away from the mic," Lucinda shouted.

"Well, I'm pretty close," the mayor said, "and I'm not sure. She said she liked the ring and then started crying, so Gabriel kissed her and then she mumbled something about Santa."

"So what is it, Mommy?" Holly asked.

"Yeah, Vixen, what is it?" Gabe asked, his voice low and rough. His arms tightened around her, one hand sinking dangerously low on her back, the other into her hair.

Regan looked at the two most important people in her world and understood that even though she and Holly made a perfect pair, with Gabe they were the perfect family.

"Yes," Regan said, loud enough for even Perkins to hear. "Yes, I will marry you."

"Thank God." But instead of kissing her, like Regan had hoped, Gabe leaned down and picked Holly up. One arm tightly around Regan, the other holding Holly. "You gonna show her?"

"Show me what?" Regan asked, smiling at her giggling daughter.

Holly reached into the pocket of her Christmas dress and pulled out a cat collar. It was green with a little red bell and had a gold tag dangling from it. "Gabe said I could have a kitty of my very own. So I was hoping you'd say yes and marry him."

"Hold it up higher," he said as Holly raised the collar above her head. "A little to your left. Other left. There you go. Now read the tag."

Collar directly overhead, Holly stuck her tongue out the side of her mouth and squinted at the name tag. "It says Mistletoe. Look, Mrs. Clauses, my new kitty is named Mistletoe."

"Well, how about that? My favorite holiday plant," Gabe said, setting down Holly, who took off toward her three grandmas. He pulled Regan close and kissed her, telling without words just how merry a Christmas it was going to be.

Read on for a sneak peek of Marina Adair's next delightful romance

SUMMER IN NAPA

Available April 16, 2013

Alexis Moreau grabbed her car keys, and headed down the rear stairs. Cracking the door open, she glanced around and smiled when she found the parking lot behind the shop blessedly empty.

She had snuck in and out of this apartment so many times as a teenager, there was no reason that her heart should be pounding out of her chest right now. It was like riding a bike, right? The only difference was that back in high school she had snuck around so that no one would know she was having sex with Jeffery, and now she was going stealth because she didn't want people to know that Jeffery stopped having sex with her a long time ago.

Lexi's heart went heavy, because erasing the past ten years wasn't going to happen. Neither was ignoring the fact that her expected arrival time was less than an hour away. She would have to face family and friends eventually. But when she did, it was going be on her terms.

Lexi took a single step, stiffening at the sound of feet pounding the pavement, followed by the instant clang of jangling metal. Both sounds were wild and hurried. And both sounds were moving.

Toward her.

"Shit!" Lexi reached back for the doorknob, twisted, and—nearly broke her wrist.

Chest tight, palms sweaty, she faced the door and gave it another try.

Shit. Shit. Shit!

It was locked. In her grandmother's quest to protect Lexi's teenage virtue, Pricilla had installed safety measures: a doorknob that was extremely loud to open, with a lock that was always engaged.

Lexi patted down the sides of her shorts as though expecting to find magical pockets containing a set of apartment keys. Sadly, she found neither.

"Come here, boy," a distinctly male, and distinctly familiar, voice called out. Followed by a playful bark that sounded much farther away.

Lexi froze and last night's pastry dinner declared war on her stomach.

"That's it, come on. Good boy." Paws clicked excitedly on the pavement—directly toward her. "Damn it, Wingman, I said come!"

This could not be happening.

Fear had her moving—and fast. Lexi would rather face her grandmother and a few customers than face *him*.

A gentle breeze blew past her and with it the smell of freshly baked choux pastry. Lexi followed the scent and found that both of the windows that her grandmother used to ventilate the rear kitchen were open a crack.

She automatically pried the first window open, her body going into adolescent autopilot as she hoisted herself through. She got that same old high school thrill until she realized she didn't have the same old high school hips and found herself, ass-up, wedged between the window casing.

"Oh, God, no." Lexi rocked, trying to gain enough momentum to tumble to the other side of the windowsill. "Please, no."

Seconds ticked by and sweat beaded on her forehead. She clawed at the sill and kicked at the planter box she stood on, mentally willing her hips back to prom night—but she didn't move, or loosen, an inch. No matter how hard she tried, she just couldn't squeeze herself through the window.

Refusing to give up, she looked around the kitchen, hoping to find something, anything that might help. But everything was out of reach—except for a fresh tray of éclairs, which sat just to her right.

Her body sank, dangling over the windowsill. It was no use. She was stuck. Trying to move forward while dodging your past was clearly impossible. So she did what any reasonable woman would do: she reached across the table and plucked a petit-éclair from the tray, shoving the entire thing in her mouth, sure to lick her fingers clean in the process.

She was reaching for her second pastry when something cold and wet poked her in the butt. She yelped. There was a bark, a sniff, and the wet nose again.

"Shoo," Lexi hissed, waving her free hand even though the dog couldn't see. "Go away."

"He was just saying good morning."

Lexi froze, considering her options. When she realized she had none, she snapped, "Well, you should teach him some manners."

"Says the woman mooning half of St. Helena," the smooth voice behind her said, as though she wasn't aware that her ass was flapping in the wind. "Plus, as far as Wingman is concerned, you were offering him up a doggie high-five."

Taking a deep breath, Lexi composed herself and went for enchanting. There was a time when she'd excelled in enchanting. Hell, she'd been cheer captain, *and* valedictorian.

But that was all before. Before the end of her marriage. Before she lost her restaurant. Before she found her husband trussed up like a Thanksgiving turkey in nothing but her award-winning *noix de coco brûlée* and a hard-on, while her sous chef Sara used a basting brush and caramelizing torch in ways that were illegal in thirty-seven of the fifty states.

And before she turned her head, looked out the window, and found herself staring up at the one person in town who had never thought Alexis Moreau enchanting. In fact, Marco DeLuca, entitled playboy and total meathead, had gone out of his way to let her know just how annoying he'd believed her to be.

Ignoring Marc's smart-ass grin and Wingman's breath on her thighs, Lexi realized that with her new diet of cynicism and foolishness, enchanting was no longer her. So she did the next best thing. She grabbed another éclair and—

"No, he doesn't do well with—"

—chucked it out the window. Barking and jumping ensued with a lot of scrambling, mainly on Marc's part.

"No, boy. Drop it. That's right, chocolate is bad. Very bad. It gives you…Aw, Wingman!"

The window next to her squeaked open. By the time she turned her head, Marc was leaning in, his forearms leisurely resting on the windowsill, ear buds dangling from his neck, and his alpha-male swagger stinking up the kitchen.

"Heard you were coming home."

The way he said it, with an added little wink for extra sting, made her wonder just what else he had heard. Damn it. This was supposed to be a covert homecoming.

She grabbed the last éclair off the table and took a bite.

"I hope you brought enough to share with the class."

She could have told him that there was another tray on the far wall, but Marc had been a permanent pain in her butt ever since she moved to St. Helena with her mom in the eighth grade. Lexi never knew what she had done to get on his bad side, a hard accomplishment since Marc loved everything with boobs.

She looked at her breasts and paused. They weren't huge, but even in her grandmother's baggy T-shirt they filled out the top nicely. Jeffery had never complained.

Then again, he had also left her for a loafer-wearing vegan who looked more like a librarian than the "other woman."

She took another bite and pondered. Whatever she'd done had placed her at the top of Marc's shit list. Not a good list to be on when the DeLucas pretty much ran St. Helena.

Even worse—for Lexi—Marc was not only loved by women, respected by men, adored by the elderly, a real hometown freaking hero. He was also her ex-husband's best friend. Had been since elementary school.

"Sorry, last one." With a shrug, she shoved almost the entire thing in her mouth, mumbling around the bits of flaky pastry and heavenly filling.

Marc reached through the window, snatched the remaining bite—the last and *best* bite.

"Give it back." Lexi's arms shot out to stop him. Only Marc was faster, and meaner. Palming her head with his free hand, he held her down while he savored the last bite.

Lexi swatted him away. "Does everyone get such a warm welcome?"

Reaching through the opened window, he wiped a glob of filling off the side of her mouth. Licking it clean, he smiled. "Only the ones who wear their breakfast, Creampuff."

"I'll be sure to pack a napkin next time. And it's an éclair."

When Marc's hand made its way back toward her lips, she quickly wiped her mouth off on her right shoulder. The white cotton came away with custard and chocolate smears.

"As great as it is to see you again, I'm kind of busy."

All traces of humor faded and his eyes went soft. "I can see that. Need some help?"

Yes, she was about to beg, already lifting her arms toward him. The offer seemed genuine enough, the last seventy-two hours had left her on the brink of tears, and for some bizarre reason Lexi wanted to give in to Marc's charm and gallantry.

Then Marc came up behind her and, pressing his body against hers, leaned over her and reached around her to scrape some leftover filling off the tray. Never one to disappoint, Marc stepped back and ran a cream-coated finger down the back of her thigh before whistling. "Come here, boy."

Not caring if she kicked Marc, Lexi started pumping her limbs like a teeter-totter. She might not be the most athletic girl on the planet, but she'd manage.

"Hold up, you're going to hurt yourself." Warm, strong, and incredibly unsettling hands rested on her upper thigh, stopping her movements and sending her heart into over-drive. Not to mention making everything below her belly button tingle. Oh, so not good. "Now push up against me and I will slide you out of there."

"Nope. I've got it."

"You sure?"

Oh, yeah. The last thing she needed was his help.

ACKNOWLEDGMENTS

To my incredible agent and fast friend, Jill Marsal, without whose support and endless belief, this book wouldn't exist. Thanks to my editors, Lindsay Guzzardo and Caitlin Alexander, for their enthusiasm and insight, and to the entire team at Montlake Romance, whose dedication and amazing contributions are appreciated.

I am blessed to be surrounded by a fabulous group of women who have filled my life with laughter, love, and lots of support on my way to publication. From my beta readers, to my coven of Roguers, my MFAers, and my fellow RWAers, I am honored to know each and every one of you.

As always, I am indebted to three very special ladies: Britt Bury for helping me plot and replot and patiently listening as I navigated through this story; Jacee James, for your endless hours of editing and advice and always being my constant cheerleader; and Hannah Jayne, for knowing how to plot me out of a corner, when I need a trip to PG and, more importantly, a stiff drink.

Finally, to my husband, Rocco, who became Mr. Mom for the weeks leading up to my deadline, never complaining when I fell asleep spooning my laptop, or when I was still in my pajamas come dinnertime. You are *my* forever home, and I would follow you anywhere.

ABOUT THE AUTHOR

Marina Adair is a lifelong fan of romance novels. Along with the St. Helena Vineyard series, she is also the author of *Tucker's Crossing*, part of the Sweet Plains series. She currently lives in a hundred-year-old log cabin, nestled in the majestic redwoods of the Santa Cruz Mountains, with her husband and daughter.